Rites of PASSAGE

USA Today Bestselling Author

CATHERINE GAYLE

Cover design by Kim Killion, The Killion Group

ISBN: 1537040006
ISBN-13: 978-1537040004

Acknowledgments

I grew up in the MTV generation, back in the days when MTV actually showed music videos. I first remember watching MTV at a neighbor's house when I was probably only five or six years old. They had cable; we didn't. My friend's older siblings were officially *cool*, and they taught us that watching MTV was part of what made them cool. Music videos like "Video Killed the Radio Star" by The Buggles, "Take on Me" by A-ha, and of course, anything and everything by Michael Jackson started to shape many of my memories. Eventually, we got cable, too, and my own fascination with MTV became a seemingly permanent part of my life.

But in my teens, MTV started to change. They became pioneers in a TV-show format that would become a television fixture in later years: reality TV. It all started with a show called *The Real World*, which was "a true story of seven strangers picked to live in a house, work together, and have their lives taped." *The Real World* had next to nothing to do with music videos, but it had everything to do with the MTV generation. Like many of my contemporaries, I watched voraciously.

The third season of *The Real World*, however, came along and hit me over the head like I never expected. The show was set in San Francisco, and one of the seven strangers picked to appear was a gay man named Pedro Zamora, who was living with AIDS.

You see, being part of the MTV generation, I was also living out my childhood and teen years at a time when the AIDS epidemic was petrifying the whole world. We knew enough about it to be terrified of this "gay man's disease," but not enough to truly *understand* the disease. Because of Magic Johnson and a few other high profile cases, we had learned that HIV and AIDS didn't affect *only* gay men, but fear and lack of information surrounding the disease were prevalent.

For the first time in my life, however, Pedro Zamora put a face on it. Yes, he was a gay man living with AIDS. But even though he was dying from it, he was still *living* with it. He was teaching people about it. I learned more about HIV and AIDS from watching that reality TV show on MTV than I had in any other arena in my life, and it was all because Pedro Zamora was determined to teach everyone he could as much as he could during the time he had left.

Today, we know even more about HIV and AIDS than we did then. Yet I find that there is still a lot of misinformation and fear running rampant. I hope that in some small way, this book can touch and teach in a similar way to how Pedro Zamora, *The Real World*, and MTV touched and taught me.

Rites of PASSAGE

Prologue

Drew

"I SHOULDN'T EVEN be here," I said. I tugged at the collar of my dress shirt and tie, wishing they did a better job of hiding my scars. That was a vain hope, though. The gash in my neck stretched from behind my ear almost all the way to my Adam's apple. Unless I wanted to wear a full scarf or something else completely out of place in this drought and heat, there was no hiding it. This ugly thing was out there for the whole world to see, whether I liked it or not.

And I most definitely did *not* like it. Especially because it still hurt like a son of a bitch, depending on how I moved. The wound had closed and the stitches were gone, but I didn't know if my neck would ever feel the same again. I could personally guarantee that taking a hockey skate to the throat was not in anybody's best interests, just in case anyone out there was wondering.

Not only that, but I felt like it branded me, my own personal scarlet reminder of the things I should have done differently in life before it was too late.

Dmitri Nazarenko rolled his eyes, one of the few features on his face not hidden behind his beard. He'd shaved it off at one point during the season, but now he was letting it grow back. At least so far, he seemed to be keeping it trimmed and tidy, unlike before, when he'd looked more like a lumberjack than a hockey player. "Why you shouldn't be here? You're my teammate. We want you here." He shrugged.

"London hardly knows me. Why would she want me at her wedding?"

"Because I want you," Dima said.

He was deliberately being obtuse. And my head was such a fucking mess I didn't even take the obvious opportunity to crack a joke about Dima wanting me.

I was one of only two guys from among our Tulsa Thunderbirds teammates who had shown up here today. Ray "Razor" Chambers and his Russian wife, Viktoriya, had stuck around for the summer—Razor had said something about his wife's citizenship status being the reason they weren't heading to Canada, not that I'd paid much attention—so they had shown up. Razor always called her Tori. Anyway, she and Dima had a weird brother-sister sort of relationship going, so their presence at the festivities wasn't too surprising.

The rest of the team had gone back to their off-season homes to spend the summer, and since Dima and London wanted to keep it small, they hadn't invited everyone to come back for the ceremony. Because most of the guys probably would have come if he'd invited them.

London's family was all present, and a few of her

coworkers had come to support her on her big day. Dima had flown in his best friend, Sergei Mironov, and Sergei's mother from Siberia. Otherwise, there were only a smattering of their friends and acquaintances.

Under normal circumstances, I would be gone, too, spending the summer with my family in Victoria and not in this hot, dry misery. But this off-season was anything but normal, and the drought that blanketed all of Oklahoma was far from the only reason. My mother would tell me I was acting like a Grumpy Gus. She'd probably be right.

There was no getting around it. I'd already been in a bad enough mood well before my injury in the final game of the regular season due to my own marriage falling apart. But now it wasn't just my marriage that was gone; it was my entire life. Or at least my life as I had always known it.

The officiant signaled to Dima that he was ready to begin, so instead of arguing with Dima any more than I had been, I got out of the way and took a seat near the back.

There weren't too many people here, but at least if I stayed away from the rest of them, I couldn't cast too heavy a pall over the proceedings. I felt like that was all I did these days. I couldn't imagine why anyone would want to be around me, because I sure as hell didn't.

Anyway, if I stayed near the back, I could maybe sneak out early without anyone noticing. It was as good a plan as any, now that I'd gone and shown up.

Stupid of me. I should've just stayed home. That had been my original plan, until Razor had sent me a *where the fuck are you and why can't you act like a decent fucking human being for once* text about thirty minutes ago, and I'd thrown on the first suit I could find in my closet and rushed out the door into the sweltering Tulsa heat.

And it was only May. The locals made sure to tell me how much hotter July and August would be at every opportunity they got. Just what I wanted to hear. Maybe by then, at least, we would get some rain. I hoped so, although I was starting to doubt it. We hadn't had any measurable accumulation since a freak snowstorm around Christmas, and that didn't look like it would be changing anytime soon. The heat was the real kicker, though. Sweat made my scar itch, which didn't make a lick of sense to me. Must be all in my head.

Everyone around me settled into their seats and the music started. London came down the aisle holding her wedding gown out of the way while her father pushed her wheelchair. I tried to smile and be happy, but it didn't work out very well. All I wanted to do was get the fuck out of there and find my way to a bar. Or better yet, the bottle of Jameson waiting for me at home. A half dozen shots might not give me the answers I wanted, but at least I wouldn't hurt so much.

For a while.

The pain always came back, sharper and stronger than ever—and this time, I didn't mean physical pain.

Before I knew it, Dima and London were making their way back down the aisle together—this time as husband and wife—and I'd missed my chance to make a silent escape. Dima caught my eye and jerked his head toward the other room, where the reception was to be held.

I hoped they would have alcohol, but knowing Dima, that seemed more than unlikely. I'd almost never seen the guy with so much as a beer in his hand.

Fuck, but this was turning into a miserable day.

The other wedding guests filed past me, some laughing, others crying, but they all looked genuinely happy to be present for such an occasion. Razor and Tori were two of the last ones to head in that direction. Razor stopped and gave me a significant look.

I shook my head. "No one'll miss me if I don't go in there." Just like no one would miss me if I never played hockey again. Not that I intended to say that out loud.

Saying the words would only hasten the likelihood of that coming to pass, and then what would I have left to live for? No marriage. No hockey. No reason to be in this fucking hellhole any longer.

"You need to get the fuck over yourself," he shot back. "Come on. If I have to go, you do, too."

I glowered, but I followed him in, finding a quiet table well away from the happy wedding-goers where I could sulk in peace. The photographer started directing people around to get her shots—not something I needed to be part of, at any rate—so I took out my cell phone and started playing a game to zone out. That should be a strong enough sign to leave me the hell alone if anyone got any bright ideas about coming over to chat me up.

Or so I thought. It worked well enough at first, but I lost track of time playing Bejeweled Blitz repeatedly, and suddenly London had wheeled up and parked her chair next to me.

"What are you doing?" she demanded.

I shot my eyes over to her, half glaring, half trying to tamp down on the anger building within me. Because it wasn't her fault I was pissed off at the world. I knew that, but she was the one sitting there in the line of fire. I had to rein it in before I did something stupid. "Just playing a game," I bit off, staring down at the screen again.

"That's not what I mean, and you know it."

Actually, I didn't know any such fucking thing. "Then what the hell *do* you mean?"

"I mean what are you doing with your life? Because you've been running off and hiding from the world ever since—"

"I'm not hiding," I interrupted.

"Bullshit you're not. Dima and I have asked you to come over for dinner at least a dozen times since the end of the season, and you haven't come once. I know for a fact that Hunter and Tallie asked you to do some things with them before they left on vacation, and you didn't go. Razor said he and Tori even went to your place and pounded on your door, but you pretended you weren't home, even though your car was in the driveway."

"So I don't want to talk to anyone. So what?"

"So everyone's worried about you."

"Why the hell is anyone worried about me? I'm still the same asshole I've always been. I'm fine. You know who you should be worried about? Zee, all right? He's the one who might be all fucked up because of this."

Eric "Zee" Zellinger was the team captain of the Thunderbirds. And he'd been the guy to put his bare hands over my gushing wound to stop the bleeding—without knowing that I was HIV-positive until it was too late.

If he ended up contracting HIV, too… I'd never be able to live with myself.

"He's not the one who nearly died out on the ice," London pointed out. She was entirely too calm and making too damned much sense for my peace of mind. I wanted to tell her to leave me the fuck alone, but that probably wouldn't go over too well. Especially since it was her wedding day. Why the hell she wanted to pester me instead of enjoying herself on a day like this was beyond my comprehension, but no one asked for my advice or opinion about how she should spend her time.

I tossed my phone on the table and shoved back in my chair, crossing my arms in front of me. Yes, I realized I was acting like a temper-tantrum-throwing toddler. No, I didn't care.

"What does it matter to you?" I shot off.

"In case you've forgotten, I had a bad accident in a hockey game, too." She raised a brow and pointed at her chair. "That's how I ended up like this. So I might know a thing or two about what you're going through."

No one knew what I was going through. Not really. Yeah, there had been other people who'd had life-threatening injuries through playing hockey. And there were lots of other people living with HIV, like I was, through no fault of their own. Hell, millions of people had gone through divorce, too. But put them all together? I was in this boat all alone. I glowered at her in response.

"What are you doing Tuesday?" she asked, ignoring my insolence.

I shrugged. The real answer was *nothing*, and I wanted to keep it that way, but I didn't feel like cooperating with her on any score right now.

"Good," she said, like I'd answered her after all. She picked up one of the napkins from the center of the table and took a pen out of the handbag on her lap, then scribbled something on it. "That's the address for my community center. Be there at nine."

"Why the hell would I want to do that? And

shouldn't you and Dima be gone on a honeymoon right about then?"

"You'll do it because I'll hunt you down and annoy the crap out of you otherwise. And we're doing our honeymoon next month. I didn't have a passport, so we had to get that straightened out before we can go to Russia."

I rolled my eyes. "If you think you're going to get me happy about life again by making me chaperone some kids' athletic event or something—"

"It's not to have you help out," London said, backing her chair away from the table. "Right now, you don't have any business helping anyone else. It's so *we* can help *you*." Then she turned and was gone before I could tell her there wasn't any help for me, and I didn't want anyone's fucking help even if there was, so she could go shove it.

Dima took a seat next to me before I could storm out of the building. "She's mouthy," he said. "And pushy. Thinks she knows everything."

"Why the hell did you marry her, then?"

He grinned and winked. "I like her mouthy. Like her pushing my buttons."

"Tell her to leave mine alone, thanks," I ground out. "I didn't sign on for this." You couldn't pick your in-laws in life, and you also couldn't pick the people your friends married. Which was too bad. Some guys made questionable choices for themselves. I should know. I'd done it.

Dima looked down at the napkin and her scrawled writing. "That's her community center. You should go. They can help."

"I don't want any fucking help."

"Too fucking bad."

"And why's that?" I demanded, my exasperation threatening to spill over and push me into causing a scene. I needed to get the hell out of here. Sooner, rather than later.

"Because you don't get help, Tallie will join London. They might bring Viktoriya in, too." He shook his head. "Three pushy women. Too much for any man to take." Then he shuddered visibly.

"You could help by keeping yours out of it," I pointed out.

Dima just laughed and got up. "Do what London tells you. Much easier than fighting with her. Besides, I always end up fucking her after we fight, and no chance in hell I'm letting you fuck my wife." Then he stalked off like a great big, lumbering, bearded bear.

Son of a bitch. All I wanted to do was waste away in peace, but the lot of them were bound and determined to force me out of my funk.

One time. I'd go to London's community center one time, prove to myself that there was no help for me, and then put it behind me.

But that was all I could promise—to myself or anyone else.

One

Drew

THIS PLACE ALWAYS smelled like it had been doused in some sort of lemon-scented cleanser. The housekeeping staff must buy the stuff in vats and drown the rooms in it every night, because when I came in first thing in the morning for these weekly Tuesday meetings, the intensity was enough to make me want to puke.

Once I sat in here for a while, the smell would start to dissipate, no longer quite as overwhelming as it started out. But until that happened, I struggled to stay put.

I had to be here, though, no matter how much I might want to be anywhere else. And, like it or not, these support group meetings had been helping me come to terms with everything going on in my life.

I knew that as well as I knew all of my pertinent

details: Andrew Nash, better known as Drew to my teammates and our fans, divorced and miserable, right wing for the National Hockey League's expansion Tulsa Thunderbirds, and future captain of the team if I ever got back on the ice. Oh, and I was also HIV-positive—a fact that, while I'd made sure the team doctors and trainers had been fully aware of the situation, I'd done everything in my power to hide from my teammates and opponents.

Until I'd been slashed in the neck by a random skate blade in the final game of last season and Zee, the team's current captain, had unknowingly put his own life at risk in an effort to save mine. At that point, I'd had to come clean.

Not that my HIV status was something I was ashamed of, exactly. But people sure as hell tended to look at you differently when they knew. Especially other guys in the league. I would've been the same if I were in their shoes, so I couldn't blame them. HIV was still one of those things that most people didn't understand, so everyone was scared of it. To say there was a lot of stigma attached to the disease would be putting it mildly.

At twenty-eight, I was too young to remember the AIDS hysteria of the eighties or the day that Magic Johnson had retired from the NBA after announcing he was HIV-positive, but I'd done enough research of my own and my parents had filled me in, so I wasn't completely in the dark about it.

But I was trying to figure out what the hell to do now that the whole world knew my health status and the rest of the guys in the league were scared to let me back on the ice. To be fair, I was scared to get back on the ice, too. Yeah, I knew that the statistical likelihood of someone else contracting HIV from me through a situation like what had happened at the end of last season was so minimal it was almost nonexistent, but that tiny fraction of a percentage chance remained. And how the hell would I live with myself if I passed HIV on to someone else through my own selfishness in wanting to continue playing a *game*, of all things, instead of just going out into the world and getting a real job, like everyone else?

I didn't know how Chelsea—my ex—could live with herself after cheating on me and then passing it my way. That was actually how I found out she'd been cheating. Hell of a thing to have the doctor tell you at a routine physical.

That was why I was here, at an HIV support group at the community center—to come to terms with what *might* have happened out there and to figure out if it was worth taking the risk again.

I'd been coming every week over the insanely dry summer, in the hope that it would help me clear the cobwebs out of my brain so I could make a logical decision. Instead, all it'd done at first was send me in a tailspin. Only in the last week or so was I starting to get a bit of clarity.

The summer had come and mostly gone, although you couldn't tell it from the heatwave covering Tulsa right now. We were still hitting the upper nineties or even triple digits every day, even though it was late August and most of my teammates were starting to return in preparation for the upcoming season. And we still hadn't seen more than a couple drops of rain since December. Everyone's grass was dead and brown, and the city was rationing water.

I fixed a cup of coffee and grabbed a pastry and a

banana from the table along the wall of windows, hoping the combination would help ease the effects of the lemony scent. When I turned around to go find my seat, it was to find London had wheeled in alongside a woman I'd never seen before. From the looks of her, I kind of doubted I'd ever see her again—she was young, pale, and absolutely gorgeous. Not something I'd normally say about a woman with lavender dreadlocks, two full sleeves of colorful tattoos that made me believe she had countless others hidden in places currently covered by her clothing, and a haunted look in her eyes, but it was the truth. She had the sort of look that said she intended to dart away to safety like a scared rabbit as soon as she saw her opening.

I tended to be attracted to women who were her complete opposite—traditionally beautiful. Confident. Sure of themselves.

Now that I thought about it, that could have been part of my problem.

London caught my eye and waved me over, her very round belly somehow even bigger than it had been when I'd seen her less than a week ago.

I supposed that meant I was the welcoming committee for the newbie. I wasn't so sure I was up to the task, but London gave me her determined brow scrunch. If I didn't cooperate, Dima would be sure to give me hell about it. Apparently, due-to-deliver-at-any-moment London was in a constant bite-Dima's-head-off sort of mood. The heat wasn't helping anything on that score, either.

I couldn't fathom how London could stand the smell if it bothered me this much. All the pregnant women I'd ever been around got sick after smelling the strangest things. It was like pregnancy sent all their senses into overdrive.

I shuffled over to do whatever she decided I needed to do this time, only dragging my feet a little bit. "Aren't you supposed to be starting your maternity leave soon? Like, a month ago?"

She let out an exasperated huff of breath and rubbed a hand over her belly in a move I recognized as one of her go-to responses to everything. I probably shouldn't have teased her right now. One more reason for Dima to bite *my* head off next time he saw me.

"We're going to induce in a few weeks if this little guy hasn't made his appearance before then. There's no reason I can't keep working right up until the big day, though."

The purple-haired chick shifted nervously, glancing surreptitiously at London's belly before shifting her eyes to the door. Ready to dart. Yeah, she wouldn't be back. I wasn't sure she'd last through the entire meeting today. She was an even bigger mess than I'd been the first time I came, and that was saying something.

"Drew, this is Ravyn Penn," London said, going back to business mode with a no-nonsense shake of her head. "She's new to the group. I thought maybe you could help make sure she's comfortable."

Fat chance of that happening, given the look in Ravyn's eyes, but I wasn't about to say anything like that in front of London in her current state of get-this-baby-out-of-me misery. I transferred all of my breakfast goodies into one hand and reached out to shake with the other. "Drew Nash," I said.

Ravyn didn't take my hand.

"Right," London said, backing out with her chair. "Well, I'll leave you to it, then."

I didn't miss the fact that Ravyn's eyes followed

London out the door, and it looked like her feet were itching to go, as well.

"First time here?" I asked, trying to keep things light. "It's not that bad. Kind of uncomfortable at first, if you're not used to talking about things with a group—"

"I don't talk about *things*," she said.

Right. Well, then. This was getting to be more fun by the moment. "No one's going to make you talk if you don't want to. You can just sit there and listen. You can still get a lot out of it that way, just by being around other people who are dealing with similar things in life."

She gave me a go-to-hell look. This wasn't going well at all. Time to change tactics.

"You want some coffee? Or they have fruit and pastries..." Without waiting for her to answer, I led her over to the table I'd just left a few moments before. Food and drink always helped ease discomfort, at least if you asked my mother. No matter what was going on, she plied everyone with food and beverages to keep them happy and out of her hair. Seemed reasonable enough in the current situation, so I ran with the theory.

For just a moment, Ravyn's eyes met mine—still full of a world of hurt, but startling in the clarity of their blue. These were eyes I could drown in if I let myself. And if she let me. Something told me that was as likely to happen as her breaking out into a Broadway-style song-and-dance routine.

As soon as I'd gotten my first good look in those eyes, she flicked her gaze away and focused on fixing herself a cup of coffee. Lots of sugar and cream. Once she had it fixed the way she wanted it, she took a sip and made a face, then went back to add more of both.

Over in the main part of the meeting space, Jack

Carson cleared his throat and indicated that he was ready to begin. He was one of the counselors here who presided over the support groups.

"I'm heading over," I said to Ravyn, who was still trying to make her coffee sweet enough. "Save you a seat?"

She gave a quick jerk of her head that I decided to take as confirmation, so I headed for the circle of folding chairs and found two together. Then I dug into my pastry and said hello to a couple of the other regulars, keeping one eye peeled for Ravyn to join me.

She didn't, though. Once everyone had settled in, for the most part, Jack got us started by asking if anyone had something pressing they needed to discuss, but Ravyn was still leaning back against the snack table, nursing her coffee with her ankles crossed in front of her.

I caught her eye and angled my head, indicating the empty seat next to me. She inched toward the rest of us, but she found an open chair well at the back.

Directly in my line of sight, though.

I couldn't help it. Instead of paying attention to what Isobel was saying about the possible discrimination she was facing in her job due to her boss discovering her HIV status, I was focused squarely on Ravyn Penn.

She wasn't paying any more attention to the proceedings than I was, both her hands wrapped around the Styrofoam coffee cup like it was her final remaining lifeline, her eyes apparently studying the vacuum lines in the carpet. Since she wasn't looking up, I didn't bother trying to pretend I wasn't checking her out, either. I stared. Hard.

She had on a bright red tank top and a pair of black shorts that were so short they might be illegal in some parts of the world. In this heat, it more than made sense to be dressed like that. If I looked half as good as she did, I'd probably do the same. The bold colors in her clothes and her ink only accentuated how fair her skin was—like porcelain.

Now that I thought of it, porcelain seemed like a very good description for her. Delicate, like she might shatter at the slightest provocation.

Some of the counselors here could push and prod and pry until a person was at the point of breaking. A lot of times, it was necessary. I doubted Ravyn would withstand that kind of questioning, though. She seemed to require more sensitivity.

I finished off my coffee in time to hear Jack say, "And I see we have someone new with us today. Care to introduce yourself, miss? This is a safe space."

And just like that, all eyes were on Ravyn, which was the last thing she wanted. She passed wild eyes over in my direction. Desperate for help. Silently begging me without words to rescue her.

There were undoubtedly a thousand things going wrong in her life that I would never be able to help her with, but this? This was something I could do. "This is Ravyn," I said, drawing the attention back to me. "London introduced us just before the session got started. It's Ravyn's first time visiting. I told her it was all right if she wants to just sit and listen today." I put enough emphasis on the last part that no one should be able to mistake my meaning.

Jack didn't take the hint, though. "So, Ravyn. Are you HIV-positive, or is it a loved one you're here to learn how to support?"

She swallowed another big sip of her coffee, her eyes boring through me. I shrugged apologetically, nodding to encourage her to answer. If she answered, maybe that would be enough for them to leave her alone for the rest of the session so she could sit and listen like I'd promised.

"It's me," she croaked. Her clear blue eyes blinked rapidly. She was fighting back tears, still staring at me as if her life depended on it.

"Is it a new diagnosis?" Isobel asked gently. At least she had some tact, but that didn't change the fact that she'd asked yet another pressing question.

Ravyn swallowed hard and, after one more silent plea for help in my direction, looked down at her cup. I supposed it was empty, because she got up and darted back to the snack table to refill.

I took that as my opportunity to go over and see if I could help.

"You said I didn't have to talk," she hissed when I reached her side.

I reached for the coffeepot before she could and filled both her cup and my own. "I'm trying to make sure you don't have to."

"It's *not working*."

"Just don't let them see that they're getting to you, and it'll all be over in no time. Promise. Tell them the bare-bones minimum, and I'll make sure they leave you alone after that."

"You haven't managed it so far," she pointed out. The disappointment in her voice, along with a hint of censure and a hefty dose of fear, was like a vise around my gut. I'd never been much of a knight-in-shining-armor type, but there was something about her that made me want to change my mind on that front. Probably because of the way she was looking at me again—like she *hoped* I'd do exactly that. Like I could swoop in and rescue her from whatever hell she'd found herself in.

Life didn't work that way, though. She was going to have to rescue herself. And I was almost positive she realized that, even if she wished things were different. I was still digging myself out of my own hole, but she could pick up her shovel and dig next to me if she wanted. Company on a journey like this never hurt anyone.

"You didn't come sit next to me like I'd asked you to, either," I pointed out. Might as well start nudging her in the direction she needed to travel if she was going to find a light at the end of her tunnel.

"I only came because my doctors insisted on it. I have to get a form signed."

Her doctors, hmm? That was an interesting tidbit. I tucked it away in my mental files for later use. "Jack can sign your form, but he won't do it until the session's over." In all honesty, I had no clue if he would or not—but it seemed like a good idea to tell her that, even if it was a white lie. One more reason for her to stay.

"You can't sign it for me? Or maybe that London lady?"

"I don't work here," I said. "And London's more of a stickler for these things than Jack is. She might not sign it unless she knew you'd talked."

She doused her coffee in tons of cream and sugar, all the while glowering at me. But she hadn't run out the front door yet. That had to be a good sign. Now I not only wanted to be sure she stayed for the rest of this session, but that she came back again.

"Come on," I said, glancing over my shoulder to see that the rest of the group had moved on without us.

"Come back and sit with me, and I bet they'll leave you be for a while. We're not here to make you uncomfortable. We just want to help each other out."

"Don't see how talking is supposed to help anything," she muttered, but this time she came along and took the open seat next to mine.

Progress. Maybe it wasn't a huge step in some people's eyes, but I knew better. I'd been down this path recently enough. I knew how hard it was to take any step at all if it wasn't a step leading further into the darkness.

As I expected, now that the group had moved on, they kept talking about the topic at hand and left Ravyn alone to stew in her own juices. If things continued in this vein, I was almost positive I'd be able to get her to stick it out for the whole session.

Convincing her to come to the next one, however, would be another matter entirely…and I had no earthly idea how I'd manage it. I only knew that it was an absolute must.

Her hands were wrapped tightly around her coffee cup again, like it was the only thing tethering her to sanity. With any luck, she had a few more connections to sanity than a stupid piece of Styrofoam. I was starting to get the sense that I might become one of those connections, and I wasn't sure how to feel about that.

Two

Ravyn

"WHY DON'T YOU let me buy you another coffee?" Drew asked as we headed out to the parking lot after that group therapy session. He'd stuck by my side through the whole damned meeting, which was both annoying and refreshing. There weren't too many people who were willing to stand by me or stick up for me in life, but he had in there. Still, why the hell did he think I needed more coffee? I'd had three cups while we were in there, and I rarely had more than one in a day. I was wired beyond belief. More caffeine was the last thing I needed right now.

Everyone else was already making their way to their own cars, ignoring me like they'd mostly done in there, thank goodness. I wished he'd do the same. But he didn't. If anything, he was moving closer, slowing down to match his long legs to my pace. I shot him a go-to-hell look, mostly because I was ridiculously attracted to him and his sexy eyes and his jagged scar on his neck, and I didn't want to be. I didn't have any business getting mixed up with anyone right now, and especially not with a hot-as-sin hockey player with brown eyes that made me want to do anything for him and biceps that made my toes curl.

He shrugged. "We could sit and talk for a while."

Sit and talk for a while. Yeah, *that* was what he wanted from me. He wanted me to open up all my ugly wounds again and bleed out all over him. I'd almost done it in there, too, because he'd been looking at me like he actually cared.

That was bullshit. No one cared.

"I don't want to talk." Talking didn't help, anyway. It only brought everything back to the forefront. Stifling me. Suffocating me. I was doing all of those things well enough on my own without trying to talk about it.

The only reason I'd come to this stupid support group was because my doctors said if I didn't make some sort of effort, they were going to shut me away in the loony bin again. That wouldn't help anything, so I'd begrudgingly agreed to attend the meetings. Rick had let me keep my space in his shop after the first time I'd had to go to inpatient therapy, but I didn't have any delusions that he'd hold on to it for me again. He might think of me as a daughter more than an apprentice, but he had to make money, too. And if a space in his tattoo shop was empty, he wasn't making any money from it.

So I'd come to this group, hoping I could sit in the back and pretend I was anywhere else, and then have the counselors sign off on my form to prove that I'd attended.

Until that wiseass counselor had decided to drag me into the conversation, and I'd freaked out. I sure as hell didn't need *this* guy trying to pull that shit with me on a one-on-one basis, and that was exactly what he was going for. I could tell from the way he kept staring at me with those deep, concerned eyes.

I couldn't deal, so I kept heading for my car.

Drew walked a bit faster, his long legs making it easy for him to overtake me. Once he was in front of me, he turned around and walked backward so he could face me. Those big brown eyes pierced me. Gutted me. Christ, the way he had looked at me in that meeting had nearly made me tell him everything, and now he was trying that shit on me again.

I had to get away from him. Now.

I walked faster, doing my damnedest to ignore how hot he was when he was pretending to be a good guy who just wanted to help me out.

He had to be pretending. I knew that with complete and utter certainty. Good guys didn't exist anywhere other than in fiction, and no one could make up the shit I'd been through. If they did, no one would believe it.

Well, for the most part, they didn't exist. Rick was an anomaly—the one truly decent man I'd ever encountered. I wouldn't bother trying to convince myself there could be more like him.

"Then what do you want?" he asked.

I shook my head. The man just didn't get it. He thought that because he was some sexy pro athlete, he could get anything he wanted. That he could make the world a better place just with a snap of his fingers. And maybe that was how it worked in his world.

I didn't live in his world, though. In *my* world, life sucked and then you died. The sooner he came to understand that was how things worked for me, the sooner he would drop the good guy act and leave me the hell alone.

"I want you out of my way," I finally said.

"Come on." He cocked his head to the side. "Everyone wants something. What do you want?"

"Doesn't matter." Life had already proven to me time and again that what I wanted wasn't important. I couldn't have what I wanted. Not in any meaningful way. As soon as I got my fingers on it, whatever *it* might be, the universe ripped it away and stomped on me in the process, making sure to keep me down where I belonged. In the gutters. The sewers. Where all the shit and piss and everything else bad gathered. I was like a magnet for the shitty things in life.

"Matters to me," he said.

"Bullshit. There's no reason I should matter to you." I clicked the button on my key fob to unlock my car doors.

He swiveled his head around at the sound, then turned back to me and came to a stop. If I kept going, I'd run straight into him. I took the path to go around him, but he reached out and put a hand on my elbow—just enough of a touch for me to recognize it, but it stopped me in my tracks.

I shot my head over to stare at him, those damned tears pricking at my eyes again. I glared in an effort to have my anger burn away the need to have a good sob fest. My chest rose and fell hard and fast from the effort to keep it all inside. That was the only way I felt safe anymore—when it was all bottled up inside me, nothing seeping out for the rest of the world to see. But it was getting more and more difficult to keep a lid on things. I was like a pressure cooker, ready to blow at the slightest provocation, and this guy was giving me more of that than was healthy for either of us. If he was smart, he'd back off.

He didn't move, not even with my death glare fully unleashed on him. I took a quick look around the parking lot. Everyone else who'd been in that meeting was already gone. There were still people in the building, though. I could go back in there and tell that London chick he was harassing me or something. She could call the cops for me. That'd probably be enough to get this Drew Nash character and his gorgeous, sexy, compassionate eyes to leave me the fuck alone.

His eyes were dangerous for me. Mainly because I was falling headfirst into them.

He put his hand back down at his side, making a visible show of *not* touching me without my permission. "You matter to me because I don't think anyone should be alone when they're…like this," he finished, waving a hand to encompass me.

"When they're as clearly fucked up as I am, you mean."

"I've been there, too. And I had friends who wouldn't stop bugging the shit out of me, even when I threatened to throat-punch them, when I was this messed up. But I get the sense that you don't have anyone in your life like that right now."

"Which is how I want it." I knew Rick cared, but he'd never been in my face about it.

"I don't buy that for a second. Maybe you think it's better for you to be all alone, but it's not. And somewhere, deep down, you don't want to be alone. You want someone to come along and demand to be part of your life even when you do everything in your power to push them away."

I rolled my eyes. "You don't know jack shit about me."

"Maybe not. Prove me wrong." And then he stood there, looking all determined and helpful and caring and sexy, with his square jaw and that purple-pink scar on his neck. Despite myself, I wanted to know how he'd gotten that scar.

"I don't want to prove you wrong. I don't want to have anything to do with you." But the words came out strangled, like I was choking on them.

"Then tell me what you want. Anything. Anything at all. And if I can make it happen, I will."

"You know what I want?" I said, without taking the necessary time to think things through. "For just once, I want to be able to feel good enough that I could forget how unfair life is, even if it's only for five minutes. That's what I want. But you can't make that happen. No one can."

I should've just kept my mouth shut, because he looked like he wanted to settle in and keep me talking, now that I'd gotten started. "I don't know." Drew leaned against the hood of my car, making himself at home. He crossed his arms in front of him, crossed his ankles, totally relaxing. It made him look good enough to eat. "What makes you feel good?"

You could, I thought to myself. Good thing I didn't say it out loud. "Nothing," I said, forcing myself to look anywhere but at him. Because looking at him was getting me into trouble. It was leading me to say all sorts of things that were better left locked up inside me.

"Nothing?" he repeated. Hell, he even had a sexy voice. It was deep and a bit scratchy, but there was a hint of laughter in it. I never found much to laugh about, so that was a complete turn-on. This guy was really bad news for me. "Not spring rainstorms? Puppies or kittens, maybe baby bunnies? Hot sex?"

I whipped my head around at his mention of sex, but he immediately looked like he wanted to backtrack.

"Sorry, I didn't mean—"

"Sex could make me feel good," I cut in. Temporarily, at least. For those few moments that it lasted, I could just let myself feel on a physical level and forget everything else that I'd bottled up inside.

"I don't— I wasn't— I'm not trying to get you to do anyth—"

"Sorry," I cut in. "I wasn't thinking." Well, hell. I didn't know much of anything about this guy other than the fact that he was doing a number on me just by existing and he'd been at this support group meeting. That wasn't enough to know that *he* had HIV, though. Some of the people in there had just been friends and family of people with HIV. I shouldn't jump to that conclusion. "I just assumed you had HIV, too, since you were in that meeting, but—"

"I do have HIV," he said, and I did a double take. "Got it from my ex. She was cheating on me."

"Oh." And now I was back to thinking about sex with him again. And wanting it. I wanted it a hell of a lot more than was good for me.

"I just don't want you to think that I'm trying to get into your pants. Because I'm not. That's not what this is about."

"Are you taking sex off the table?" I demanded. "Because think about it. How often will either of us ever be able to think about casual sex again? We don't have to worry about infecting each other." I shrugged, trying to convince myself that anything about this was casual, even though everything inside me was going haywire. I hadn't had sex with anyone since I'd gotten the courage to leave Jax even though I didn't have anywhere to go, and I *definitely* hadn't had sex since I'd gotten the diagnosis.

There weren't too many people out there who wanted sex—casual or otherwise—with someone who was HIV-positive, and I wasn't in any shape emotionally to get involved with someone for more than a fling or a one-night stand.

The idea that I might be able to have a physical connection with someone, once it had gotten into my head, had quickly taken over all my thoughts. Now it looked like I was bound to be disappointed again. Just one more thing to add to my list of things about life that sucked. "If you're not down—"

"I didn't say that," Drew cut in. "It's just… Are you sure? You don't even know me."

And I didn't intend to *know* him, either. Not the way he meant. I only wanted to know him for a night. Or an afternoon, I supposed. "You said if you could make it happen, you would. So are you a liar or what?"

For a long minute, Drew stared at me with that piercing gaze. It went on so long that I rolled my eyes and made for my car door.

But he put out a hand and grabbed hold of my elbow. Even that small touch was more than I'd had from another human in so long it almost choked me up again, but somehow I swallowed it down.

"Come with me," he said.

If I couldn't even handle this man taking hold of my elbow without nearly losing it, how the hell was I going to get through the sex I'd all but demanded of him? But now that it was within my grasp, I couldn't pass it up.

I nodded. "I'm coming."

He moved his hand down to take hold of mine, and I knew, without a doubt, that I was making a massive mistake.

Damn if I did anything to stop myself, though. One more thing I could add to my list of mistakes I made when I was young and stupid. Of course, I wasn't sure I'd live to see old and wise.

Three

Drew

WHEN WE PULLED up in front of my house in the Brookside neighborhood of Tulsa, Ravyn was clutching the double-folded strap of her purse so tightly that her knuckles had turned white. She hadn't said much the whole way back to my house, and now I was starting to think she'd changed her mind about coming back to my place, after all. I probably shouldn't have gone along with her suggestion so readily, but she'd finally started talking to me a bit and I'd been willing to go along with almost anything if it meant learning more about who she was and why she was so nervous.

Besides, she had a point about casual sex. I hadn't dated at all in the two years since my divorce. I'd come a long way in terms of accepting my new lot in life as far as how living with HIV affected *me*, but I hadn't made any strides at all in the direction of determining what sort of woman would be willing to risk contracting it in order to have a relationship with me. Most of the other attendees of the support group were either gay or already in relationships, so Ravyn was my best option—at least in the short term.

So, other than a somewhat protracted moment of hesitation, I hadn't thought twice about it once she'd thrown the idea out there.

Probably a bad idea, and I knew it, but I hadn't listened to my gut. Sex wasn't the answer for anything. I should know. It hadn't fixed my marriage. If anything, it had put the final nail in the coffin.

I put the car in park in the driveway and faced Ravyn. "I'm sorry. This was a bad idea. I shouldn't have—"

"Are you seriously trying to back out of this again?" she demanded, eyes flashing blue fire. "If you're not into me, just say so and take me back so I can get in my car and go home, all right? I seriously don't need this kind of blow to my ego right now, so—"

"I didn't say I'm not into you."

She scowled and raised a brow. "You didn't say you are, either. Which is fine. I get it. The tattoos. The purple dreads. We won't even mention the piercings. I completely understand that I'm not everyone's—"

"I'm into you," I interrupted, my curiosity piqued by her mention of piercings.

I gave her another once-over. She had a couple of piercings in each ear, but nothing too shocking or surprising. They were all I could see, so I could only imagine she had other piercings hidden in places her clothes kept covered.

"I am," I insisted when she didn't look convinced. I

was a hell of a lot more into her than I understood, to be honest, so I could completely understand why she was so skeptical right now. Especially since I had to be coming across as hesitant. But my reluctance was only because I didn't want to push her into something she didn't want. "I just— You seem nervous. And why shouldn't you? I mean, you don't know me, so—"

"I know what I want," she cut in. Her lips were in a thin line, the hot pink of her lipstick seeming even brighter against her porcelain skin than it would on most of the overly tanned women around here. "I'm not having second thoughts or anything. That's *you*."

If I was having second thoughts, it was only because she was acting like she'd rather be anywhere else. "You're sure?"

"I'm sure I don't want to keep sitting here in your driveway with all your neighbors looking at me."

At that, I blinked in surprise and took a quick glance around. No one was out and about. It was a Tuesday around lunchtime. Almost everyone who lived near me was at work. There weren't any cars on the street or people walking their dogs on the sidewalk. "No one's looking," I pointed out.

"Not where you can see them, no." She rolled her eyes. "But I promise, they'll notice some chick with purple dreads and piercings and tattoos lurking around outside your house. People like me aren't welcome in neighborhoods like this. So can we go inside or something? Or just take me back to my car, because they'll probably call the cops soon."

"But you're with me," I said. It was true, she didn't exactly look like the upper-middle-class suburban housewives of my neighborhood, who wore designer yoga pants to walk their toy-sized dogs, but that was no good reason for anyone to call the police.

My argument fell on deaf ears. Ravyn tightened her grip on her purse and wrapped her arms across her chest.

Fuck me, this wasn't going well. I hit the button on my remote to raise the garage door, making sure to close it again once I had the car parked inside. "Come on," I said, waiting for Ravyn to come around the front of my car to join me. I held out a hand for her, but she kept hugging her purse to her body instead of reaching for me.

This wasn't going to be easy. Something told me nothing involving Ravyn would be easy. Maybe that was why I was so intrigued. I'd never been one to pass up a challenge. It wasn't in my nature.

I led her inside and headed for the kitchen, making a beeline for the fridge. "You hungry?" I asked. "Or need a drink? I don't have anything with sugar in it, but I've got some cold water in the fridge. Not much of a cook, but I can put together a sandwich easy enough. Or I have some chicken I could toss on the grill…" I took out a couple of bottles of water, popping one open for myself and taking a swig.

She didn't answer right away, so I turned around to find her checking out the open kitchen and living room in obvious awe. It was a big house, to be sure, but it wasn't like I lived in a mansion, so I wasn't sure what the fascination was. I made a good living from playing hockey, and my lawyer had managed to reduce Chelsea's alimony award due to the fact that her cheating had brought HIV into our marriage—something she and I would both have to live with for the rest of our lives—so she hadn't walked away with too much of my earnings. But no matter how nice my house was, it wasn't anything to gawk at. Or at least I didn't think it was. Maybe in Ravyn's world, things were significantly different.

"Ravyn?" I asked again, holding out one of the bottles of water. "You hungry?"

"I didn't come here for you to feed me," she said, shaking her head like she couldn't believe what I was saying.

"No, I don't suppose you did." I couldn't help but feel a bit disappointed, too, which didn't make any sense. We both knew why she was here.

She took the water from me, though, and loosened the lid. When she took a sip, she eyed me over the top of the bottle. "You don't have to keep playing the good guy, you know."

I didn't know what to make of that response. At all. "What are you talking about?" I wasn't playing at being a good guy. Hell, I'd only met her a few hours ago, and I'd brought her back to my place for sex. What kind of good guy did that? None that I knew of, which only made me feel worse about the fact that I'd done it.

But she shook her head and looked out the windows into my backyard and the pool. "So where's your bedroom?"

She sure didn't seem to mess around with anything, did she? That said, her bluntness was refreshing. I hated being given the runaround. Chelsea'd given me more than enough of that to last a lifetime. I didn't get the sense that would ever be a concern with Ravyn. She might not be forthcoming with every tiny detail of her life, but why should she be? There was no reason for her to open up the closet of her past and give me the proverbial tour, tossing a welcome mat down at my feet.

Keeping a few things close to her chest was normal. It was smart. But in other ways, she laid everything out there, for me to take as I would. Too bad there weren't more people in this world who did that.

I took my water with me and headed down the hall. "Come on. I'll show you."

She didn't waste any time, following close on my heels as I led her to my bedroom. Once we got there, I set my water bottle on the nightstand while she looked around, kind of like she'd done in the kitchen and living room. I apparently hadn't closed the closet door this morning when I'd left, so she could see all the way in there. I took a moment to chuckle to myself over the irony of the situation—me, leaving my closet open so she could see all the skeletons in there. Not that there was anything she could truly learn about me from my closet. It was a big walk-in that wasn't even close to being full since Chelsea's stuff had never been moved in.

Then her eyes landed on the *en suite* bathroom. Admittedly, it was enormous, with a separate shower and garden tub, his-and-hers sinks, and a separate room for the toilet. That had been one of the selling points for Chelsea when we'd bought the place. All the space and separation meant we could both be getting ready without one having to wait for the other to get out of the way. But we'd divorced before she ever moved in. With it being only me, it felt like overkill. But it was mine.

I tried to read what was going on in Ravyn's mind while she checked out my things, since she wasn't talking, but she was an impenetrable wall, her face a perfect mask of nothingness. Was it nerves that had her so silent now? Or was it something else?

But then she turned so she was fully facing me, stripped off her shirt and let it fall to the floor next to her feet.

Not gonna lie. My mouth watered at the sight of her bare torso and her breasts straining to come free from her bra. "Not wasting any time, hmm?" I said, trying to keep things light.

If she was already feeling jumpy, then the last thing I needed to do was add to her anxiety. There was no stopping my eyes from roving over her body, though. There was a silver ring with a purple jewel in her belly button. So I'd found at least one of her hidden piercings. My mouth watered as I wondered how many others I might find and just how deeply hidden they might be.

I stopped my inspection for a moment, landing my eyes on a colorful Japanese dragon tattoo down the side of her ribs. When I moved on, it was to discover more colorful ink peeking out from beneath the cup of her bra. I couldn't tell what that one was, though. There wasn't enough showing. But damn if I wasn't curious as all hell.

Unlike most of my teammates, I didn't have any ink. My parents were pretty straight-laced, and a lot of their conservative, traditional values had rubbed off on me. I'd thought about getting a tattoo a couple of times, but I'd always chickened out before actually going through with it.

And now that I was HIV-positive, I didn't know if I even *should.* I mean, yeah, they used clean equipment and whatnot, so theoretically I shouldn't be putting anyone at risk. But still. There would be a needle puncturing my skin over and over again. In a situation like that, there's bound to be blood. Better safe than sorry, right? Some risks just didn't need to be taken, and I'd already put too many peoples' lives at risk out of my own selfishness. No need to add to that list over something as silly as getting ink on my skin.

She shrugged, deflecting my attention for the moment. "Don't see the point in wasting time. This is what we're here for, isn't it?"

"I guess so," I said with a wink. For now, she seemed to be relaxed enough. I wanted to keep things that way, so I reached overhead and drew my shirt up from behind, the way I'd always done.

Now it was Ravyn's turn to check me out. She wouldn't be finding any ink on me, but she seemed interested enough, anyway, her gaze landing on my biceps for a bit before skittering across to take in my shoulders and down to my abs. She licked her lips. I had to assume she liked what she saw, especially with the way her chest was starting to rise and fall with greater frequency.

She reached behind her back to undo her bra, but I didn't want to rush this.

"Wait," I said, inching closer.

She dropped her hands to her sides like she'd just been caught raiding the cookie jar, chest heaving. "Is something wrong?"

I closed some more of the distance between us, trying to figure out what I wanted with stopping her. "Not wrong, no. I just thought…I could help you." My gaze fell to her chest again, and particularly to that tattoo that was peeking out from over the top of her bra. I reached out a hand to trace a finger along the delicate fabric.

When I glanced up, her eyes had darkened, and her lips were slightly open. Her desire was palpable, thickening the air between us. Mine wasn't far behind. "What's the tattoo of?" I asked, my fingertip teasing the black outline surrounding the bold pinks, purples, and greens.

She hesitated. It wasn't just something I'd imagined, either. Her jaw had dropped for a flicker of a moment, at the same time as something flashed in her eyes. It was gone as soon as it came, though, and she said, "Why don't you see for yourself?"

Was I wrong about my earlier assessment, then? Maybe she wasn't going to be quite so upfront about things as I'd initially thought. But then again, tattoos could be very personal. I knew that, even though I didn't have any of my own. Just talking to a few of the guys about theirs was enough to educate me on the matter. And while Ravyn's tattoos could just be for decoration, something told me there was a hell of a lot more to them than simply making a fashion statement.

Which meant I needed to not make a big deal out of them if I ever wanted to learn what they were. Time to turn on the charm. My lips curled upward in a seductive smile as I slipped the strap off her shoulder and tugged the cup down, revealing a pink heart entwined with a purple and green triangle. The symbol of adoption. I'd recognize it anywhere since it was all over my sister's house. Melody and her husband, Shawn, had adopted two toddler girls a little over a year ago after several failed attempts with fertility treatments.

The tattoo covered quite a bit of Ravyn's left breast, falling directly over her heart.

She attempted to distract me, flicking a finger over her taut nipple and drawing my eye to the piercing there. It didn't quite work the way she wanted it to, even though I liked what I saw a hell of a lot more than

I expected to. But she didn't do a damned thing to explain the tattoo. Probably hoping I didn't know what it meant, I'd guess.

But even though I knew what it was a symbol for, I didn't know why she'd have it etched onto her body. Had she been adopted? Or maybe someone she knew? There was no way to know unless she told me, and it didn't appear she was in the mood to do so.

I traced over her ink with the nail of a finger, leaving a path of goose bumps behind on her skin. Her tit puckered even more, and she sucked in a breath.

"What does it mean?" I asked softly, nudging the other strap down so I could free her other breast—also pierced, my dick was happy to report. Not that I expected her to answer. Still—I wanted to know. Wanted her to tell me. To trust me enough to let down some of her guard. I knew it was crazy to want that. Hell, I didn't know her. Didn't know a damned thing about her, really. But there was no denying I was drawn to her.

But she didn't answer me. Instead, she wrapped both arms around my neck, stretched up onto the tips of her toes, and kissed me.

I let out a surprised moan, but it didn't take me long at all to get with the program, picking her up by the waist and crushing her against my chest. She hardly weighed a thing. Her breasts and hips were full, but the rest of her was thin as a waif. But she didn't give me the chance to linger on that, kissing me with an intensity I hadn't known I was missing until right this moment.

Our lips met with almost bruising fervor, then our tongues tangled and teeth clashed. She dug her fingers into my traps, rubbing those pierced tits up and down my chest until my skin felt raw, but I still wanted more.

Faster. Harder. Christ, that was hot.

I kneaded her ass, grinding her softness against my cock. She responded by biting my lower lip and suckling it into her mouth to soothe the ache. Her hands were everywhere. Exploring my chest and arms. Dragging my head down to wherever she wanted me. Reaching for the waistband of my jeans.

"Fuck me," she said, her voice husky. "Please. I need you to fuck me."

There wasn't a chance in hell I could tell her no.

Four

Ravyn

HE'D KEPT LOOKING at the tattoo on my chest and asking questions—about it, about me—but I didn't have any way to answer him. That was why I'd thrown myself at him. At least at first. But now his big, strong arms were all around me, and he was so damn hard all over, and it wasn't about avoiding awkward questions anymore.

It was about scratching an itch I didn't believe, at least up until a little while ago, I'd ever have properly scratched again. It was about letting this Greek sculpture come to life do what he'd told me he could do and make me *feel good*, or at least try to. It was about escaping from the hell that was my life for a little while since everyone knew escaping it permanently wasn't an option, outside of ending things.

Drew might be a lot more vanilla than any of the men in my life, considering his lack of ink and piercings and his perfectly naturally colored hair, but that was probably for the best. My judgment, when it came to men, was worse than poor.

Now, if he could fuck even half as well as he kissed, I thought we might get on all right. At least for this one afternoon hookup.

Because that was all this was. A way to blow off some steam and let go of some tension before real life reared its ugly head again and dragged me back down.

He carried me a few steps and set me on the bed. He'd barely let go of me before I grabbed at his jeans—I'd already undone the button and fly while we were making out—and dragged them down his hips along with his briefs.

When he stepped out of them, though, he moved out of my reach. I started to go after him, but he shook his head and held out a hand to stop me. "I'm coming right back," he said with a wink as he headed for the bathroom. A moment later, he returned with a condom.

Yeah. Probably good thinking. I really shouldn't be allowed to make adult decisions sometimes, because the thought of protection had never crossed my mind. We might not have to worry about giving each other HIV, but that didn't mean there weren't plenty of other reasons to practice safe sex.

Not the least of which was pregnancy. Of all the people in the world, I should have thought of that.

I pressed my eyes closed, silently remonstrating myself for sheer and utter stupidity.

"You okay?" he asked. And damn if he didn't sound concerned. *Again.* Why the hell did he have to keep up with the good guy act? Good guys didn't exist in the real world, and even if they did, I didn't want him to be one right now. I wanted him to do dirty, dirty things to me, and good guys didn't do dirty, dirty things to anyone. They *made love* and other bullshit like that.

I fluttered my eyes open again and met his gaze, slipping my shorts free from my hips and kicking them away. "Fine. Amazing," I forced out. At least, I intended to be amazing very soon, even if I wasn't there yet. This guy had better not be a bad lay, because I needed a good orgasm right now more than I needed my next breath. I hadn't had decent sex, let alone mind-blowing sex, in so long I wasn't even sure it was possible for me anymore, and there was no telling when I'd have my next opportunity.

"I'm clean, other than the HIV," he said. "But you already know about that. Still, no point taking chances."

I blinked. Again with him thinking like an adult and acting like a good guy. I didn't know what to do with him, other than knock his legs out from under him so we could get on with the dirty stuff. His good guy act was only serving to remind me how bad I was, not to mention how stupid I was acting by coming home with him. I didn't like it. "I'm clean, too," I said, reaching for him.

But he nodded and stayed out of my grasp like a pro. What the hell? Still, even I had to admit it was crazy that either of us would just take the word of the other over something like STDs, but that was exactly what we appeared to be doing. At least we were using protection. We weren't being complete and total idiots. Only mostly idiots.

If we ever got on with it.

He might not be letting me rush him, but a moment

later, his attention dropped to the space between my legs. Or, more specifically, to my piercing.

"No fucking way." His cock had already been at full attention, but it jerked and bobbed a couple of times as he stared. "Doesn't that hurt? That's got to hurt."

"Life is pain, Highness," I replied, the words slipping out before I could stop them.

He quirked up a grin, so at least he was taking it well. "You just threw a *Princess Bride* reference at me?"

"Guess so." I winked. But I damn sure wasn't going to slip up and say anything like *As you wish* to him on accident. No reason to let the guy get any crazy ideas about things, and if he knew one quote from that movie, he was bound to know what they all meant. "Besides," I said, "everything worth having in life hurts." And a hell of a lot of other things hurt, too, if truth be told.

He shot those big, brown eyes up to meet mine, his brow etched with unease. I should've kept my damned mouth shut after the movie quote. I didn't want him to keep pretending to be sweet and caring and all that bullshit.

"It hurt at first," I hurried to say before he could delve any deeper. No need to dig into the past when I only wanted sex from him. A good fucking orgasm, damn it. That was what I needed, nothing more and nothing less. "Now it just makes everything feel better."

"Everything?" he repeated, cocking a brow.

I tugged him toward me, urging his hand down to my pussy. He explored the piercing with his fingers, spreading my natural wetness around. I let out a moan, somewhat surprised by how ready I was despite having barely gotten started. I dropped my head back against the mattress. "Makes me more sensitive. There's always pressure on my clit from the bar, always contact, so I feel every touch just a bit more than I would otherwise." Or a lot more. Whichever.

"Is that why you pierced your nipples, too?" He kept swirling the pad of one finger around my clit in gentle circles, with just enough tension for me to know he was there but not enough to really get me off, easing his other hand toward my tit. He caressed my breast with the slightest pressure, like he was afraid he'd hurt me.

"They're more sensitive now, too," I said, having a hard time remembering to breathe because he was driving me to distraction, trying to carry on a conversation while working my body to a fever pitch. If I wasn't careful, I'd end up saying something I'd regret.

"Mm hmm," he murmured, continuing to torment me with delicate caresses. Hell, he hadn't even tried to slip a finger inside me yet, but I was so wet and swollen I could probably take his whole hand without straining.

Apparently he was in the mood for a slow tease, not hard and fast, wham, bam, thank you, ma'am. I didn't want slow, careful, cautious sex. I wanted rough, filthy, wild sex. His current pace didn't line up very well with my plans for how this should go. Not at all. It gave him too many opportunities to try to get past my defenses, and I couldn't allow that to happen.

I sat upright on the bed, grasping his erection firmly in my hand. And then, before he could voice a complaint, I took him in my mouth.

He groaned, but it definitely didn't sound like a complaint. Not only that, but he put a hand on the back of my head. Not forcing me to take him deeper but softly guiding my efforts as I worked him over.

Everything with him seemed to be firm but gentle. Fuck that. I wanted to drive him crazy. I wanted him to lose the thin rein of control holding him back. Nothing turned me on more than a man who was so fueled by lust that he forgot to be careful with me, and right now, Drew was being far too considerate.

His cock was already weeping, the pre-cum salty on my tongue. I swirled my tongue around his head a few times, drawing carnal sounds from his throat. Then I took him as deep as I could, using my hand to stroke the base of him while I sucked like my life depended on it.

It didn't take too much of that before I could sense the difference in his response. A bit more of this, and he'd be like putty, willing to just get on with things like I wanted.

The hand at the back of my head fisted around some of my dreads, growing more demanding by the moment. I gave him a gentle tug on his sac. His balls drew up, tightening like he was about to come, so I backed off and tightened my fingers into a circle around his base, like a cock ring, and kept sucking and swirling my tongue around his head. Sure enough, he swelled even more, and he added his other hand to my hair, directing my movements more vigorously. But my pressure at the base of his cock also held him off from coming too soon.

"Fuck, baby, that's too good," he rasped.

No such thing as too good. Especially not if it got me what I needed—and this was having the desired effect, so I had no intention of changing what I was doing.

But then something…shifted, I supposed was the right word. I couldn't be sure *what*, exactly, but he released my hair and ran his hands over my body while I continued to work him over. My neck. My back. The dip of my shoulder. My breasts. His touch was firm but gentle, just like always, exploratory yet knowing at once. His fingers grazed my nipples, which were already taut and peaked.

I shuddered, my moan a strangled whimper over his length.

A few more touches like that, and I'd lose whatever control I might have over the situation—I'd become his to mold and do with as he would. A dangerous thought. I refocused my energy on driving him mad with need, but too late.

Drew backed away, one hand cupping my cheek, the other putting firm pressure on my shoulder. "Lie down for me," he said, his voice gruff with need.

I didn't want to do that yet unless he planned to climb on top of me and screw me into oblivion. But I did what I was told—a bad habit that I intended to figure out how to break one of these days. Then again, the one time I'd broken it, I'd probably made the biggest mistake of my life. Maybe I should keep doing what I was told and forget about trying to rebel. Was twenty-three too old to be rebellious? I wasn't sure.

When he kneeled between my legs and lowered his mouth to the space between my thighs, all thoughts raced out of my head like a Kenyan marathoner in the Summer Games.

I still didn't have any clue about his skill with his dick, but the man could compete in the Cunnilingus World Championships and probably come away with the win. He shifted my body around, drawing my thighs up over his shoulders so he could perform his magic. When he worked a couple of fingers inside me while his tongue flicked over my clit, it was all I could do not to leap off the bed. My breaths came in sharp, whimpering bursts, and I white-knuckled the blankets beneath me with both hands.

He sucked the barbell between his lips and held it there while he lashed my clit with his tongue, over and over again. All the while, he kept curling his fingers up inside me, brushing them against my G-spot.

And then I cried out, erupting into climax as my toes curled in toward his shoulder blades and the rest of my bones went limp. But still, he didn't stop. Yeah, I was a goner. I only hoped he kept going with the sexcapades and didn't decide it was time for a good ol' talk.

After an orgasm like that, I wasn't sure I could handle another right away. When I'd gotten my piercings, I'd meant it to heighten my sensitivity. When I'd been with Jax, I'd always assumed the reason I rarely reached orgasm was my body's slow build combined with his inability to care about my pleasure in his drugged-out state—or his inability to keep it up, also due to his drugged-out state—and so I'd decided to take matters into my own hands as often as possible. The piercings had certainly helped, and I found myself in a sexual state of nirvana when we were together at least occasionally. It happened a lot more often when I was alone than when I was with him, but at least it sometimes happened when I was with him. But I would never have assumed myself to be multi-orgasmic. Not in a million years.

Drew took away all my doubts on that score, not allowing me to come down too far from my initial crest before building me up for the next one. Maybe the problem hadn't been my lack of sensitivity, after all, although I wouldn't complain about the enhancements now. Not when I was reaching heights I'd never imagined possible.

By the time he finally crawled up my body with a shit-eating grin, he had me on the verge of a second powerful climax. Seriously, two or three good thrusts, and I'd explode again. I was starting to think my decision to come home with him had been a good one, after all, even if on the surface it seemed like I was being stupid.

Drew tore open the wrapper to the condom and unrolled it over his length before settling his hips between my thighs. He reached between us to fit himself to my entrance, and I drew up my knees so I could take him deep.

We both moaned in sync as he filled me. Then he stilled for a moment, both of us taking some time to adjust to the sensation.

"You're so damn tight," he said.

I made the mistake of looking into his eyes. His brows were drawn together, creasing his forehead in concentration, like he was still trying to hold himself back.

"Fuck me," I begged, sure that now he would finally forget all about his efforts to take things slow, to treat me gently.

But he didn't. He kept staring down at me, those brown eyes probing me and forcing me to look away. I ground my hips against him, raised my legs higher to take him deeper, raked my nails over his ass, and drew him closer. Everything I did was meant to drive him out of his mind with need. None of it mattered. The only one out of their mind was me, and that was nothing new.

When he finally moved, it wasn't in the way I wanted or expected. Instead of drawing back to thrust home repeatedly, he shifted his angle, crawling up my body so his pelvic bone was positioned immediately over my clit. Then he rocked back and forth, grinding against me. He lowered his mouth to mine and kissed me, his tongue swirling lazily around mine, his teeth taking small nibbles out of my lips until I broke into a thousand pieces, stars shattering behind my eyes. It was more exquisite than anything I'd ever felt—and more intimate than I could afford.

But damn if I could do anything to stop him from breaking me. Not right now. All I could do was bask in the reverent way he touched me and try my best not to lose any of the pieces of my heart he had chipped free. Maybe later I could glue myself back together again. Sometime when he wasn't trying to stare his way into my soul and kiss his way into my heart.

My body was still tremoring from my latest climax when he buried his face against my neck, pressed himself deep, and went still, an erotic groan tickling my ear.

Both of us breathing hard and covered in a sheen of sweat, we lay like that for a few moments. I pressed my eyes closed, determined not to lose myself in what had just happened. It was sex. Nothing more.

But then he pressed a soft kiss to the spot just behind my ear and rolled off me, dragging me back against him as though to spoon with me.

Cuddling was not part of the deal.

I eased myself out of his arms and off the bed.

"Not yet," he complained, reaching for me.

There wasn't a chance in hell I would let him drag me back into his embrace right now. Not while my hormones were going haywire like this. "Bathroom. Have to pee," I muttered before rushing in there. Which, admittedly, I did need to pee. Besides, it was only smart, if I wanted to avoid yet another UTI. That was true for all women, whether they had HIV or not, and he didn't need to know that there was more to my rushing off than that. Since he was HIV-positive, too, he probably knew I had the potential of being more prone to them than the average healthy woman, anyway, so we could just leave it at that.

Once I was alone, I pressed my forehead against the cool surface of the closed door and tried to gather my wits.

Just sex. That was all it was. That was all it *could* be, even if this guy seemed determined to make it more. I took a few deep breaths and straightened away from the door, then took care of my business. I found a clean washcloth and cleaned myself up some and washed my hands when I was finished.

When I went back into his bedroom, Drew was sitting up in his bed, still naked and looking like absolute perfection. He'd disposed of the condom, but he didn't look like he was in any big hurry to do anything else.

He grinned at me—slow and sexy and natural—and he patted the spot next to him, encouraging me to sit next to him. "I was starting to think you'd fallen in."

If I joined him, would he try to snuggle with me again? I couldn't rule it out, and I couldn't let it happen. I shrugged. "Just needed a minute. Girl stuff." Then I bent to the floor to pick up my clothes.

"You have somewhere you have to be?" he asked. Damn if he didn't sound disappointed, too.

"Not right away, but I've got to work later, and I need to run a few errands beforehand." Which was a complete and total lie. Rick's entire shop was closed on Tuesdays, and I took Wednesdays off, too. The only thing I needed to do was get away from Drew.

"Damn," he said. "Do you have time for me to make you lunch? Or we could go out somewhere. I could—"

"You don't have to feed me," I cut in. "We already went over that. This was just about sex. Nothing more. You don't owe me anything for a fuck. It was given of my own free will." I didn't even attempt to hide my aggravation.

"All right." He sounded hurt, damn it all. But he got up and started gathering his clothes off the floor, too.

I turned around to slip into my panties and bra, not because I was feeling shy or anything like that but because I couldn't deal with the way he was *still* looking at me. Like he wanted to fix me or some shit. The sooner he understood I wasn't fixable, the better off he'd be. But once he got me back to my car, I probably wouldn't ever have to worry about it again. I'd gone to that stupid meeting and my form was signed for my doctor. I could take it back and tell him that I wouldn't be returning, so he'd have to come up with some other option. Not that I had a clue what it was, but whether I could deal with the group therapy or not, there was no chance I could handle facing Drew again.

He wanted to undo me. I could feel it. The problem was, I'd already been broken apart so many times there wouldn't be any chance of putting me back together again before too long. I was a regular ol' Humpty Dumpty in ink and dreads, and Drew was only a single guy, not a whole slew of horses and men.

I slipped my tank top over my head and eased into my shorts, trying not to let myself think too hard. About anything. By the time I had my shoes on again, Drew was fully dressed.

He shoved his hands into his pockets. "So you want

me to take you back to your car, then?"

I nodded. Didn't trust my voice right now. The way he had been treating me since we'd first met was doing crazy things to me, and I didn't think I could hold it together if I started talking.

The whole way back to the community center, we were both silent. There wasn't anything to say, as far as I was concerned.

"You coming back next week?" he asked as he turned into the parking lot. I didn't miss the fact that his voice cracked a bit over the words. I shot my gaze over to him, trying to figure out what he was upset about, but I couldn't read anything in his expression.

I shrugged. "Maybe. Not sure yet."

"You should. Why don't you give me your number? I could come and pick you up."

Make sure I came—and stayed—more like. "That's my car over there," I said in response, pointing to my beat-up Ford that was as old as I was. But at least it ran.

"I remember." He pulled into the spot next to it and put his car in park. "Is that your way of telling me to fuck off and leave you alone?"

Yes. But I had to admit, I felt like a bitch for it. My mouth was half-open, the words on my tongue refusing to come out, when I saw that pregnant London chick wheeling out of the front doors of the community center like she was in a wheelchair race. "What…" I couldn't finish the sentence, but I pointed to send Drew's attention in her direction.

A couple of other people rushed out of the building behind her, but she didn't slow down, making a beeline for one of the cars parked in a handicapped spot out front.

Drew's eyes nearly bugged out of his head. "What

the fuck?" he shouted, throwing his car door open and rushing over to find out what was going on.

I couldn't seem to stop myself. I followed him, running almost as fast.

"She's in labor," a woman called out across the parking lot.

London had jerked open the door to the car and was trying to transfer her very pregnant body inside the driver's seat.

"What the hell do you think you're doing?" Drew growled at her.

"Going to the hospital. Water broke."

He sighed and turned to the other people who'd followed her out of the building. "I've got this. You guys can get back to work."

"You sure?" the woman asked, looking wary.

He nodded, but he didn't look happy about it. Not at all. "Well, how far apart are the contractions?" he demanded.

"Hell if I know." She had forgotten to use the brake on her chair, and it was moving too much for her to complete the transfer. I grabbed hold of the handles in the back to hold it steady so she wouldn't go careening across the parking lot. She didn't even spare me a glance. "I can't feel much down there, in case you forgot."

Drew rolled his eyes and moved to block her from getting in the car. "You can't drive yourself to the hospital while you're in labor."

"Get the hell out of my way, Nash," she bit off.

"If I let you do this, Dima'll kill me. Come on. Let's go back inside, and we can call Dima and an ambulance—"

"I might not have time for Dima or an ambulance."

She tried to back her chair up, but I was in the way. I flashed wide eyes at Drew, not sure what to do, but he didn't even spare me a glance. His focus was squarely on London, and hers on him. And…well…I wouldn't want to be on the receiving end of the glare London was sending his way. "My doctor told me to get to the hospital as soon as I knew I was in labor. That's what I'm doing. So unless you want me to run you over, I'd suggest you move your ass."

"How about we compromise?" he replied, leaving me in awe of the fact that he was able to keep his cool in a situation like this.

"What kind of compromise?"

"We go right now, but we leave your car here and you let me drive you."

She hesitated, so I assumed that meant she was at least thinking about it. That was a good sign. I agreed that she needed to get to the hospital as soon as possible—a lesson I'd learned the hard way. But I'd also learned the hard way that I couldn't drive myself while in labor. Add in the fact that she was in a wheelchair, and she might as well have a neon sign flashing *Hell to the no* at her.

"Where are we going to put my chair in your stupid little two-seater?" she demanded.

"In my car," I said before I could think better of it.

Both Drew and London shot surprised looks in my direction.

"I'll follow you and I'll bring your wheelchair. But he's right. You have to let someone else drive you."

"Come on," Drew said, trying to force us both backward so he could close the car door. Surprisingly, London allowed it. "You can call Dima on the way. Which hospital are we going to?"

"Hillcrest."

"Got it. Meet us there," he said to me, looking at me until I nodded my understanding.

Hillcrest. How on earth could I walk in there? I hadn't been back since… No, I couldn't let myself think like that. Not right now. It'd only make me cry, and I couldn't very well drive if I was crying.

Instead of letting her transfer herself into his car, Drew picked her up and put her in. She rolled down the window and shouted directions to me about how to dismantle the thing so I could get it in my car. She was still shouting as he pulled out, but at least I'd heard enough to figure out how to take the wheels off.

A minute or two later, I had the various parts of her chair tossed in my backseat, and I was heading toward the very same hospital where I'd surrendered my son.

Five

Drew

"TOOK TOO SLOW, *mudak*," Dima growled at me as soon as he threw open the passenger door of my car. He'd been at home when London called. Their house was closer to the hospital than the community center was, so he was there and waiting for our arrival by the time I squealed to a stop in the women's center drive, an orderly with a wheelchair at his side, and a combination of fear and excitement making his heavy Russian accent even more undecipherable than normal.

I was fairly certain he meant that I'd taken too long, even though I'd made the twenty-minute drive in less than fifteen, but I gave him a pass since he was a nervous, expectant father.

He didn't mess around with waiting for me to respond, unfastening London's seat belt and lifting her out of the car to a chorus of curses coming from her mouth. Let's just say she wasn't a fan of the fact that he and I had both decided to take matters into our own hands instead of letting her take care of herself.

Then another guy came up to us—I recognized him from London's sled hockey team—and tried to help, too.

"I'm fucking pregnant and in labor, not dying. All of you just *stop*."

"Why you're here?" Dima demanded of London's teammate.

"Because she's having a fucking baby," the guy bit off.

"And I'm going to have it right here if you two don't stop with your pissing contest and get me inside. Goddamn fucking macho jerks. The both of you! Wade's my friend. Dima's my husband. Both of you need to fucking deal with it."

I bit my tongue to keep from laughing at her infuriated litany. Once she was properly settled in the hospital's wheelchair, I reached across and pulled the door closed so I could find somewhere to park. I might have been a miserable friend at their wedding, but I was almost positive I'd made up for it just now.

The three of them headed inside, still arguing.

On my way inside, I passed Ravyn trying to reassemble London's wheelchair behind her car. She didn't seem to be having much luck, either, since she had plopped down on her ass on the hot concrete and was working on tying her dreads behind her head with a bandana, an adorable scowl creasing her brow. Never would've thought I'd find her adorable, especially after she all but gave me the brush-off after we'd essentially used each other for sex—insanely good sex, I might add—but it appeared I had no control over my attraction to her. Not a good sign for me since she didn't want anything more than a hookup.

This was the first time since my divorce, though, that I'd *wanted* something more. I still hadn't settled on how *much* more I wanted, but damn. A one-night stand or a quickie wouldn't be enough to satisfy me.

"Want a hand with that?" I asked, dropping into a crouch next to her and resting my elbows on my knees.

She shot me an annoyed look, but then recognition dawned in her eyes. "Yeah, if you can. I managed to get it apart, but now it doesn't want to go back together."

"Don't think it'll be much use to London that way," I said, cracking a grin. Not that I expected my smile to have any effect on her at all. Ravyn seemed completely immune to my charm. "Although I think it wants to go together just fine, as long as you put everything where it goes."

"Did you…get her here in time?" she asked, ignoring my attempt to flirt.

Maybe I was more out of practice than I realized.

I took the base and one wheel from her and gave them a once-over to determine how they connected. "She didn't give birth in my car if that's what you're asking."

Ravyn nodded, looking more relieved than I could understand. She'd only spent a grand total of five minutes in London's presence, as far as I knew. Why was she so worried?

Once I had the first wheel in place, I reached for the other and repeated the process. "There we go. All set now. I'll get Dima to make sure we didn't miss anything before she uses it, but I think the two of us have successfully put a wheelchair back together." I straightened and reached out a hand to help Ravyn to her feet.

"Not sure I had much to do with that," she said.

I winked. "Our little secret. No one else has to know it wasn't all you."

She didn't take my hand, though, pushing herself to her feet on her own and wiping her hands on the butt of her shorts. Damn, back to the cold shoulder.

"Why don't we take this in and find out where they've taken her?" I suggested.

But Ravyn shook her head. "Like I said earlier…I've got to go. I just— I thought I'd help you get this here. But I can't stay." She kept passing anxious looks toward the entrance where I'd dropped London off moments ago.

So much for hoping I'd get a bit more time with Ravyn to wear her down. "Right," I said. "You've got to work and run errands."

"Exactly." Her gaze was transfixed on the hospital entrance.

"So I'll see you next week at the support group meeting then?" I asked, despite the gnawing suspicion that I'd never see her again.

Her throat bobbed as she swallowed hard, and damn if there weren't tears in her eyes. What the fuck was that about? But she nodded and backed away from me, and I knew it was a total lie. She wasn't coming back again.

I pushed London's chair out of the way and waved as Ravyn drove off. I hadn't made it three steps before Razor and Viktoriya Chambers claimed Ravyn's empty parking spot.

"What the fuck were you doing on the ground with my tattoo artist?" Razor demanded as the two of them caught up with me.

"Your tattoo artist?" I repeated dumbly. I had no idea what Razor was talking about, but that was nothing new. The guy lived in his own world, and the rest of us were merely spectators to the train wreck.

"Yeah, dipshit. Ravyn—purple dreads." He put an arm around his wife's back and tugged her to his side before giving me a cocky grin.

So Ravyn was a tattoo artist. Not really a huge surprise, I supposed, considering she was covered in ink. But it rankled that Razor knew more about her than I did, since I was the one who'd just had her in my bed about an hour ago.

No point getting worked up over that now. I shrugged. "She was at the community center when London went into labor," I said, leaving out all sorts of details that were none of Razor's business. "She helped me out by bringing the wheelchair, since there wasn't room for it in my car. We were just putting it back together."

"Hmm," he said, but he sounded distracted.

"Hmm?" I repeated.

"Guess she had to get back to her babysitter or something. She was about to pop back in December when I got her to do a new tat for me. Guess her kid's eight months or so, now? Something like that. Anyway, we'd better get in there before one of them kills the other. Dima was such a mess when he called, I couldn't understand a fucking word he said. Tried to get Tori to interpret for me, but she swears he wasn't speaking Russian, either."

I came to a stop, pretending I needed to re-tie my shoe. Razor looked back over his shoulder, but I waved him on ahead because I needed a second to wrap my head around the bomb he'd just unwittingly dropped on me.

Ravyn had a baby.

She was HIV-positive, she was single—as far as I knew—and she had a baby.

I never would've put it together on my own, but it made sense now that I thought about it. Her body had all the telltale signs—bigger, darker nipples that I'd stupidly assumed had something to do with her piercings, wider hips that I'd just been thrilled to get my hands on. She'd had some stretch marks, too, but how many women *didn't*? So the idea that she'd had a baby had never crossed my mind.

But now I wondered if her baby was HIV-positive, too.

No wonder she didn't want to talk about anything. But all of this just led me to believe she needed to talk more than ever.

How the hell was I going to make that happen, since she likely had every intention of making sure the two of us never ran into each other again?

Six

Ravyn

A FEW DAYS later, I was in the middle of designing a custom watercolor tattoo—my specialty—for a new client when Rick popped into my room and peeked over my shoulder. Rick was the owner of INKredible Ink, the tattoo shop where I'd done my apprenticeship and where I currently rented a space. I'd apprenticed under him for several years, back when I was really just a kid. Actually, my apprenticeship had lasted longer than most do because I was still too young to get my license at the end of my two years, since I'd lied to him at first about how old I was. Granted, he'd known I was lying to him, but he'd wanted to help. Rick had always been able to see through me like that.

He'd become something like a father figure to me in

those days—much more so than my real father had ever been. So much so that when I left Jax before the baby was born and didn't have anywhere to go, Rick had let me stay in the apartment over the shop for a while, until I got my feet under me. Oh, yeah. And he was also the person who delivered my baby upstairs in that very apartment, after I'd waited too long to get to the hospital and realized there was no way I could drive myself. I'd called him in a panic because the 9-1-1 operator told me all the EMTs near me were already busy dealing with a fifteen-car-pileup on the interstate, and I didn't have a clue what to do. Rick had done what he always did; he came to my rescue.

The plan had been for him to drive me to the hospital, but the baby didn't want to wait that long. Granted, as soon as Rick had delivered the baby, on the phone with the 9-1-1 operator talking him through it, he'd tried to convince me there was no reason to give up the baby. *Shannon and I can help you out,* he'd said. *You can find a way to make this work. You're a hell of a lot tougher than you give yourself credit for, you know.*

Bullshit. I wasn't tough. He had to realize the truth now, all these months later, after seeing just how badly I'd fallen apart. That little boy was a hell of a lot better off without having a basket case like me for a mother. I knew that even *before* I'd found out about being HIV-positive. I could barely take care of myself, so how the hell would I have been able to take care of a kid?

I couldn't, plain and simple.

"What colors are you going to use?" Rick asked, doing his best to sound merely curious, even though we both knew there was a lot more behind it than curiosity. So far, my design was only in pencil, which made it a fair question. But then there was the fact that I'd been out of sorts lately, and my work had been suffering from it. My designs were usually full of bold color choices. These days, I'd been working a lot more than normal in black and gray. Even my canvas paintings were coming out in a muddled mess that reflected the state of my mind.

I shrugged, trying to play it off and looking down at the cherry blossom outline. "Pinks, greens, a pop of yellow, maybe a touch of purple. The usual. She wants it to be relatively traditional, even if it's a watercolor design."

"Relatively traditional, hmm? So she wants some black in it?"

"Some. Not a lot. I'm going to do most of the outline in color, then blend it in. Just a few touches in black."

"Well…I'm glad you're going to use some color for her," he said.

I didn't respond. Because there was nothing to say. I'd tried using color lately, but somehow I ended up doing everything in black and gray, or only with a little pop of color. My art was all coming out as ugly and dreary as my soul.

"Where's it going?" he asked, changing the subject somewhat.

"Ribs. She wants a branch to curl up around a breast."

He let out one of his silent chuckles. I could only tell because of the huff of breath from his nostrils hitting the back of my head.

It made me grin. "You think I have a problem tattooing a woman's girly bits?"

"Nope. Just thinking about the fact that she wants it on her ribs. You sure she can handle it? You could be setting yourself up for a hell of a difficult time."

I rolled my eyes, not that he could see it. "You know I learned from the best, right?"

"Damn straight, you did."

"She's sat through a lot before, just not for me. So we'll see if she can be still long enough. No matter what, I'm going to give her a tattoo she can be proud of, though." When my new client had come in a few hours ago and told me what she wanted, I'd counted no fewer than a dozen other tattoos already on her body, and those were only the ones in visible places. She had enough piercings to put mine to shame, too. This was a woman who used her body as art. I was just glad she was giving me a pristine canvas on which to work, a large space that didn't have any other ink on it. A blank sheet, mine to fill with our combined vision.

"If anyone can make that work, it's you," he said, sobering.

Watercolor tattoos were still a relatively new technique in the tattooing industry. Some tattooists refused to do them because they said the ink wouldn't hold up well. There was definitely some truth to that. Black lasts better than color. There's a reason traditional tattooists use solid black outlines on all of their work, after all. But there's a certain art to the watercolor technique, even if the recipient would need to get more touchup work done over the years to keep their ink looking the way it should. The watercolor style was a natural fit for me, though, since I had been painting in watercolors my whole life. I was one of the few watercolor tattooists in Oklahoma, so I had a steady stream of clients coming in to INKredible Ink, looking for me to produce their vision.

Under Rick, I'd studied all sorts of styles. He was a

new school specialist these days, but he'd spent a number of years honing his skill doing black-and-gray portrait work. Talk about diversity. It was hard to find two tattooing styles more different than those, but somehow he made it work. When I'd told him I wanted to try my hand at watercolor tattoos, he didn't bat an eye—especially not once I'd shown him a few of the canvases I'd painted at home with actual watercolors. He might not do them himself, but he was one hundred percent behind me mastering the technique.

I bent my head over my sketchpad, adjusting the angle of the table lamp so the light shone on a particular section of my page, and worked on getting the tiny details of a few blossoms just right.

"You've been acting strange the last couple of days," Rick said after a moment, and I stiffened. So he was finally revealing his reason for hovering. "Since you went to that group session."

Little did he know, it had a hell of a lot less to do with the group therapy session and everything to do with the things that had gone down afterward. Going to the hospital. Getting a glimpse of a nurse in the distance and thinking it might have been the one I'd handed off my son to. Having a panic attack as soon as I got back in my car. Needing to pull off the road for about twenty minutes to calm down. Not to mention the insanity of going home with Drew before that.

I'd already lost all my marbles a long time ago, but on Tuesday, the few I'd relocated had probably left me for good. It had taken every bit of willpower I possessed to keep it together and not end up back in the loony bin after all of that, so there was no wonder Rick sensed I was *a little off,* as he'd put it.

I set my pencil down and spun around on my stool

to face him. "I'm not going to flip out," I said, staring deep into his eyes and hoping he'd see the truth of my words in mine. Yes, I'd started to lose it, but I'd reined the crazy back in before anything bad happened.

I could do this. I could function as a normal person in the real world without Rick hovering constantly to be sure I wasn't cutting myself again. Or worse.

The look he gave me said he wasn't quite buying it.

I sighed. "It was just… That meeting threw me off. But I'm fine. Or I will be fine, but either way, it's not something for you to worry about, okay?"

One corner of his mouth curled up, although it was hard to see behind his mountain-man beard. If I didn't know him so well, I might have missed it. "You know it's impossible for me to stop worrying about you, right?" he said. "I mean, I know you've been getting your shit together lately, but I still worry. Shannon does, too."

"I know you do. Wish you wouldn't."

He winked. "We wouldn't know what to do with ourselves if we didn't have someone to worry about."

Wasn't that the truth? Back when I was still his apprentice, the two of them had spent a lot of time and effort trying to bail their youngest son—who was a few years older than me—out of the mess he was making of his life. Robbie had finally started to straighten up and fly right at about the same time my world started falling apart.

"Well, maybe you should adopt someone new to focus it on, then. Give me permission to get my shit together, you know?"

"Baby doll, you've got permission to do that anytime you see fit. Not that you need permission. You just need to do it. Grab the reins of your life and go. Don't let the two of us factor into anything."

I chuckled and shook my head. "Get out of here and let me do my work."

He pressed a kiss to the top of my head, which damn near shattered me. "Need to go yell at Billy, anyway. I spent four hours last night fixing one of the shittiest tattoos he's ever given." Then he backed out of my room and left me to do my work.

But now, Drew was back in my head again—another man who'd damn near shattered me. Those muscular arms that he wrapped around me. The deep, brown eyes always trying to see through me. The way he'd given me exactly what I'd asked him for, everything that I'd needed, even though he had no good reason to do so.

For the past four days, anytime I wasn't freaking out about my baby—whether he had parents who loved him, if they had tested him for HIV, if they were treating him for it whether the tests came back positive or not, whether he would hate me someday—I had been thinking of Drew.

But that was another door I'd closed. Yeah, I could go back to that meeting, so I was sure I could run into him again if I wanted to. It wasn't that I didn't know how to find him.

The problem was that I'd used him and then given him the cold shoulder. The rejection that had filled his voice and creased his brows when I'd insisted on leaving that afternoon was unmistakable. And he hadn't done anything to deserve me treating him so coldly and callously.

I just didn't think I could bring myself to return to that support group. It might mean running into London again. Talking about her baby. That was something I couldn't bear at this point, because it would only make me think about my own son. Even without that, I wasn't ready to tell a room full of strangers anything about myself, and listening to them talk about their own issues wouldn't do a damn thing to help me get past all the shit in my head. The only positive would be running into Drew again—but would he want to have anything to do with me after the way I'd treated him?

And even if he did…he'd be better off without me in his life.

Just like everyone else.

Especially my little boy.

I finished up the line work on my drawing and reached for my colored pencils, hoping that this time, I could get out of my head long enough to give my client what she came to me to get. Bold, rich, abstract color. Shading. Color washing.

Not a black-and-gray mess.

I'd only been working on the colors for this design for a few minutes when there was a soft knock at my door, and Dagger stuck his spiky-haired head through the door. He ran the front and did most of our piercings.

"Walk-in's asking for you."

Automatically, I closed my sketch pad and set it aside, already standing to go out and greet my new client. The woman who wanted a cherry blossom on her ribs wouldn't be back to see the artwork for a week, so I had plenty of time to finish it later.

"Any idea what they want?" I asked.

"Just that he wants you. He's a virgin," Dagger added.

I couldn't help raising a brow. Most male tattoo virgins didn't ask for me, specifically. I got the chicks who wanted watercolor tattoos or butterflies or other *soft* images like those. Most men getting their first ink wanted something hard, black, and tribal—and they definitely wouldn't come to me for something like that.

My curiosity was more than simply piqued.

I followed Dagger out into the lobby, but then I immediately stopped cold. Because, standing there looking expectantly in my direction was Drew, alongside another man I remembered coming to get a tattoo months ago.

Suddenly, I couldn't breathe.

Then Drew winked, and I doubted I'd ever be able to take a full breath again.

Seven

Drew

RAVYN LOOKED AT me like I'd just run over her puppy—not exactly a stroke to my ego, but I hadn't come here for a boost in confidence.

I also hadn't come for a tattoo, but if it meant getting the chance to talk to her again, I'd absolutely take a seat in the chair and let her etch something into my skin. The place seemed clean—I'd seen a couple of the other tattoo artists taking needles out of packaging—and she and I both knew about my HIV status.

If I was ever going to get a tattoo, this was the place, and she was the artist. I didn't even need to see any of her work to know it, either.

But she looked like she was about to bolt, her blue eyes shifting between me and Razor before she turned to stare toward a door in the back.

Today, she had on a pair of jeans that hugged her ass in ways that sent my brain into a tailspin along with another brightly colored tank top. I could get used to seeing her in tank tops like that. They showed off her curves and made my mouth water.

Probably not what I should be thinking about at the moment, but I couldn't help it. Just like I couldn't stop myself from getting hard from thinking about curling myself around her sexy body again.

Fuck, I was a mess.

"Long time no see," Razor said, his tone relaxed and cocky, just like always.

The guy was a smooth operator. I was still in shock that he was settled down and married these days, because he'd always been such a player until his Russian ballerina had come onto the scene last summer.

He walked over and planted a kiss on Ravyn's cheek, a move that startled her enough to keep her from running off. Then he turned her around, one steady hand on the small of her back like he was her best friend in the world, and started leading her into the room she'd just come out of. "My buddy here needs to get some ink, and I told him there was no one better than you."

Cool as a cucumber, that one. Maybe it wasn't a bad idea to bring him along, after all.

I followed them in and closed the door to her room behind me.

"What are you doing here?" she demanded once it was just the three of us and no one else could overhear. Or so I assumed. I took a quick glance around, debating the thickness of the walls, not that I could do anything about it if someone overheard us. She was staring straight at me, ignoring my teammate, even though he was the one who'd guided her back here.

I shrugged, trying to play it off. Too bad I'd never been as cool and collected as my teammate. "Getting a tattoo, like Razor said."

"You don't have any tattoos."

Razor popped up a brow. "How does she know that?" he asked. "You said you just met her once, at that meeting you go to."

I ignored him. He didn't need to know that I'd fudged the truth. I was only trying to protect Ravyn, anyway. Why should my teammates know I'd hooked up with her? "I don't have any," I agreed. "*Yet.* You can help me correct that."

"Why do you want a tattoo?"

"Do I have to give you a dissertation on my motivations in order to prove I'm a worthy candidate? I want one. I want you to do it."

"Bullshit."

I rolled my eyes. This wasn't working out the way I'd imagined it.

"Why are you here?" Ravyn asked again.

Hell if I knew, other than the fact that I hadn't been able to get her out of my head since the moment I'd watched her drive away from the hospital a few days ago. "Don't tell me I'm the first person who's ever come in here asking you to get their first tattoo."

"That's not what I mean."

"I know it's not."

Razor plopped down on the chair in the middle of the room, propping his elbows up on the metal supply table next to it and resting his chin in his hands, settling in like we were his own private soap opera. He passed his eyes back and forth between us like he'd never witnessed anything more entertaining. Bastard.

"I just…" I dragged a hand through my hair and let out a frustrated sigh, much to Razor's amusement—there was no missing the delighted gleam in his eye. "I got the sense that you wouldn't be back to the community center."

Ravyn blinked a couple of times, her face an unreadable mask.

"And I wanted to see you again."

Still nothing.

I glared in Razor's direction, angling my head toward the door in a not-even-remotely-subtle indication that he needed to get the fuck out of here. He wasn't supposed to stay. I'd only asked him to show me where Ravyn worked so I could come talk to her, but he was supposed to go home to his wife once he brought me here and was sure it was the right place.

He winked in response, his grin as wide as the Mississippi, but he didn't move an inch. Fucker.

Ignoring his presence was my only option. I'd clean up whatever mess I created later. If needed, I could threaten to rip off his balls and shove them up his ass if he said a word to any of the guys. Something like that.

For now, I focused entirely on Ravyn. "What we did the other day… That's not my MO. I don't jump in bed with women I don't know—"

"Wait, you two hooked up?" Razor cut in, somehow grinning even wider than before.

"—and I definitely don't just move on like nothing ever happened," I finished, pretending the son of a bitch wasn't here. Easier said than done, though.

"You fucking hooked up with a single mom?" Razor continued, but now he sounded kind of pissed. I vaguely remembered his mother had raised him on her own—his father wasn't in the picture. Of course, he would feel strongly about something like that. Hell, I did, too. Like I'd told Ravyn…that wasn't the way I did things, single mother or not.

"I didn't know she was a single mom," I said feebly.

"I'm not," she cut in, and both Razor and I turned to question her with our eyes. She didn't give us the answer we were looking for, though. "You don't have to feel guilty. It was my idea. No strings, remember?"

The thing was, guilt played no part in this. I *wanted* there to be strings, not that I could explain that desire. I could blame it on the way my parents raised me, but there was something more to it than simply that. I wanted the chance to get to know her better. To understand what it was that drew me to her.

Don't get me wrong, the sex had been phenomenal. Better than any I'd had in years, and surely miles better than anything I could expect to have for a long time to come. But it wasn't just about sex.

The frightened-rabbit look in her eyes—especially during those moments when I'd been inside her and she'd been on the verge of orgasm, and again when we'd arrived at the hospital—was such a startling contrast to the image she presented to the world, with her purple dreads and using her body as an artistic canvas.

But then again, maybe her look achieved the desired effect with most people. She seemed as if she wanted people to stare, to see her boldness, and cower away from her, thinking they could never have the confidence she possessed in spades.

Something told me the bold look was nothing but a show, a front to keep people away. If so, it was having the opposite effect on me.

"No such thing as sex without strings when there's a single mother involved, sweetheart," Razor said, and Ravyn's gorgeous blue eyes shot over to him for the first time since I'd closed the door.

"I'm not a single mother," she said, but then she clammed up, refusing to explain.

Which was all the explanation I needed. "So you're with someone," I bit off. "You cheated with me." I felt sick to my stomach all of a sudden. For so long, I'd been furious with Chelsea and the son of a bitch she'd had her affair with during our marriage. That had eventually fallen off to a sort of numbness. But the idea that I had in any way been on the wrong side of that equation made me hate myself.

Ravyn blinked at me a few times, struggling with keeping her emotionless mask in place. The frightened-rabbit look was inching back into her expression, which left me feeling like an ass. I didn't want to scare her, damn it. But I sure as fuck didn't want to be used, either.

I shook my head and ripped open the door, ready to leave without getting either a tattoo or answers, but Ravyn put a hand on my elbow and I stopped. It was just a simple touch, not nearly enough to prevent me from leaving if that was what I really wanted.

But I didn't turn around.

"I'm not with anyone," she said quietly. It felt like an eternity before she said anything else—so long I was sure Razor would break out with some stupid wiseass crack to break the tension, because the guy couldn't handle awkward silences. In fact, there was a part of me hoping he'd get on with it already, because I wasn't doing so well with the silence, myself. But Ravyn spoke again before Razor could get to it, her voice carrying a hell of a lot more emphatic strength than I could ever recall hearing out of her before. "I'm not a mother."

"Bullshit," Razor said, and I spun around to search Ravyn's eyes. "You were so pregnant you were about to pop when I was here before."

"I was." She nodded. "But I'm not a mother. Now, are you here for a tattoo or not?"

I supposed that was the end of that, at least for the time being. If she was willing to give me a tattoo, though, I needed to stay and get one. There was no telling what I might get out of her if given enough time. "Let's do it. Show me what you can do."

Suddenly, she was all business, moving over to remove a portfolio from a drawer and hand it to me.

Razor gave me a questioning look that was on the verge of being comical, but I gave him a slight shake of my head. I sure as hell wanted to get the story, probably a hell of a lot more than he did, but pushing wasn't going to get us any answers.

I needed to chip away at her, a bit at a time, or else she was going to push back so hard there'd be no more forward progress. I flipped through Ravyn's portfolio, taking it all in. Her work was gorgeous, but not exactly what I had in mind for my first tattoo. It was all too…

"Flowery," Razor muttered. "Soft colors and shit."

Not something I could walk into the locker room wearing on my skin, unless I wanted to hear about it for the rest of my life.

"What did she do for you?" I asked.

With no hesitation at all, he dropped his shorts and pointed to the angel with phoenix wings on his thigh. It was a hell of a lot less flowery and…well, *pretty*…than the ones we'd been looking at in this photo album.

Ravyn took a quick look. "Healed well. So did he tell

you the right Russian words, or did you have to rearrange his face?"

He winked at her. "Tori swears Dima told me the right words. No need to murder him. I'm sure his wife appreciates that, too, since they've got a new baby and all. But you know all about that."

She blinked a couple of times and shook her head.

"London's his wife. The one whose wheelchair you took to the hospital the other day?"

With that, she sobered up instantly, giving a curt nod. "I can do other styles, too," Ravyn said, back to business.

I wished she still had that playful tone she'd had only moments before, and I wondered what I could do to bring it back.

"Those at the front are all done in the watercolor style, which is what I'm best at. But if you look back here"—she flipped back to the midway point of the massive photo album—"you can see some of the other work I've done. My mentor taught me a bit about nearly every style imaginable. I can do traditional, new school, even some trash polka…"

"Trash polka?" I asked, more curious than interested. I'd never heard of it before, and I had no earthly idea what it meant.

Ravyn flipped a few more pages and pointed to some wacky, bold designs in black and red. "They're similar to my watercolor work in that there aren't necessarily hard lines and edges, but there's a lot of saturation. They're strictly black and red, though, and kind of abstract."

And they were very appealing to my eye. "You did these?" I asked, running my finger over a combination of a raven, a clock, a gun, and some bold lettering on some guy's back.

She nodded.

"So could you do something along these lines for me? I'm thinking about a red ribbon…"

"For HIV? Yeah, I could do something with that." Before she'd even finished speaking, she took out a sketch pad and a pencil and started drawing. "Where do you want it?" she asked, not looking up.

"My biceps?" I suggested. Because I sure as hell hadn't thought this through. I wasn't entirely sure I wanted to get a tattoo, but I did want to spend more time here with Ravyn. And maybe see more of what she was all about.

She glanced my way, her gaze falling on my upper arm. "Lift up your sleeve and show me how big you want it and where."

I did as she asked, and a slow grin came over her face.

"What's that smile about?" I asked.

"Just got a great idea on how we can show off those guns." Then she ducked her head down and went back to scratching her pencil over the paper.

Razor snorted, but I didn't care that he was getting a kick out of this.

Because I'd gotten Ravyn to smile.

Eight

Ravyn

I'M NOT A mother.

My own words haunted me while I silently bent my head over Drew and inked the design onto his arm. Haunting or not, they were true. To be a mother, you had to have a child. One that you were responsible for.

Getting pregnant didn't make me a mother.

Giving birth on the apartment floor on Christmas Eve didn't make me a mother.

Walking into a hospital and passing my newborn baby into the arms of a nurse before walking out again *definitely* didn't check the boxes needed to put me into the *Mother* category.

I was glad that Drew and his friend were busy talking while I worked, because it meant they were ignoring me, and there was no need for me to keep up a conversation with them. I worked better when I didn't have to talk, anyway. That allowed me to focus on the art I was creating and not on idle chitchat with someone I might never see again.

"Hunter and Tallie are supposed to be back in town tomorrow," Razor said, now straddling a folding chair in the corner with it turned around backwards so he could face us, his muscular arms folded over the back providing him with a chin rest.

"How soon do you think Tallie'll be dragging your wife to garage sales?"

"Tori doesn't need to be dragged." Razor winked at me when I made the mistake of glancing up at him. "But I'd guess they'll be at it by tomorrow if Tallie can find one that soon. And I'm sure Tori intends to take Svetka with them, too."

"She and Sergei are still here?" Drew asked.

With all of these Russian names, they had to be related in some way to the Russian friend who'd come in with Razor months ago. The new father. Or maybe in some way related to his wife, since apparently she was Russian, too. I had hoped I could just listen in on their conversation and zone out to do my work, but everything they were talking about kept reminding me of London. And the baby. And the hospital. All things I'd rather banish from my mind.

"Tori says they're going to stick around for about a week before heading back to Siberia. She's trying to talk Svetka into staying longer."

"Hell," Drew said. "They might as well just move out here. Then Svetka could play the full-time grandmother. Dima and Sergei could go back to being best friends. Sergei could play with London's sled team…"

"Good idea all around, but no one asked the two of us. They should really do that," Razor added, catching my eye and winking again.

I dipped my head lower and focused on the chunky, solid black plus sign I was filling in, doing my best to tune their words out.

"Spurs said a couple of the new guys should be in by next week," Razor said. He didn't seem affronted that I was studiously paying him no attention, or at least doing my best to do so.

But my efforts at ignoring them had come too late, because now my thoughts were racing through my head at breakneck speed. Babies. Hospitals.

Memories.

"Wait," the nurse called after me. "Come back."

So I slowed down and let her catch up to me, tears streaking down my cheeks and threatening to freeze to my skin.

We'd had a freak snowstorm just before Christmas. The whole city had shut down for a few days. That was how it always went when there was any frozen precipitation anywhere in the South. Since it usually only happened once or twice a year, it was safer for everyone to stay home than to try to go out in it—southern cities didn't have the snowplows and other equipment needed to handle it.

The roads had been beyond awful, which was just one more reason I hadn't made it to the hospital in time. That was the cause of the massive fifteen-car pileup on the interstate, which prevented the ambulances from getting to me. I'd only arrived at the hospital now because Rick insisted on bringing me.

So there I was. In the snow. Trying to get away before my emotions got the best of me, and I allowed them to change my mind for me.

"I have to ask," she said, huffing for breath in the cold winter

air, holding my little boy tight in her arms. I'd wrapped him up in two big, fluffy towels to keep him warm, and she tucked the ends tighter, a natural, motherly move, like it was something she did every day. For a moment, I wondered if she was a baby nurse. That single action was enough to make me breathe somewhat easier. He would be safe here. Safer than he'd be with me.

"This is legal," I spit out, choking up before I could even finish the single sentence. "A hospital is supposed to be a safe place to—" But then I cut myself off, unable to force out the words surrender a child *without falling apart.*

But I'd done my research. There were safe-haven laws all across the country. In Oklahoma, I didn't even have to answer any questions. I could just leave the baby with an employee at the hospital or any of the other designated drop-off zones.

Before I'd handed the baby over to her, I'd asked her if she was an employee, even though I'd seen her name badge. Tricia Patterson, R.N., *it read, along with other credentials for the hospital. As soon as she'd answered in the affirmative, I'd passed him over into her waiting arms and told her I was surrendering him, my voice cracking so badly on the words that they were almost indistinguishable.*

And now, she wanted to ask me more questions. I had to leave. Right away. Before I took that little boy back into my own arms and took him home with me.

"I know it is. And you're right, this is a safe place. I'm not trying to get you in trouble," she said, clearly trying to calm me down. There couldn't be any doubt that I was just this side of losing control. "But can you tell me anything about yourself? Or the baby? Anything at all? When was the baby born?" Maybe she was trying to help me, too, not just learn as much as she could about the situation.

I hadn't intended to say anything. My plan had been to hand over the baby and make my exit as fast as possible. Because the longer I stayed there, the longer I could see him, the more I could think about changing my mind. But before I could stop myself, the words tumbled out of my mouth. "He was born about three hours ago. Just before midnight."

"So he's a Christmas Eve baby," she said with a soft smile. "And a boy?"

I nodded, too emotional to get any more words out without running the risk of completely breaking down.

"And you're the mother?"

I couldn't allow myself to think of him as being his mother. That was a dangerous idea. I blinked back more tears and bit down on the inside of my cheek, trying to hold it together. "I gave birth to him," I said, in lieu of calling myself his mother. "About three hours ago. Like I said."

"Did you give him a name yet?"

The tears spilled over then. Naming him was something I couldn't allow myself to do. It would only bring on a fresh wave of tears, and I just… I couldn't go there. So he didn't have a name. So I shook my head and tried to leave again before I completely lost it.

But that nurse put a hand on mine, and I froze. "Can you tell me anything about your medical history?" she asked. "Or the baby's father?"

Already, the urge to take him back into my arms and forget all about the whole idea of surrendering him had grown so strong I wasn't sure I could fight it off much longer. So I shook my head. "There's nothing to tell."

"Will the father be looking for him?"

"The father probably doesn't even remember he was going to be a father." With that, I broke down into a sobbing mess, collapsing into a pile of snow that had been shoveled out of the driveway.

"Why don't you come inside?" she suggested, looking panicky. "We can help you. We can have the doctors check you out, too." She even bent down, cradling my baby in her arms to keep from

dropping him, and reached for my hand to help me to my feet.

But I picked myself up and brushed the snow off, and I shook my head again. "It's best this way."

"No one's going to try to make you—" Her words dissipated into the black night as I walked back to Rick's car.

I probably should have gone inside and gotten checked out that night. It would have been the smart thing. I *had* just delivered a baby on the apartment floor, after all. Maybe if I had, I would have learned I was HIV-positive a lot sooner than I did. But if I'd gone inside that building that night, I was almost positive I would have walked out again with that little boy in my arms.

Even now, those same arms ached to hold him one more time. I knew he was better off wherever he was now. Newborn babies get adopted fast, so he wouldn't have spent much time in the system waiting for a home. He probably had two parents who loved him, who could provide for him…maybe even siblings. And he wasn't living in some tiny, run-down efficiency apartment with no father and with a mother who kept ending up in the loony bin. He *was* better off now than he would have been with me.

But it still broke my heart every time I thought about the fact that I wouldn't be able to see him grow up.

"Hey," Drew said, brushing a tear off my cheek with the pad of his thumb and startling me out of my pity party. "You okay?"

I sat up straight and blinked a few times, trying to get my tears under control. I *never* did that. I didn't lose it in front of my clients. Typically, I reserved my moments of acting like a crazy person for when I was completely alone, or at worst, when only those people who knew me best, like Rick, were around.

"Sorry," I said. "I'm fine."

"Call me crazy," Drew said, "but I don't know that I can believe that. I mean, it's not every day that a woman cries all over me for no reason…"

Razor let out a snort, but he got up and walked out of the room, leaving me alone with his friend.

I got up and grabbed a tissue, quickly drying my eyes and tossing it in the bin. My gloves followed the tissue, and then I washed my hands again so I could glove up all over again. "I'm all better now," I said. "It's not going to affect your tattoo at all."

He followed my every movement with his eyes. "I'm not worried about my tattoo, baby. I'm worried about *you*."

"Well, there's no reason for you to worry about me. I'm fine."

"Do people who're fine start crying for no reason? Wait…I know. It's because we were talking about the T-Birds' upcoming season. We're still going to be awful, I know, but—"

I laughed out loud. Couldn't help it. The things he was saying were so ridiculous that there was no other option.

He nodded solemnly. "Probably better to laugh it off. That's how bad we're going to be. I always feel shitty for Zee and some of the other older guys. They deserve a shot at winning the Cup, but sticking around here, they'll never get it."

"What are you even talking about?" I asked, picking up my machine again and settling in to get back to work. I dipped the needle into the cup of black ink and set it in place over his taut skin.

"The Thunderbirds?" He raised a brow. "Razor and I play in the NHL."

"The NHL?" I murmured, focused on the line I was filling in. "Not a minor league or something? Isn't it hard to keep the ice frozen around here?" I'd remembered him saying he played hockey, but that was as far as I'd gotten with figuring out who he was.

He winked. "I don't imagine the crew has an easy time of it, but that's their problem, not mine."

"I didn't realize we had a pro hockey team in Tulsa."

"You're not alone." He let out a sigh that I felt all the way to my toes. "And if we don't get our shit together, that won't change any time soon."

"You're not any good?"

"Well, *I* am. We're all good hockey players. We're just not quite there as a team, you know?"

With his free hand, he reached over and brushed a finger along the top of my left hand, where I'd rested it on his chest to steady myself. I shot my gaze up to meet his, my breath catching in my throat.

"What?" I asked, because he was looking at me with an expression I couldn't allow myself to interpret.

Drew shook his head. "Nothing. It's just nice to see you smile. And I kind of like the thought that you weren't after me because I'm a hockey player." Then he winked, and I cracked up even more than before.

"Do women throw themselves at you because you're in the NHL?"

"Nah. Not anymore, at least."

"Anymore?" I shouldn't have asked. I didn't want to get to know him better. That would only lead to me thinking about him more than I already was, and my head was too fucked up for me to risk getting involved with someone right now. Too late, though, because the question had already come out.

"Not since the world found out I'm HIV-positive.

I'm kind of surprised you don't already know all about that, actually. It was all over the news last April."

I dipped the needle into the ink again before pressing the tip to his skin, trying not to focus on the way his warm hand had settled over the back of mine, holding it to his chest in an almost possessive manner. Because it felt good. Too good. My breaths fluttered through my lungs. "Well, I've never been one to follow sports much. Besides, in April I was—"

In the loony bin. I barely cut myself off in time. A massive knot formed in my throat.

"In April, you were what?" he asked.

"I wasn't paying any attention to the news," I said evasively.

But then Razor came back in, carrying three cups from Starbucks in one of their cardboard drink carriers, saving me from having to explain further.

I didn't need Drew to know I'd been in a behavioral health facility in April. Or again in June. I didn't need him to know anything at all about me.

All I needed was to finish this tattoo so he could leave, and then I could find a way to put him out of my mind.

He should be a hell of a lot easier to forget about than my baby, at least.

Razor handed me one of the cups, grinning and winking at me as I took my hand out from under Drew's, thankful for the excuse for breaking that contact. "Loaded it up with tons of cream and sugar. I asked the guy up front—the one with the spiky hair. Let me know if it's not sweet enough, and I can take care of it for you, sugar." Then he peeked over my shoulder and handed Drew another cup. "Looking good. You won't have to wear a Band-Aid over it to show yourself in the locker room, after all."

I sipped from my coffee and kept working. The two guys started up their banter again, which meant I could go back to doing my best to ignore them and stop attempting to carry on a conversation.

But I couldn't help but wish Drew's strong, soothing hand was still covering mine.

Nine

Drew

TO MY UTTER shock, Ravyn was already in the conference room at the community center on Tuesday morning when I walked in for the support group meeting. I was so unprepared to see her there, despite the fact that I'd done my damnedest to convince her to return, that I did a double take when I walked in, guarding my senses against the overpowering lemon scent, not to mention the overwhelming draw I felt toward Ravyn.

But I hadn't made a mistake and I wasn't seeing visions. She was really there, already nursing a cup of coffee in a seat at the back, head ducked down, as if that would keep anyone from realizing it was her. This time, her dreads were pulled back and tied together behind her head. No tank top. Too bad. Instead, she was wearing a black men's Ramones T-shirt that was three sizes too big. I couldn't help but think it must have belonged to an ex, which made me jealous in ways I didn't want to explore.

We'd moved into September now, but still no rain. I found myself hoping for one of the random fall thunderstorms we'd had in my first couple of seasons, but for some reason, I didn't think we'd get one.

Since we were getting closer to the start of training camp and more of the guys on the team had started returning to Tulsa, yesterday a bunch of us had gotten together to work out, which meant I had to be a lot more conscientious about how I was eating again. I'd already had an egg-white-and-veggie omelet this morning before coming in, so this time I just grabbed a coffee. No more pastries for me, no matter how tempting.

Except…I still wasn't sure if I should get back on the ice. Hockey was the only thing I'd ever known. It was the only future I'd ever envisioned for myself, until that game at the end of the last season, when I'd nearly bled to death on the ice in front of friends and fans alike.

When Eric Zellinger had ignored my warnings and jumped into action, putting his bare hands on the gash in my neck. The freaking guy had risked his own life in order to save mine. I still didn't know how to process that. And I didn't want to put anyone else in that position ever again.

All of that was racing through my head as I took my coffee over to sit next to Ravyn. "Wasn't expecting to see you here," I said quietly.

"Wasn't expecting to be here."

"So why are you?"

She shrugged. "My doctors told me that if I didn't

keep coming, they were going to put me back in inpatient care."

I raised a brow in question.

"I've been in and out of the loony bin a lot lately."

"The loony bin…"

"It's my pet name for the county behavioral health facility. For some reason, when you get caught cutting yourself and other things like that, they seem to think you're not fit to be among the general population."

"*Cutting* yourself?" I repeated, trying to take it all in. "Like, you tried to hurt yourself?"

Again, she shrugged. "I'm not suicidal, if that's what you're thinking. I don't want to die. I just… I don't know how to deal. If anything, I'm trying to remind myself that I really, truly *am* still alive. When all the shit's running around in my head, I have to do *something*, you know? So I cut."

"And when you get caught doing it—"

"They toss me in the loony bin, yeah." She gave me an annoyed look. "There are all sorts of people who end up there, you know, and that doesn't make us crazy. Some of us do self-harm. Others are addicts. Lots are bipolar or deal with anxiety disorders. Damn sure makes me *feel* crazy when I'm in there, but I'm not actually insane."

"I never said you were."

She narrowed her eyes, studying me for a moment. "No, I suppose you didn't. Sorry. I get kind of defensive when I have to talk about this shit."

"No one's making you talk about it," I pointed out. It didn't escape my notice that, forced or not, she *was* telling me, though. That was definitely progress. And I liked the fact that it was me she was telling, out of all the people she could have gone to.

A *hmph*-ing sound came from her as she crossed her arms in front of her and leaned back in her chair, resting her coffee cup on her thigh. That move pushed her breasts up higher, which, of course, got me thinking about her breasts again. And how much I liked them. And how I'd like to see them again.

"Careful with that coffee, now," I said, dropping my voice when she lifted the cup for a sip. I waited for her to look up in question. "There's a shortage of perfect breasts in the world. It would be a pity to damage yours."

She snorted in laughter, which drew a few eyes from around the room. "*Princess Bride* again?" But then she sobered up again. "Pretty sure that's what my doctors think is going to happen if they make me come to these stupid meetings. That I'll have to talk about it."

"You don't have to do anything you don't want to."

"Says the guy who isn't being threatened with a stint in the loony bin." But she laughed.

I could get used to hearing her laugh. It was rich and husky, reminiscent of the sounds she made when we'd been in bed together. Addictive.

Damn, I was a fucking mess.

While we were sitting there, the rest of the room had filled in. Now, Jack Carson took a seat in the center of the room, across from the two of us. He cleared his throat and took a sip from his coffee before setting the Styrofoam cup on the floor by his feet. "Good to see everyone again." He nodded in our direction, catching Ravyn's eye. She slumped lower in her seat, trying to be invisible, but he kept looking around the room as if he hadn't noticed her disappearing act. "I don't have anything on the agenda today, so I thought I'd open it up for anyone who needs to talk. Any takers?"

A few people shifted in their seats, mumbling things to their neighbors. It was always this way if we didn't have a speaker coming in or a specific topic to get us started. No one wanted to have the spotlight focused in their direction.

Normally, I didn't, either. But today wasn't normal. I leaned forward, resting my arms on my knees with my coffee warming both hands. "Actually, yeah," I said before I could think better of it and stop myself.

Ravyn flashed worried eyes in my direction, but she didn't need to be anxious. This had nothing at all to do with her and everything to do with me.

"So I think you all know I've been struggling lately. Debating my future and shit. I mean, the team's been great about everything that went down. The guys are all acting like they want me back this season. They say they want me playing with them. Even Zee, which is nuts, since he's the one I could have infected."

I paused for a moment, taking in the eyes staring my way, the heads nodding empathetically. It was Ravyn's attention I felt more acutely than the rest, though. We might have been intimate, but that didn't mean we knew a damn thing about each other. She hadn't even heard the news when I'd taken a skate blade to the throat last spring, and it had been *everywhere*, not just on ESPN and other sports outlets. But she'd opened up to me somewhat, revealing that she harmed herself and had spent time in "the loony bin," as she put it. This was a way I could turn the tables, so to speak. It didn't escape my notice that she was eating it up.

"I've got a meeting scheduled later this week with the general manager and coaches," I said. "I'm supposed to give them my answer. I'm under contract, but they'll let me out of it if I decide I want out. I can officially retire as a player, maybe take on some other position within the organization. Or just leave professional hockey entirely, I suppose. And they've given me a hell of a lot longer to make my decision than they needed to. I mean, if I wasn't going to play, the fair thing for me to do would be to fill them in before July, when they could have made some moves in free agency and whatnot. But they told me I could have until now, just before training camp starts up."

"I get the sense that you still haven't made up your mind," Jack said, his voice calm and measured, just like always.

"Not in the slightest. I don't know who I am if I'm not a hockey player. I don't know who I want to be or who I *can* be. I mean, I don't have any skills to speak of outside of what I can do on the ice, and I never finished high school. Who's going to be stupid enough to give me a job?"

"You have to have a lot of dedication to get to where you have with hockey," Darlene said. She was a business owner if I remembered correctly. Maybe a restaurant? Hard to recall. "That's better than a lot of workers out there."

In these support group meetings, we all went by first names only, kind of like at Alcoholics Anonymous. I was a special case, though. Everyone knew exactly who I was—first and last names, plus my career.

There'd been no point in trying to keep any of that secret since my story had ended up all over the news well before London had badgered me into attending. Everyone here knew as much of my story as the rest of the world did. The only part of it still a secret from them at that point was that my cheating ex-wife had been my means of contracting the disease. Not that it had remained a secret for long. Apparently, I had no qualms about opening up and spilling my guts to these complete strangers. It had been a hell of a lot easier to tell them than my teammates.

"But there's no reason you can't still go out there and play hockey," Chuck said. He was one of the first guys I'd met when I'd started coming to these meetings. The guy had been HIV-positive for well over a decade after contracting it from the partner he was still with. "I mean, unless you decide that's what you want. But they can't legally prevent you from playing. And there's a higher risk of someone getting hep-B from playing sports than there is of transmitting HIV between players."

"Yeah, but those numbers are looking at *all* sports," I pointed out. "And in most sports, you don't have guys out there moving at thirty miles an hour, wearing knives on their feet, wielding sticks that they're actively using to strike things, and slamming each other into unforgiving boards all the time. And that's not even taking into account the hundred-mile-an-hour slap shots launching a piece of frozen rubber at guys' heads."

"So you're saying there's more blood in hockey," Chuck shot back, grinning to let me know he was joking around with me.

But it wasn't a joke. Not to me. "There *is* more blood in hockey. I mean, maybe in boxing and MMA you get a bit more, but—"

"But nothing," Chuck cut in, and most of the heads around the room nodded in agreement with him. "The facts are the facts. Once your blood hits the air and is no longer contained within your body, the virus dies fast. So the chances of anyone contracting HIV from you—whether you're in a fight on the ice or you get some teeth knocked out by an errant puck or someone slashes your throat open with a skate again—are so slim as to be statistically irrelevant. Your doctors are in a lot more danger of contracting HIV from you than your teammates or opponents are, so that shouldn't even be one of the things you consider when making your decision. Now, if this is just about the stigma since your secret is out—"

"I don't care about the stigma," I interrupted, even though that was bullshit and everyone in this room knew it.

"Right," Darlene said, scowling at me. "Sure you don't. Never mind the fact that you've got to face more of it than the rest of us combined."

Chuck nodded. "Look, none of us in here is going to pretend we have a clue what it's like to be in your shoes. Because we don't. For most of us, maybe our family and a few friends know that we have HIV, plus our doctors and a few other key people. Maybe for a handful of us, there are a few dozen people in our lives who know. But it's not like we've got millions of people looking at us the way you do. But don't try to lie to us and say that's not playing a factor in whether you keep playing or not, because no one here's gonna buy that."

"Everyone knows that's why Magic Johnson stopped playing back in the '90s," Bill added. Bill was a high school biology teacher who'd been living with HIV almost as long as I'd been alive.

"We don't *know* that," Darlene said.

Bill rolled his eyes. "Yeah, we do. Even back then, we knew enough about HIV to know he wasn't likely to spread it from playing sports. It was just because other players were scared. They wanted to listen to fearmongering, not to facts. Fear is what ran him out of the NBA, and it would be a damn shame if Drew were to allow fear to run him out of the NHL more than two decades later."

The discussion kept bouncing around like that for the rest of the session. By the end of it, I still wasn't sure what I'd tell the team. I knew all the arguments for continuing to play, but I couldn't shake the sensation that I should quit.

The big positive to come out of the meeting was that this time, Ravyn stopped me before I could leave instead of the other way around. I'd started to unfold myself out of the chair, stretching my back after sitting in such an uncomfortable position for so long, when she reached out a tentative hand and placed it on my forearm. Her touch was so soft I almost didn't feel it—more of a tickle than anything—but I glanced down to find her staring at me. And smiling.

Her smile nearly buckled my knees. "You were right," she said. "I didn't have to talk."

"No one's going to make you talk if you don't want to." Not if I had anything to do with it, at least. For whatever reason, I felt the need to protect her.

The corners of her mouth quirked up again. I could get used to seeing her smile.

"How's the arm healing?" she asked.

Without hesitation, I dragged up the sleeve of my T-shirt to show her. "No itching yet."

She looked it over with critical eyes. "What are you putting on it? And how often?"

"Udder balm, just like you told me to. Two or three times a day."

She nodded, apparently satisfied with my answer. "It'll probably start itching in a few more days. Don't you *dare* scratch it."

"Yes, ma'am." I started heading for the door, and thankfully, she walked alongside me. I wanted to get out of there, but I wasn't ready to leave her company yet. "You hungry?" I asked, hoping she'd let me buy her lunch this time.

"Not hungry, no."

Yeah, my heart dropped a bit on hearing that. There wasn't any point in denying it. We walked out the main entry and into the parking lot, where the sun threatened to blind me. I should've brought my sunglasses inside, but they were sitting on the dashboard of my car. I kept walking that way, trying to figure out what else I could do to get more time with Ravyn.

Because I *wanted* to spend more time with her. She'd started to open up to me—even if it was only a bit—and the more she revealed, the greater my curiosity grew.

But then she surprised me again by placing her hand inside mine and stopping. On a physical level, there was no way that could have stopped me. But on a visceral level, there wasn't a chance I could take another step. Not without her coming along with me.

Even though we were standing in the middle of the fire lane cutting in front of the community center, I stood rooted to the ground and faced her.

"You still don't need to feed me," she said. "But there's something else I want from you."

The heat in her gaze made it clear exactly what that something was, and I'd be the biggest idiot on the planet if I even dreamed of telling her no.

Whatever this thing between us was becoming, I didn't have the first clue what to call it. Friends with benefits? Fuck buddies? I didn't know. It wasn't what I wanted, but it was still a hell of a lot better than the alternative.

"You're sure?" I asked, my voice thick with lust.

She licked her lips and nodded.

Well, fuck me.

Ten

Drew

WE'D BARELY GOTTEN through the door leading from my garage into the kitchen when Ravyn threw herself at me, kissing me like a starving woman. She dragged my T-shirt free from the waistband of my denim shorts so fast it was a miracle she didn't rip the fabric. Not that I would have cared. What was a torn shirt compared to a sexy-as-sin woman wanting me badly enough to rip my clothes off me?

I picked her up by the thighs, reveling in her demanding kisses. She wrapped her legs around my waist, holding on to my shoulders as I carried her into my bedroom. I kicked the door closed behind us and tried to lay her back on the bed, but she gave me a tug, and I practically fell on top of her.

She gave a sexy squeak of surprise, as if that wasn't what she'd intended, but I swallowed the sound up with another kiss. She smelled like a fall thunderstorm—fresh rain and crackling electricity. I could get drunk on her, especially the way she writhed beneath me, trying to get our bodies closer. But there were too many clothes in the way, and we were both in too much of a rush to slow down and take them off properly.

I shoved her shirt and bra up, freeing her breasts, then fought with the button and fly on her jeans. Fucking skinny jeans. They looked hot as hell, showing off every curve of her body to absolute perfection, but they were a nightmare to peel away from her skin. I dragged them down to her knees before my frustration got the better of me. Denim wouldn't give as easily as my T-shirt had.

"Let me," she panted, wiggling her hips beneath me to shift the material free. "You get rid of those," she added with a meaningful nod toward my shorts.

She didn't need to tell me twice. I stood up, undid the fly, and discarded the rest of my clothes before I could think too hard about what we were doing. She was still struggling with her jeans, so I threw open the drawer of my nightstand, took out a condom, and suited up.

Ravyn finally had one leg free. Instead of working to finish the job, she reached for me again, bringing me down on top of her and shoving her tongue into my mouth.

I knew I should slow things down. If we kept going like this, I wouldn't last very long at all. But damn if I could think clearly enough for that with Ravyn digging her fingers into my ass and clasping her legs around mine, writhing beneath me like a woman possessed.

Still, I had to try. I grazed my hands down her sides, then up again to caress her breasts. She hissed against my lips when my thumbs brushed over her taut nipples and teased the bars piercing her there, which made me chuckle.

"You like that?"

She raked one hand down my hip and reached for my cock. "I'd like it better if you'd fuck me already." She captured me in her small hands and stroked a couple of times, and my hips rocked into her almost involuntarily. That brought a sexy grin to her lips and a dark, lusty look to her eyes. "We're both ready. Christ, Drew, I'm so fucking wet."

And she wasn't kidding about that, either. I slipped a hand between our bodies, and it glided effortlessly along her core. I choked out a groan that was full of need.

"I've been wet almost since you walked into that room," she said, her hips grinding up against me while she squeezed my dick and rubbed her thumb over the head. "Kept trying to pay attention to what people were telling you, but all I could think about was how much I wanted you inside me."

"Fuck, that feels good." I buried my face in the hollow between her shoulder and neck, breathing her in. One of her dreads flitted over my face. I shivered with a jolt of desire. Her dreads were surprisingly soft to the touch, and they smelled like coconut.

"This'll feel better," she whispered, her lips brushing my ear. Then she fitted me to her entrance.

I surged forward, finding my way home. And she was right. It did feel better, especially because of the soft whimpering sounds she made with every thrust, which she almost always followed with more dirty talk.

"Harder," she demanded. "I want to feel every inch of that big cock."

So I lifted her knees up until her ankles were over my shoulders, and I gave it to her harder and deeper. Which only made her tighter. Which felt like heaven to me. Which made the base of my spine tingle, like I was about to come.

I couldn't keep going like that. Not for long, and I was absolutely *not* ready for this to be over yet.

I flipped us around, resting my head on the pillows and lifting her over me. She straddled me with her knees resting on either side of my hips, her hands braced on my chest to hold her steady while she rose and fell above me.

Those gorgeous, round breasts bounced with every movement. I helped myself to a handful, swirling my thumb around the hardened nub. "Perfect fucking breasts," I murmured.

"Don't you dare stop that," she said, dropping her head back with a look of sheer bliss claiming her features.

"I have no intention of stopping." And my dick hoped she wouldn't be stopping what she was doing anytime soon, either. She'd taken up a motion that was a mixture of bouncing over me and grinding against me, and I was about as close to heaven as I expected was possible this side of the grave.

Ravyn kept changing things up, which turned me on more than I could have ever imagined. One minute she relaxed above me, going soft and pliant as she leaned down for a sloppy kiss. Then in the next moment, every muscle in her body would tense. She'd throw back her head, straining to get closer to me. To touch me in more places. To take me deeper.

I got caught up in watching her ride me and feeling the way she squeezed me, and even though I was still on the verge of coming, it became even more important to me to be sure she came first.

When she arched her back, I sat up and dipped my head so I could take her breast in my mouth and suckle her tit, shoving her bra and T-shirt up again, since we'd never managed to get them fully off. She let out a moan that made my heart stutter. Then later, when she leaned over me, her hair like a coconut-scented, lavender waterfall around my face as she kissed me, I held her tight around the waist and slipped a hand between us to thumb her clit.

That slight contact was all it took to send her crashing over the edge. But this time, her climax was almost silent. Her sexy sigh was like a shot of adrenaline that went straight to my cock, especially with the way she shuddered in my arms and collapsed against my chest, spent and sated.

And then, I didn't even try to hold myself back anymore. I held Ravyn close and pumped into her with a shout, my whole body tingling with my release.

We lay in a heap, tangled limbs covered in a sheen of sweat and lungs playing catch-up. After a while, I knew I *needed* to move, but I sure as hell didn't *want* to move. Because Ravyn wasn't trying to close herself off to me. She was as relaxed as I'd ever known her to be, her cheek resting on my shoulder, her full breasts pillowing against my upper abs.

I stroked her back, trying to cling to the moment for as long as I could. Once one of us moved, the spell would break. She'd go back to pushing me away, only coming to me for a physical release.

Sex was supposed to be more of an emotional experience for women than for men, but I must be the exception that proved the rule. In every relationship I'd ever been in, it had been these quiet moments after sex when I'd felt the most connected to my partner.

That seemed to be happening again with Ravyn, only she and I weren't even involved. Were we? Could two afternoon quickies, a week apart, be the basis for something more? Probably not, and I knew I had to be the world's biggest idiot for wanting it.

But I did.

I didn't understand it, and I sure as hell would never be able to explain it to another living soul, but it was the absolute truth. I wanted more than a weekly hookup.

I wanted to learn all the sounds Ravyn made.

I wanted to unearth the secrets she was keeping—about the baby that didn't exist and about the meaning behind her adoption symbol tattoo and about any number of other things that hadn't come up in any way yet.

I wanted to find out how she made her hair so soft and kept it smelling so good.

I wanted to watch her work so I could witness her artistry taking shape.

I wanted to discover how long she'd been hurting herself and why she did it, and I wanted to help her stop.

Damn if I had a clue how to go about making any of that happen.

After a few minutes, the hand she'd been resting on my abs inched upward until she could fit it between her cheek and my body. "Your heartbeat is loud," she said.

I laughed so hard I nearly dislodged her. "My heartbeat is *loud*? Seriously?"

"Yeah. Loud and steady. It's going to put me to sleep if I'm not careful."

I didn't want her to be careful. I wanted her to stay just like this, maybe fall asleep on me, trusting me enough for that if nothing else. I knew that would be asking for too much, but it didn't stop me from wanting it. "Would it be the end of the world to take a nap right now?" I teased, trying to keep things light. "It's not like you have to go to work today."

She tensed. It was just a slight change, almost imperceptible, but I caught the tightening of her previously languid muscles. "How do you know that?" she demanded.

"I saw the hours posted on the door. The whole place is closed on Tuesdays."

"I didn't mean to lie to you last week," she rushed to say.

I blinked a couple of times, but then I understood. Last week, she'd told me she couldn't stay afterward because she had to go to work. That was why she'd run off from the hospital as soon as she'd dropped off London's wheelchair.

Well, hell.

"I wasn't trying to catch you in a lie," I said, but it was too late. The damage was done. She was already peeling herself off of me and sitting upright on the edge of the bed. I felt the loss immediately, so I sat up, too, and wrapped my arms around her from behind.

She was still rigid.

"You don't have to explain yourself," I said. "You don't owe me anything, least of all a reason for not wanting to stick around last week. Hell, we'd only met that morning."

"I don't normally lie about things," she said.

I wished she'd soften again, maybe lean back against me, but for now I'd settle for the fact that she wasn't pulling away from me. "Well, I'd say that lying about having to work, to a guy you'd only known for about two or three hours, is pretty low on the scale of awful things to lie about," I teased.

She let out a chuckle. Progress. But then she moved out of my arms and stood up. Damn it. I wasn't ready to let go of her, and now she was probably going to tell me she needed to leave even if she wouldn't use the excuse of getting to work this time.

"Bathroom," she mumbled as she headed that direction, tripping over the skinny jeans that were still hanging off a single leg. She made it a few steps, but then she actually tripped herself and took a tumble.

"Shit, are you all right?" I was off the bed and at her side in a hurry, helping her up.

But instead of crying, she was laughing. Hard. So hard that I couldn't help but follow suit.

"We really should've taken these all the way off," she said once she caught her breath, giving the denim another tug. "Now they're all sweaty and stuck in place and gross."

"Let me help you." I sat on the floor and tugged while she leaned the other direction. Eventually they came free, and we both fell backward, laughing even harder than before. Once I could breathe again, I pointed to her T-shirt and the bra still shoved up around her shoulders. "Give me those things, too, and I can put it all in the wash if you want. I mean, if you're not in a hurry to get out of here…" I left that hanging between us, hoping she'd agree but resigned to the fact that she probably wouldn't.

She was still laughing as she dragged them both overhead and passed them over to me.

I wasn't laughing any longer. Because now I could

see the marks on her upper arm from where she'd cut herself—a meticulous row of angry red lines, evenly spaced. The sight hit me like a punch to the gut.

"What?" she asked, suddenly self-conscious and wrapping her arms in front of her.

My tongue was thick and my mouth had gone dry. I cleared my throat, debating exactly what to say and how to say it. But nothing seemed right, so I just spit it out. "When you said you cut yourself, I assumed you meant past tense. A long time ago. Not now."

She sat there on the hardwood floor of my bedroom, completely naked and vulnerable, staring at me. But a bit at a time, her mask settled back into place.

Fucking hell.

Eleven

Ravyn

THE LAUGHTER HAD all fizzled away. So had any lingering sexiness. All that remained was a crap-ton of uncomfortable silence.

Combine that with the way Drew was looking at me—some odd combination of sadness, pity, and curiosity—and all I wanted to do was grab my clothes out of his hands, throw them on, and get the hell out of his house.

I didn't even care if I had to walk all the way back to the community center to get my car. It might take me the rest of the day to get there, but a good, long walk would do wonders for my state of mind. It'd give me plenty of time to think through all the things racing through my head, if nothing else.

But that would be running away. *Again.* Seemed like all I had done for the last year or so was run away from things instead of facing them. Actually, I'd been running a lot longer than that. I'd run away with Jax back when I was only fourteen years old.

Getting the hell out of whatever shitty situation I found myself in by fleeing was apparently my MO. I couldn't keep going like that forever. At some point, I had to grow up. Dig in my heels. Confront life instead of letting it crush me.

So instead of giving in to that urge, I swallowed hard and nodded in his direction, indicating my clothes in his hands. "I'd absolutely appreciate it if you'd go wash those, like you suggested."

He took such a deep breath it made me think he'd been holding on to it for a while. But he nodded and got up. Before leaving the bedroom, he stepped into his closet for a moment. When he came out again, he'd pulled on some ratty, old sweatpants, and he tossed a T-shirt and a pair of boxers in my direction. "They're way too big for you, but it's better than nothing." Then he ducked out of the bedroom and disappeared.

It was a hell of a lot better than nothing. Offering to wash my clothes and then giving me something to cover up with was incredibly thoughtful. And kind. It was something a good guy would do, if good guys actually existed.

I wasn't sure what to do with Drew. What box in my mind was he supposed to fill?

I carried the clothes into the bathroom with me, where I took care of my business and cleaned myself up. I took another longing look at that enormous tub. My apartment didn't even have a bathtub. Just a tiny, cramped shower. I hadn't had a good bath in so long I almost didn't even remember what it felt like to climb in and soak my muscles. But Drew didn't bring me here so I could indulge in his bathtub, so I needed to just get that out of my head.

I tugged his clothes into place. The boxers wouldn't stay up unless I was sitting, and the T-shirt hung down almost to my knees, but they were softer to the touch than anything in my closet.

I'd never understand why women's T-shirts couldn't be made out of the same super-comfy fabric as men's T-shirts. Like the T-shirt I'd worn today. It was one of Rick's, originally, but he'd given it to me several years ago one night when I'd needed a place to crash and ended up at his house. Why did women have to get the short end of the stick all the time?

When I left the bathroom, Drew still hadn't returned to his bedroom. Plenty of time had passed for him to start a load of laundry. I'd never been one to go snooping around someone else's house, and he hadn't exactly taken me on the grand tour before. Both times I'd been here, we'd had a single purpose in mind, and the only room required to accomplish our goals had been the bedroom.

I took a seat on the edge of the bed to wait for him to come back, but after a minute or two, I got the sense he wasn't planning to. That sense turned to absolute surety a couple of minutes later when I heard banging coming from the direction of the kitchen and smelled something distinctly like garlic and onions.

Well, then. It was the middle of the day, and since my clothes were in the wash, there wasn't much chance of us going somewhere else. It made sense that he would need to eat, but damn if it didn't make me uncomfortable to think that he probably intended to feed me, too. Walking with an awkward Hop-Along-Cassidy gait in order to keep his boxers up, I followed my nose to join him.

"You like pasta?" he asked, popping his head up when I emerged from the hallway. He flashed me a knockout grin.

Good lord, he was too sexy by half. Never mind the fact that he'd just given me a wild, sweaty orgasm; my girly bits were already coming back to life.

"You don't have to feed me," I reminded him. Which was probably bitchy of me. No, it was *definitely* bitchy of me. Whether it was an act or not, he was trying to do something nice for me, and I was acting like he was trying to pay me for sex.

He kept chopping stuff and tossing it into a skillet, though, and didn't seem to mind that I didn't know how to behave when someone treated me with kindness. "I know I don't have to feed you, but unless you want me to pass out later when I should be driving you back to your car, I do need to feed *me*. And it's easier to cook for two than it is to cook for one. So… Pasta? Yes or no? I've got some potatoes I could do something with instead if you'd rather. Oh, wait." He set down the knife and looked up at me, raising a brow. "You're not a vegetarian, are you? Because I was planning to sauté some shrimp to throw in there. But if you don't—"

"Shrimp is fine," I cut in, fighting off the bitchy urge once again. "Pasta is, too."

He winked with a wide smile. I could get used to him smiling at me like that if I allowed myself. Scary thought.

"You look hot in my clothes, by the way," he said.

Then it was my turn to grin. "I feel like I need a belt

to keep the shorts up."

"You could lose them if you want. The shirt covers enough. And even if it didn't..." He waggled his brows.

He was right about the shirt, and I'd never been much of a prude about my body. Seemed like a good plan to me, so I shimmied out of them.

"Just toss them in the hamper in my closet," he said, focusing on the task of cooking again.

I did as he suggested, but on my way back into the main part of the house, the doorbell rang. I froze, panicking. Did he have guests coming over? But maybe it was just someone selling things door to door. People still did that, right?

Drew didn't seem anywhere near as concerned as I was. He set down the knife, gave the stuff in the skillet a quick toss, and headed toward the door. I did my best to find a corner of the living room to disappear into, somewhere I wouldn't be seen. Short of literally ducking behind a piece of furniture or hiding in another room, there weren't any good options. I settled for taking a seat on the chair closest to his bedroom, where I could make a hasty escape if needed.

"Hi, Drew!" a little boy shouted. A dog's bark punctuated his greeting. Actually—it sounded more like a puppy than a fully grown dog.

"Hi," Drew replied, sounding confused.

Without another word, the boy and puppy raced inside, heading straight for the living room. Where I was. Holy shit. I was so freaked out that they were in front of me that my muscles decided not to work. I couldn't get up and run off to hide in another room. All I could do was hope they didn't see me.

Yeah, no luck with that. Not when you have purple dreads and tattoos on nearly every available patch of skin. I tried to sink further into the background because I was only wearing one of Drew's T-shirts. And because, whoever they were, they didn't know me. And…well…why on earth was I here? I hadn't been counting on this at all, and at the moment, there was nowhere I wanted to be less than where I was.

The little boy, who might be six or seven, had dark brown hair and an impish grin. He was wearing swim trunks and had already-inflated floaties secured around his biceps and bright orange sunglasses falling off his nose. The yellow lab puppy couldn't be more than about six weeks old, based on how tiny it was and how it seemed to be moving faster than its feet could keep up, causing it to run at a sideways angle.

Apparently, I hadn't done a good enough job of hiding myself. The boy skidded to a stop in the middle of the living room and grinned at me. "Did you have a sleepover?"

I could only blink in response, shock and embarrassment keeping me tongue-tied.

"I'm Carter," he said. "And that's Snoopy." The puppy yapped a few times, running circles around him before racing toward me. The next thing I knew, I had an overly excited puppy in my arms, licking my face and wiggling like crazy.

I'd never spent much time around animals before. Definitely not around puppies. Even though I was more than just a little bit freaked out, I also kind of liked it. This puppy had never seen me before, but he was already showering me with more affection than I knew what to do with.

"I'm Ravyn," I managed to say without getting puppy tongue in my mouth. But barely.

Carter giggled. "I want purple hair, too." Then he

crossed over to me and petted Snoopy on the back. He nodded, a serious look in his dark brown eyes. "He likes it when you rub his ears. Like this." Taking one of my hands in his, he closed my thumb and forefinger over one of Snoopy's floppy ears and gently rubbed.

I'd only thought Drew's T-shirt was soft before. This puppy's ear? I'd never felt anything softer in my life. It was like velvet against my skin. I rubbed again.

That puppy damned near let out a sigh of contentment before squirming to get closer to me. I honestly couldn't figure out how I'd ended up nearly naked in Drew's house with a little boy teaching me how to rub a puppy's ears. But despite myself, I liked it. What the hell was going on in my life?

"Sorry," another man said, still in the hall, his Canadian accent thick in the way he pronounced the single word. "Trying to get everything moved in today, but it's not easy to do with these two underfoot. I tried Razor first, but he's got a thing with Tori's little ballerinas this afternoon. He suggested dropping them off here since you're closest. Said maybe you'd let them swim while I unload the truck? It'll just be a couple of hours."

"You didn't think about calling first?" Drew said, but he didn't sound all that upset. "I don't know what to do with kids. Or puppies."

"You've got nieces," the other man said.

"Yeah, but I've never been alone with them."

"Just keep these two outside, where they can't ruin anything." Whoever he was, I didn't miss the fact that he hadn't apologized for not calling first. He'd just brought a kid and puppy over and assumed it would be all right.

Was that how things worked in Drew's world? I'd

never experienced anything like that before. My life had always been far too complicated for someone to just drop in with no warning. Probably because I was always dropping out before they got close enough for that.

"I brought mac and cheese and Kool-Aid," the other man continued. "He doesn't normally get to eat that stuff, so between that and the pool… I'm hoping he won't be too much hassle for you."

The men kept talking in the hall for a few minutes, and I tried to carefully tug Drew's T-shirt down so it wouldn't reveal quite so much while I sat here with Carter and Snoopy. Especially because I still didn't know who, exactly, they were.

"Why does your hair look like rope?" Carter asked me, reaching out a sticky hand to touch one. He giggled again. "It tickles."

"They're dreadlocks."

He nodded solemnly. "You gotta get the key, then."

"The key?"

"To unlock it."

"Ah," I said. Not that I understood. Not in the least. And I was too busy studying his small hand and memorizing the velvet-soft feel of the puppy's ears to try to make sense of it, even if a small smile was working its way to my lips.

Carter climbed up onto my lap, like there was nowhere else he should be. He kept toying with my hair while he told me how they'd found Snoopy in a black garbage bag on the side of the road, and his dad told him they could keep him, and he was going to have to leave Snoopy here with his dad when he went back to Minnesota in a couple of weeks because his mom was allergic to dogs, but none of it registered in my mind. Because all I could think about was how soft the puppy's ears were and how trusting the little boy was, and how I hoped that somewhere, right now, my son was curled up on someone's lap just like this, with a puppy of his very own.

And then my chest clenched, and I thought I might cry.

The front door closed, and Drew came back down the hall. He looked over at the three of us, a grocery bag in his hands and a sheepish expression on his face. "Sorry about that," he said, grinning again as he tossed the bag on the counter and stirred the food in the skillet. "One of my teammates. Everyone's coming back into town for preseason. Looks like it's not just the two of us this afternoon. Hope you don't mind?"

I didn't have it in me to mind. I shook my head, still in a daze at how fast everything was happening.

"You feel like having some mac and cheese before we head out to the pool, little man?" he asked.

Carter leaped down from my lap, nodded, and ran into the kitchen. "I like mac and cheese." He reached into the bag on the counter and took out the blue box. "Can I help?"

He left Snoopy with me, probably because the puppy was about to fall asleep in my arms. The pup was all tuckered out, and rubbing his ears seemed to have helped him relax into a much-needed nap.

"How about you help by sitting down at the table and drinking your Kool-Aid while I take care of the hot stuff?" Drew suggested. "Looks like your dad put a coloring book in here for you, even." He might not *think* he knew what to do with puppies and kids, but it seemed to me he was a natural. But he had said something about nieces, and it seemed natural that at least some of his teammates would have kids he'd be around sometimes. Could things like that rub off on a person?

Drew got Carter settled at the table with his drink and the coloring book. Then he checked on everything on the stove again before coming into the living room and sitting on the arm of my chair. With a finger, he stroked the puppy's forehead. Not too long ago, he'd been stroking me in much the same way, only in a far more intimate spot. Damn if I hadn't melted into his touch exactly like Snoopy was now, too.

"Cute little guy, isn't he?" Drew asked me.

"Snoopy or Carter?"

He shrugged. "Both, I guess. Sorry. I didn't know they were coming over."

"You do realize I'm sitting here practically naked, right?" I hissed. "With a small child right there."

"Trust me, I'm aware." Drew chuckled softly, but Carter was completely focused on his coloring book and oblivious to us. "But what his father doesn't know won't hurt *me*. I'll check on the laundry. Maybe I can move your things into the dryer now. And I'll see if I can find you something better to wear while we wait. Can't scar the kid by flashing your bits around. I'd never hear the end of it, because there'd be no chance he wouldn't blab it to his father first chance he got."

He headed off into the laundry room, and all I could think was that I should've run away after all. This was feeling entirely too domestic for my sense of comfort.

Especially because I liked it.

Twelve

Drew

ALL THE PUBLIC pools had closed for the season after Labor Day yesterday, but the weather was still plenty warm enough to take a swim. All summer long, I'd spent more time in my pool than I should, particularly since we were in a drought, and I never had a problem with any of the guys coming over to join me if they were in town. Not too many of them stuck around Tulsa over the off-season, anyway, so it wasn't like they were throwing a massive party at my place every night or anything.

Having Ethan "Huggy Bear" Higgins drop off his kid and a puppy I didn't even know they owned for a swim date was a first, though.

I didn't exactly mind. Or at least I wouldn't under normal circumstances. But today wasn't normal, and this wasn't quite how I'd seen the afternoon going.

I'd been hoping to get Ravyn in the shower with me after lunch, for one thing…and then if we'd ended up back in bed afterward, all the better. I was starting to learn that she was a lot more willing to share bits and pieces of herself with me when she was sexually sated, so that seemed like a good plan for getting to know her better. More than anything, I wanted to learn more about this whole cutting business. Why she did it. What she thought she could do instead that wouldn't cause her physical harm.

But we couldn't quite turn the afternoon into a sex marathon with Carter and his puppy hanging around.

Other than that, I didn't mind having the kid here. He and Snoopy were actually a hell of a lot of fun. I'd only met Carter twice before. Because the kid was so young, he stayed with his mother most of the time, and Bear got a month with him over the summer, when he could be back in Minnesota, close to his ex-wife.

But Carter was old enough to fly alone now, so this year was going to be different. Which meant his father had to have an actual house and furniture and all that jazz, instead of living out of a hotel like he'd been doing. Since the house he'd bought was only a couple of blocks away, something told me I'd be seeing an awful lot of Carter this season.

And apparently Snoopy, too.

At the moment, the two of them were doggy-paddling around in the shallow end of the pool. Shallow was a relative term, of course, as my pool went from four feet on one end to seven feet at the other end, all of which was far too deep for a six-year-old boy to be able to touch the bottom.

After feeding everyone and finding a pair of shorts with a drawstring she could tie around her waist so they'd stay on for Ravyn, I'd slathered the kid with sunscreen and brought everyone out back. Carter wasn't a bad swimmer. He probably didn't need the floaties, but he felt more confident with them on, and it meant he wasn't hanging all over me, so why give the kid a hard time about wearing them? That puppy, though? I doubted he'd ever been in the water before other than the bath Carter claimed they'd given him last night in the hotel room, but Snoopy was swimming like a champ.

Those two were playing full tilt and had been for a while. Something told me that both of them—hell, you could even add me into the equation—would need a serious nap later. My nieces were a few years younger than Carter, but I doubted there was much difference when it came to how hard he'd crash after this kind of fun and exertion.

Ravyn still hadn't gotten into the pool with us, which disappointed me like nobody's business. She had her hair tied up on top of her head, either to keep her neck cool or to prevent her hair from getting wet, I assumed. She'd tied a knot in my T-shirt, slightly above her waist. No, it wasn't exactly a bikini, but it would do since we hadn't planned on taking a swim when I'd brought her home with me.

She said she could swim, so that wasn't the problem. No matter how many times I'd invited her into the water, though, she still hadn't joined us, choosing instead to sit in one of the deck chairs under the big umbrella.

"You really shouldn't be in the pool right now if you want that tattoo to heal properly," she called out to me after Carter made a flying leap into my arms.

I released him and let him paddle over to the ladder

to climb out. He'd been jumping into the water repeatedly at various points during the afternoon, and I kept moving farther away from the edge. So far, he hadn't complained that I was too far away or the water too deep. I tossed a ball for Snoopy before turning my attention to Ravyn.

God, she looked sexy as hell right now. The thought of that T-shirt being wet and plastered to her breasts was all it took to get me hard. Good thing I was in the water so no one could see. I checked my watch again, wondering how much longer Bear would be. Three o'clock already, and no more word from him, damn it.

But I winked in Ravyn's direction. "I know. I remember the rules, but sometimes a guy has to break the rules, you know?"

"If you break the rules, you get a yellow card!" Carter shouted. "Then you have to sit in the quiet corner."

He'd almost reached the ladder, so I figured I had about thirty more seconds before he launched himself toward my head. "I'll be sure to let your dad know you completely understand how that works," I replied, never turning my attention from Ravyn.

Because holy hell, I liked looking at her. Too much for my own good, I was almost positive.

"So what do the three of us have to do to convince you to join us?" I asked. "Promise not to splash your hair?" I didn't have the first clue what went into taking care of dreads. Chlorinated water probably wasn't the best thing ever for them, though, and I doubted all the pool chemicals would be good for the color, either. It didn't take a genius to figure that much out.

But she shook her head, crossing her arms in front of her. "Don't think it's a good idea today."

Today? But it might not be a horrible idea some other day? Color me confused about that, but Carter launched himself into the water with a delighted cackle, splashing water all over the place—especially in my eyes—distracting me from Ravyn's answer. I blinked the chemicals away and made a grab for him since he was flailing like a drowning cat. Once I had him, I realized what the problem was—his arms were bare.

"Where'd your floaties go, little man?"

"I took 'em off," Carter said, like it was no big deal. "Wanted to swim all by myself." Never mind the fact that he had both arms wrapped around my neck so tightly he might cut off my airway and his legs were holding on to me in a monkey-boy grip.

Snoopy paddled for us, yapping up a storm, but he was getting tired. The puppy was swimming a lot more slowly than he had been only a short while ago. I swooped out an arm and fished him out of the water, settling him in Carter's arms. Snoopy shook and sprayed water all over both of us.

"How about next time you want to try to swim by yourself, you give me some warning first?" I suggested.

Carter giggled in response.

I swam him over to the side and set him on the edge. "Go get those for me, so we can put them on again." I pointed toward the floaties.

Then I took Snoopy out of his arms, setting the pup on the concrete. He stayed, at least for the moment. Something told me he'd be back in the water in three… two… one…

Splash. Should've put money on that one. I watched the puppy out of the corner of my eye.

"I don't wanna wear them," Carter said with a pout that would do my nieces proud.

"Well, here's the deal." I looked him straight in the eye, talking to him like he was a man. "Your mom and dad don't let you swim on your own yet, do they? You have to have your floaties on if they're with you." I waited for him to nod his head. "Right," I said. "So that means I need to have both eyes on you if you don't have your floaties on. But Snoopy hasn't ever gone swimming before, either, so I need to have at least one eye on him, too. I've only got two eyes, and I'd need at least three for that to work out."

"Ravyn could help," Carter said. "She's got eyes."

True enough, but there was a possibility that she couldn't swim and she'd only told me she could to save face, not that I'd care one way or the other. Why else wouldn't she get in the pool with us? And if she really couldn't swim and she came out with us, then I'd need more than three eyes, because I'd need to be watching her, too.

But what I told him was, "She's a guest. She's not here to act as a lifeguard." Although I wouldn't mind practicing a variation of CPR with her later… Thoughts like that weren't helping right now, though, so I shook it off. "Go on. Grab your floaties for me so we can put them on again."

He rolled his eyes like a well-rehearsed teenager, but he got up and went to fetch the floaties. I settled them back in place—without a single iota of help from Carter, I might add—and gave him a wink. "Good to go. Now you can jump in to your heart's content. How far out do you want me to go?"

"*Way* back!" he said, pointing toward the opposite side.

"Like, to the middle?"

"Farther."

I laughed, but I swam out into the middle of the pool. "Think you can jump this far?"

Instead of answering, he backed up a few steps, then ran for me, pinching his nose and squeezing his eyes shut. I had to close some of the distance because, of course, he couldn't make it anywhere near as far as he wanted to. I scooped him out of the water, and Snoopy came paddling over to us with a miniature tennis ball in his mouth.

"They'll keep you doing this all day, if you let them," Ravyn called over.

And wasn't that the truth…

I pried the ball free from Snoopy's mouth and tossed it a couple of feet in front of me—sending it toward Ravyn, actually. He took off after it, and Carter followed. Which meant they were both between me and Ravyn, so I could actually look at her again.

I gave her a sheepish look and mouthed, *Sorry*. Because there wasn't a doubt in my mind this wasn't how she'd imagined spending her afternoon. It wasn't what I'd planned for, either, but I was enjoying myself a lot more than I ever expected to.

"You don't need to be sorry," she said quietly.

"No?" I raised a brow. "But you still won't get in with us."

She shook her head, but there was a hint of a smile on her face.

Carter reached the puppy's ball first, and he gave it a toss, sending Snoopy off in a different direction. Those two were having so much fun it should be illegal, if their excited barks and infectious laughter were any indication.

But I was focused on Ravyn's eyes. She was laughing, too, and it completely changed her face. She looked so relaxed and carefree right now, and something in my gut clenched. I'd do just about anything to see her laugh like this more often—a realization that nearly stole my breath.

My phone started ringing. It was sitting on the table next to Ravyn.

"Who is it?" I asked.

She peeked over, and her expression turned comical. "Someone named *Huggy Bear*?"

"That's Carter's dad. Answer it for me." I picked both Carter and Snoopy up in a single swoop, setting them on the edge of the pool before dragging myself out.

Despite an uncomfortable pinch of her eyebrows, Ravyn answered the call. "Drew's coming," she said. "Hold on just a second."

Snoopy was about to dive back in, so I put him under my arm like a football and turned to Carter. "Stay out for a minute while I talk to your dad, okay?"

He pouted. "Okay…"

When I got to the table, I handed Ravyn the puppy, ignoring her look of shock, and dried my hands on one of the towels we'd brought out before taking the phone from her.

"Hey, how's it going?" I said.

"You didn't tell me you had company," Bear grumbled.

"You didn't give me the chance."

"True. Anyway, I'm done. On my way over, but I thought I'd see if you wanted me to grab some beers. But since you've got company—"

"Beers are good," I cut in. "And maybe some steaks for the grill?" I covered the mouthpiece and caught Ravyn's eye—which wasn't easy, since she was thoroughly distracted by the way Snoopy was trying to climb her and lick her into submission. "Do you like steak?" I asked.

"I…" Then she shrugged. "I guess?"

That was as good as a yes, as far as I was concerned. I mean, it was only steak we were talking about. And I wanted her to stick around. Having her over for dinner seemed like a good plan, even if it meant having Huggy Bear and Carter around, too. "Yeah, beer and steaks. We're just about to put on more sunscreen, so no rush."

"Got it. Be there in twenty." Then he hung up.

"Can I get back in the pool?" Carter shouted. He'd stayed on the edge, his feet dangling in the water.

"Not yet," I said. "You need more sunscreen first. And a drink."

"And a snack!" he added.

"Right. So come over here so we can deal with all of that." I held out the towel, and he raced into it. While I dried him off and covered him in another heavy dose of sunscreen, Ravyn dug in the cooler for one of his Kool-Aids and a string cheese.

"You ever going to get in the pool with us?" I asked, trying to sound casual. "No one cares that you're not in a swimsuit."

"It's not that," she said, and she sounded like she really meant it, which surprised me.

I cocked a brow at her, spinning Carter around so I could lather up his back now that I'd properly covered his face and chest with the lotion. "Then what is it?"

She licked her lips, glancing at Carter before meeting my gaze. "The cuts on my arm," she said quietly. "I just… What if they haven't closed enough yet?"

And then it all made sense. "You haven't known

about your diagnosis very long, have you?" I asked.

She shook her head. "Five months?"

"Weren't you listening this morning in the session? Everyone was repeatedly pointing out to me that I wouldn't be putting anyone at risk if I started playing hockey again."

"I wasn't able to focus," she admitted with a sheepish expression.

"Well, that's what everyone was telling me. And they're right."

"But you're still nervous about playing hockey."

"I am. But my nerves are unfounded."

"Seriously?

"Completely. Let me put your mind at ease. If you're not bleeding so badly that you should be in the hospital because you're about to die, there's not much chance of you passing it on to someone. Once the blood leaves your body, it dies faster than you think. And when you're in the pool, the chlorine's probably going to kill the virus even if it wasn't already dead. So it's fine."

"Yeah? Promise?" The look in her eyes was full of hope.

"Promise."

"So are you gonna come swimming with me now?" Carter demanded. "I wanna splash you!"

"Guess I'd better put some sunscreen on."

There was no wiping the grin off my face after that, especially because I was imagining how sexy she'd look with my wet T-shirt plastered to her chest. I didn't even care that my teammate and his kid were going to be here to see it, too. I was just glad that at least for a while, Ravyn was going to step outside of her head and allow herself to have a good time.

And later, once the others left, I could get her out of

that wet T-shirt.

That was my plan. And I fully intended to stick to it.

Thirteen

Ravyn

AS SOON AS Carter's father came out lugging a few cases of beer, I knew I was in well over my head—and I wasn't talking about the water level.

I still didn't fully understand why Ethan Higgins was called Huggy Bear by Drew and the rest of his teammates. When I'd questioned him, Drew had mumbled something about it being a play on the last name, but the way he'd kept his voice down made me think he didn't want to say anything in front of Ethan's son, like maybe he didn't want to embarrass the kid. I might be reading too much into it, though.

The *bear* part I got, no problem. Ethan was massive—probably six foot six, at the very least, with a muscular build that made Drew seem almost scrawny in comparison, and I knew firsthand that there was nothing even remotely scrawny about Drew. But Ethan looked like the sort of man who'd bite your head off if you tried to hug him, and he could definitely crush me like a bug if he had a mind to.

Even if I was a hugger, I'd steer clear of this guy. Good thing I wasn't overly affectionate by nature, because that meant there was a zero percent chance of me getting any silly ideas like that in my head.

We were all in the pool, and both Carter and his puppy were chasing me when Ethan arrived. Drew got out to help his teammate unload everything.

They spoke for a minute—too quietly for me to hear anything they said, especially with all the noise coming from Carter and Snoopy—while unloading the beers into a small refrigerator in an outdoor storage shed. Then they headed back into the house together through the kitchen door. When they returned, they had enough steaks to feed a small army, and Lord only knew how many other snacks and side dishes. They made a third trip, bringing bottled water, more Kool-Aid, and other nonalcoholic drinks…as well as Razor and a woman I could only assume was Razor's Russian wife.

Apparently, there was going to be a party. Now I wished I'd never come. Or that I'd insisted on having Drew take me back to my car before all of this had gotten started. Or that I'd just put my clothes back on and ventured out on the walk back to the community center, like I'd debated doing earlier.

But I hadn't done any of those things, and now it appeared I was stuck.

I stared at them longer than I should have since I was supposed to be on child-and-puppy safety duty, but my thoughts were racing. Just exactly how many people were coming over? Looked like dozens, based on the amount of food and drinks Ethan had brought with him. What was Drew planning to tell them about me? What was I supposed to say to them about…well, about *anything*?

The four of them stood near the grill, talking and laughing like old friends—which, yes, I realized that was exactly what they were, but that only made me feel more out of place than I had initially—and I saw Drew say something while pointing in my direction.

Cue my panic.

But Snoopy and Carter made a diving, giggling, barking leap for me, combining to dunk me under the water. It was enough of a distraction to get me out of my head for a moment.

Not for long. I came up spluttering in time to see the back door of the house opening again and more strange faces streaming out, adults and children alike. It was too late for me to streak out of the pool, race inside, find Drew's laundry room, throw on my own clothes, and head home, wasn't it? Yeah, it was, but that didn't stop me from trying to estimate the time it would take me to do exactly that.

The urge to run was so strong it was almost overwhelming.

But before I could do anything, Carter's father stripped off his shirt, kicked his sandals to the side, and belly flopped into the pool like a champion. Carter laughed so hard he took in water and started choking, but he still couldn't stop laughing. I tried to pat him on the back, but Ethan was there in a flash, taking over.

"Thanks," he said to me. No smile. No wink. Just a gruff *thanks* and he took his son away from me. Which was probably for the best. I didn't have any experience with kids beyond the few short hours I'd held my son, and it wouldn't do me any favors to get attached to someone else's kid now.

I nodded, all too aware of Ethan's size now that he was right next to me, and backed away to let him deal with Carter on his own. Ethan pounded him gently on the back while the boy held his arms up in the air. In no time, the choking had stopped, but not the giggling.

"Do it again," he begged.

Before I could get out of the pool and find something to cover myself with, though, it was like the floodgates had opened. Drew's backyard filled with what must be the majority of his hockey team, along with their wives, girlfriends, and kids. Even London showed up, her husband wheeling her out to a place under the shade of an enormous umbrella while she bounced their tiny baby, and my lungs closed up completely.

I couldn't do this. Being around Carter had been more than enough already, but being around a newborn…

I wasn't ready.

I doubted I'd ever be ready.

Tears stung my eyes, but the last thing I needed to do was start crying. That would only draw more attention to me, when all I wanted to do was disappear into the background, slip off of their radars so I could *really* disappear.

There were so many people, and I didn't know any of them but Drew and Carter, and honestly, how well did I know either of them? But there was nowhere for me to hide. Any chance for running I might have had before the arrival of so many strangers had already slipped through my fingers.

More of the men and kids were making their way to the pool, so I grabbed Snoopy's ball and guided him toward the shallower end, since it looked like they were starting up a human cannonball competition in the deep water. I figured I could keep him out of harm's way, and maybe—if I was lucky—they wouldn't notice me.

I didn't know how realistic it was to think they wouldn't all be staring at my purple dreads, but I was going to do my damnedest to pretend I didn't exist.

One of the mothers—a tall, athletic-looking blonde—brought a couple of smaller children over near me, fitting floaties on their arms and putting a couple of inflatable, kid-sized rafts in the water.

I tried to melt into the pool. So far, so good. She was more focused on the children than she was on me.

She put the youngest one—a boy, who looked to be about a year old—on the first raft.

The older boy wasn't having it, though. "I can *swim*, Mommy," he shouted. "Wike Emmy."

"Mm hmm. Emily is a lot older than you, and she's been taking swimming lessons for two summers already," she said, calm as could be. She picked the little boy up again and tried to set him in the second raft, but he kicked too hard for the mother to complete the transfer.

Before the blond woman could sort it out, Snoopy took the opportunity and ran with it. He swam out of my reach and climbed onto the inflatable toy, then curled up in a ball like it was meant to be for him.

The mother took one look at that, burst out laughing, and gave up trying to get her son onto the contraption. "Guess you're going to have to figure it out on your own, Ryan. Somebody stole your raft."

I reached for Snoopy, but he barked in complaint. "I

can get him—"

"No, it's fine," she said, shaking her head. "My husband seemed to think it was a great idea to skip nap time and come out for a pool party, is all. I think that makes today a *great* time to turn this little stinker over to his father." She glanced in the other direction before turning back to me and angling her head toward the younger boy, who was happily floating along with a tiny pair of shades protecting his eyes and a Tulsa Thunderbirds baseball cap covering his head. "You mind keeping an eye on Patrick for me? It'll just be a minute. I'll be right back once I drop Mr. Cranky Pants off with my husband."

In too much shock to do anything else, I shrugged. She took that as my agreement. But then I was alone with a baby. A little boy. He was much bigger than my son had been the last time I'd seen him, but I couldn't help but think they'd be similar in age right now. My son was probably a few months younger.

Did his family take him to the pool and let him float on a raft? Would he be scared of the water? The weight of my guilt acted like an anchor and threatened to pull me under. If I didn't snap out of it, and fast, I'd flood the pool with my tears.

The mother returned only moments later, just as she'd promised. She leaned against the edge of the pool and gently splashed the water onto her son's raft.

He giggled, and something strangely fuzzy took root in my chest. I'd heard more giggles today than I could remember hearing since I was a child. That only made me want to run even more than before. Because I loved the sound of his laughter and that of the other children here, and it was more than I knew how to handle.

"Thanks for that," the blonde said before I could

make my escape. "I'm Dana Zellinger. Eric's wife." The way she said it made it seem as if I was supposed to have a clue who she was, but Drew and I didn't have that sort of a relationship. I wasn't sure what, if anything, he'd told them about me, but I didn't know a damned thing about any of them.

We'd have to mean something to each other to talk about our lives outside of the bed. Obviously, things hadn't progressed to that point, and I doubted they ever would.

But she kept looking at me with an amused expression and a raised brow. Right. Because, after introducing herself, it would make sense for me to do the same.

"Ravyn," I choked out, hoping that was enough. Because I didn't think I could form more words than that.

And besides, what was I? Drew's…friend with benefits? Although, I wasn't sure we were even quite to the stage of friends. We mainly had sex and nothing else.

But she smiled, not demanding an explanation, and went back to playing with her child.

And he kept laughing. God, his laugh was like a vise around my chest. My heart ached, and my lungs collapsed, and I didn't think I would ever hurt worse than I did at this very moment. The pain was both physical and emotional, made worse by the fact that I was empty inside. There was no softness in me to absorb the blow. I consisted solely of jagged edges and rusty gouges.

I blinked hard, trying to keep my tears at bay. The older kids and the men at the other end of the pool appeared to be having a belly flop contest, which kept them occupied. Snoopy was already fast asleep, soaking up the sun as he floated along in his raft. No one was paying any attention to me at all, which, as far as I was concerned, was perfect.

With one more glance around to be sure no one was watching, I carefully climbed out of the pool and headed back toward the house. On my way, I snatched a dry towel from the table where London was seated.

She'd been smiling into the face of her newborn, but her head whipped around as I darted past her. "Hey, Ravyn," she called after me, but I didn't slow down.

I couldn't do this.

I. Could. Not. Do. This.

Not any of it. I couldn't be around Drew's friends as though I belonged with people like this, who had big family gatherings and pool parties with friends and cooked out, who could smile and laugh and go on with their lives as if the world wasn't a shitty place to be, who were healthy and happy. I couldn't sit and watch all these perfect families with their perfect children and listen to them having a good time. I couldn't look after someone's baby and pretend I was normal and sane and whole.

Because I wasn't.

I wasn't normal. I definitely wasn't sane. And I didn't think I'd ever been whole—certainly not anytime in the last decade—and there was no way I ever would be now. How could I be, when a piece of me was somewhere else, and I'd never know how he was or if *he* was happy and healthy and whole?

Wrapping the towel around me, I hurried through the kitchen, hoping the laundry room was somewhere in that direction. The tile floor was cold beneath my wet feet, and I shivered from the blast of air conditioning that wrapped around my limbs and seeped under my skin. I opened what I hoped was the right door and said a silent prayer of thanks that it was.

Drew had apparently taken my clothes out of the dryer already. My T-shirt and jeans were on hangers, and my underthings had been folded and set on a shelf. I grabbed the bra and panties, then tugged the other things off their hangers and headed back through the kitchen. I could change in his bathroom, find my shoes wherever I'd kicked them off in his bedroom, bring the wet clothes back into the laundry room and leave them in the washer, and then slip out the front door.

But Drew's voice stopped me before I could close the door to his room. "Ravyn," he called after me. "You okay?"

That was exactly the problem, which was why I was getting out of there as fast as possible. I wasn't even remotely okay, and I didn't have any reason to believe I ever would be. Definitely not the sort of okay that would allow me to fit into his world, if that were even something he'd want.

For some reason unknown to me, though, I slowly turned so I could face him, water dripping from my clothes to puddle on his hardwoods. Damn. I'd need to dry that up before I could leave. I opened my mouth to tell him I was fine, but nothing came out but a puff of air.

Then he closed the distance between us, concern etching a line across his forehead. He reached up and tucked one of my dreadlocks behind my ear, like it was the most natural thing he could ever do, and I had to fight off the urge to lean my cheek into his touch and rub against his palm. But that wouldn't help anything. It would only make walking out of his life more difficult.

So I stood there, trying to remember how to speak.

"I didn't know they were all coming," he said. "It was as much a surprise to me as it was for you. I'm sorry. I know you didn't sign up for this, but they're not going to stick around too much lon—"

"I can't be here," I cut in, my panic taking over. "I have to go." But my legs refused to move. It was like the water was freezing solid as soon as it left my body and landed on the floor, turning me into an ice sculpture. I couldn't move, not even an inch.

Drew studied me for a long moment, like he was trying to figure out what was going on in my head. But even *I* didn't know what was going on in my head. And then he nodded. "All right. If you need me to take you back—"

"No, you need to stay here."

"I can leave for a bit to drive you to your car or wherever you need to go. It'll be fine. They can manage on their own. They don't need me."

But it wasn't fine. And there was nothing that could make it fine.

Because I didn't know anything about my baby other than he wasn't with me. No matter what I did, no matter how I tried to plug the hole in my heart and fill it up, new leaks would spring and the stuffing would melt and drain back out again faster than before. So what was the point in trying anymore?

"I'm just going to walk," I said, swallowing past the lump in my throat. "It'll be good for me."

"Walk?" Drew repeated. He shook his head. "The community center is eight miles from here. That's a hell of a lot more than just a walk."

I shrugged, trying to back away from him. But apparently I didn't think about the fact that I was moving farther into his room. He followed me in and closed the door behind us, and then we were alone.

Despite knowing that wasn't what he intended, I felt utterly and completely trapped.

Which left me jumpy.

Not what I needed right now.

I'd been trying to hold the dry clothes away from my body so they wouldn't get soaked, but I kept bringing them closer to me as he closed the distance between us. Apparently, I'd just have to walk home in wet clothes, because I couldn't stay here long enough to dry them again.

"Something tells me this isn't about my teammates showing up without warning," he said quietly. "Wanna talk about it?"

If I spoke right now, I'd just fall apart. So I shook my head.

He sighed. It sounded resigned and pained at once. "Can you let me help you with whatever it is?"

There was no help for me. I knew that better than I knew my own name.

Drew dragged a hand down his face, frustration bunching the muscles of his shoulders. "Do you have someone who can be with you, at least?" he finally asked. "I don't think you should be alone right now."

I shrugged again. The truth was, there weren't that many people in my life these days. When I'd run away with Jax as a teenager, the only friends we'd had were *our* friends, not *my* friends. And they had all been part of the problem, taking him deeper and deeper into the drug-induced haze where he now existed. When I'd left him, I'd left all of them behind, too.

I had Rick and Shannon, but they had their own family to worry about, and I didn't like to keep showing up and asking them for more help. They'd already done more than enough. More than most people would. They didn't need another burden, and that was all I could be to them.

I'd thought about keeping in touch with some of the other people I'd met in my stints in the loony bin, but they were just as fucked up as I was. Probably not the best people for me to lean on if they couldn't look after themselves any better than I did.

"I'll be fine," I bit off, determined to make him believe it. To make myself believe it.

But I didn't, and neither did he.

Drew kissed me on the forehead. "Go put on your clothes and give me ten minutes. I'm driving you home, and then I'll stay with you."

"You'll what?" I asked, but he'd already left the bedroom and closed the door behind him, leaving me numb with shock.

Fourteen

Drew

RAVYN'S APARTMENT WAS tiny and tidy. There wasn't any need for a grand tour, because I could see everything in a single sweeping glance. One wall housed her hyper-organized closet, her impossibly small bathroom, and what passed as a kitchen. There wasn't a door to the closet, but she'd hung a curtain on a tension rod to provide some privacy. Apparently she hadn't thought to drag it closed before leaving, though, because I could see the stacks of canvases and bins that undoubtedly housed art supplies. The rest of the apartment consisted of a single room. Every piece of furniture appeared to serve multiple purposes. The bed was a futon, so it doubled as a couch. The coffee table had drawers all around. A shelf along one wall had several cabinet-style doors and a number of those cloth baskets that slid in and out so she could store things within easy reach but still keep them out of sight.

I was a big guy in general, but seated next to her on the futon, I felt gargantuan.

She was still vibrating, much like she had been when I'd followed her inside after my teammates' arrival for an impromptu convince-Drew-he's-still-part-of-the-family-and-we-need-him-on-the-team pool party.

I appreciated the gesture, but they had the shittiest timing ever.

Right now, they might think I was trying to run and hide. Not too many months ago, I had been doing exactly that, but this time that wasn't the case. I would've stayed—and I would've enjoyed hanging out with them—but Ravyn needed me, and that was more important.

Well, she needed *someone*. And I was available. And willing. So I'd nominated myself, because I didn't get the sense she was in the right frame of mind to come up with someone on her own. Assuming she had someone she could turn to. I wasn't convinced.

She hadn't said a word the whole way back to the community center to pick up her car. In the parking lot, she'd tried to convince me to go back to my guests, but I hadn't given in. I told her I'd left the keys with Huggy Bear and instructed him to lock up when everyone went home. He could hold on to my keys for the time being.

Only a couple of days ago, things had apparently been bad enough that Ravyn had felt the need to physically harm herself; I wasn't going to be the asshole who left her alone so she could do it again. What if she did more than cut herself this time? What if she went too far, and there was no one close enough to come to her aid? What if she didn't get help in time?

There were too many what-ifs, and I didn't like the potential answers to any of them. Maybe that meant I already cared more about Ravyn than I should. Sue me. The only person who was likely to get hurt from caring too much in a situation like this was me.

So I'd ignored her arguments and followed her back to her apartment, and now we were sitting on her couch in silence.

It wasn't the silence that had me on edge, though. I could deal with not talking.

The problem was that Ravyn was just this side of a complete breakdown. I knew because of the way she kept fighting back tears and the way she jumped any time I moved.

I knew because I'd been there myself, and frankly, it hadn't been all that long ago.

I wanted to wrap her up in my arms and tell her everything would be okay. But that was a promise I couldn't make—no one could—and I didn't want to feed her lies. Chances were high that she'd already heard more than enough of those to last a lifetime. They were even higher that she was the one lying to herself more than anyone else ever could.

But I *could* wrap her up in my arms.

So I did. I drew her onto my lap and held her close.

Ravyn went as rigid as a board at first, but after a minute she relaxed into me, nestling her face in the space between my shoulder and my neck and letting her hands rest on my ribs. The scent of the chlorine was still strong in her hair and on her skin. It tickled my nose when she snuggled closer to me.

I traced soothing circles on her back and arms, needing to comfort her in order to calm myself. At first, she melted, all the tension oozing out of her body as she fell against me. We fit together like two perfect puzzle pieces, her curves seamlessly filling the empty spaces of my body, my angles blending with her curves. But then she was touching me, too—her small hands raking my abs with increasing urgency, her hips relentlessly shifting over mine.

That was all it took to get me hard as a rock.

But sex would be the easy way out, and I knew it. If I gave in, wouldn't I just be allowing her to run away from whatever was haunting her? Turning a blind eye to it?

Yeah, I realized that went directly against everything I'd decided earlier, with the whole she's-more-likely-to-open-up-after-sex idea, but it seemed like my best option. If all we ever did was jump in bed together, we'd never get anywhere.

And I wanted to get somewhere. I wanted to get to know her. To be with her, and not just on a physical level.

This was the first time I'd felt that way about anyone since I'd kicked Chelsea out. Our divorce had taken place almost two years ago—not long after I'd found out that the Thunderbirds had picked me up in the expansion draft.

And to be honest, I'd never thought I'd get into another relationship again. The idea of trusting someone else that much didn't seem like a possibility, and considering the HIV diagnosis, I couldn't imagine any woman who'd want to trust *me*. Why should she believe I'd gotten it from an ex who'd been cheating and not the other way around? Professional athletes weren't exactly known for their great skill at monogamy, after all.

But the more time I spent with Ravyn, the more I

wanted to spend with her, and that didn't seem likely to just go away anytime soon.

Call me a romantic, but I'd always wanted the sort of relationship my parents had. They'd been together since high school, and I'd never seen a couple more perfect for each other in my life. They worked hard at it, of course, but they knew it was worth working for. That was what they'd shown me and Melody throughout our childhoods, and they were still showing us today.

Because of that, I'd never felt like a bigger failure than the day I'd called to tell them my marriage was over. But now I was starting to feel the urge to try again, only this time, with Ravyn. Call me crazy, but something told me we'd be good for each other, if we could both find a way past our hang-ups.

I wanted to give it a go.

She lifted her lips toward mine, but I angled my head and kissed her on the cheek. That wasn't enough to stop her. With a sort of determination I hadn't seen from her before, she took the opportunity to place wet, openmouthed kisses along my jaw and neck. It felt so right, the temptation not only to let her continue but to join her was overwhelming.

I had to put a stop to it now or there wasn't a chance in hell I'd avoid giving in. "Ravyn," I said, kneading the nape of her neck.

She let out a contented hum but kept kissing my jaw.

"Stop, baby."

"Want you to fuck me," she murmured, her lips locked to my skin.

That was never in doubt. "*I* want you to *talk* to me," I insisted.

But she dropped a hand and found me hard as a spike, then rubbed over my shorts to get me even harder. "You want to fuck me, too."

"No point in denying it, but now's not the time."

She didn't give up easily. At all. Before I knew what hit me, she was tugging at my clothes and trying to get me naked, and my dick was absolutely on board with her efforts.

"Ravyn," I said more insistently, putting both hands over the tops of hers to still them. "We need to talk."

"Why do we need to talk?" she demanded, her lips hovering over the jagged scar on my neck, tickling my skin.

"Because I need to know what we are to each other. And I need to understand why you flipped out when Dana left her baby with you for a minute. And why you couldn't even look at London's baby because you were in full panic mode and ran straight past them."

With every word out of my mouth, she grew more and more tense until she was nothing but a knot of rigidity on my lap, her cheek resting on my chest.

At least she'd stopped grinding against me. Maybe now we could actually talk and make some progress.

But when she finally spoke, her voice was terse. "I was in the pool, wearing your clothes and nothing else when a bunch of people I've never met before show up, and you want me to just be happy-go-lucky? Sorry, but that's not who I am."

"I didn't say anything like that."

"Might as well have."

I sighed. This wasn't going like I'd hoped. Ravyn's hackles were raised, and now I was in damage-control mode. I stroked my hands over her back, hoping the action would soothe her and not set her off even more than she already was. "I was asking about your reactions to the babies. Because it seemed like you reacted especially strongly to them."

"I'm not a kid person."

"You seemed to be doing fine with Carter when it was just the three of us. Well, and Snoopy, but I don't know that the puppy counts as a person."

"Fine, then I'm not a baby person."

"Is that why you've got that adoption symbol tattooed on your chest?" I asked before I could think better of it.

Whatever small amount of tension had started to melt away from her limbs returned full force, and she pulled away from me, crawling off my lap to put as much distance between us as possible while still sitting on the couch.

I felt her loss immediately, but now that I'd gone there, I couldn't unsay the words. I had to keep going. "You never denied that you were pregnant," I pointed out. "You only denied that you were a mother. So did you give the baby up for adoption? Is that what happened?" Because the alternatives—that she'd miscarried so late in her pregnancy or that the baby had been stillborn—were too awful to contemplate.

Ravyn wouldn't look at me. She stared at her lap as if it held the answers I was seeking. But it was her tears that shattered me. They fell one at a time, making slow tracks down her cheeks and leaving dark indigo stains on the denim of her jeans.

"It's not as simple as that," she finally choked out, and I took a shaky breath.

"Then tell me what it is. Let me help you."

She shook her head. "It's too late for that. I'm beyond help."

The certainty in her voice broke me. I couldn't stop myself from brushing away her tears with the backs of my fingers. Hell, I didn't *want* to. I *needed* to touch her as much as I needed my next breath.

And then she looked up and met my eyes, hers filled with so much pain that it ripped me in two. "I surrendered my baby," she choked out. "I couldn't take care of him, so I walked into the hospital and turned him over to a nurse. I don't know anything about him—if he has a good home or if he's stuck in foster care, or if he's really better off than he would have been with me. There's no way for me to ever find out, either. So I'm stuck with not knowing. And I probably gave him HIV, because I didn't know I had it."

With those words leaving her lips, she dissolved into a flood of tears. So I did the only thing I could. I lifted her onto my lap again, and I held her close to me, letting her cry on my shoulder for as long as she needed. She didn't fight me this time. I doubted she had it in her to do so.

All I knew was I didn't have it in *me* to let her go now. And I wasn't sure I ever would.

Fifteen

Ravyn

I DON'T KNOW how long we sat like that, Drew stroking my back and running his hands over my hair, me with my face buried in the crook of his neck and my tears staining his shirt dark orange.

Long enough for me to wish I'd never opened my big mouth and said a damned word, because he was playing the good guy again and I knew there was no such thing unless they were named Rick. At least not in my life.

Long enough to realize I had never allowed myself to tell someone the awful truth of what I'd done, outside of the doctors who were always on my back. Surrendering a baby like I had wasn't illegal, but that didn't make it any less horrible—a truth I was going to have to live with for the rest of my life.

Long enough to understand that as soon as Drew walked out the door of my apartment, I'd never see him again, because I sure as hell wasn't ever going back to that support group now that he knew the truth, and there was no chance he'd fabricate another meeting with me like he had when he'd walked into Rick's shop. Why would he want to spend time with someone who could walk away from her baby like that? I wasn't an idiot. The fact that I could do such a thing said a hell of a lot about me, none of it good, and no man in his right mind would ever want to have anything to do with me once he knew the truth. He'd probably just held on to me as long as he had because he needed a moment for reality to sink in. To realize how utterly disgusted by me he was.

Long enough to come to the realization that I'd never felt so protected before as I did with his strong arms around me, holding me in the sort of embrace that said I was precious.

Long enough to know that I'd never feel this way again, because it was all a big, fat, stinking lie. I wasn't precious. Anything that told me otherwise was nothing but bullshit, and the sooner that sunk in and stuck, the better off I'd be.

Drew couldn't be as nice as he was acting. He couldn't care about me or want to protect me, and even if he *did* want to, there was no way for him to do such a thing. How could someone protect me from myself? How could anyone forgive what I'd allowed myself to become?

It would be far better to disabuse myself of this notion right away. Allowing myself to fall into the trap of thinking this *thing* between the two of us was about anything more than sex would only make me hurt worse when Drew walked out of my life. Because he'd never return.

It was amazing how many tears a body could produce. Sometimes over the last year, I'd thought I was all cried out, that there were no more tears I could possibly cry in a single lifetime because it simply wasn't possible to have more fluids leak out of my eyes. But then something like this would happen, and a new flood would drag me back under like a riptide.

The knowledge of my guilt smothered me like a wet, woolen blanket, and a thousand what-ifs threatened to eat me alive.

What if I'd gone to a health clinic during my pregnancy, even though I didn't have insurance?

What if I'd learned I had HIV before giving birth? They could have potentially given me drugs that would have lowered the risk of passing it on to my baby. The doctors had told me this now, which only increased my sense of guilt.

What if I'd left for the hospital as soon as my labor pains had started instead of convincing myself it wasn't truly labor since I wasn't due for several more weeks? Again, there were ways they could have minimized the baby's exposure. And I could have been sure the baby had the best care possible. Hell, I could have started taking care of myself a lot sooner than I did.

But who was I kidding? I wasn't even taking care of myself now.

And what-ifs didn't help in the present. They only kept me in a downward spiral with no chance of pulling myself out of it any time on the horizon.

If ever.

People kept telling me things would get better, that

I'd find my way out of the darkness if I just kept putting one foot in front of the other, moving forward. Hard to think they weren't all liars, full of a bunch of bullshit that someone had fed them for so long that they'd started to believe it.

I wasn't anywhere near gullible enough for that.

Somehow, the reminder that things were just as bad as they'd ever been and I didn't have any chance to come out on the other side of it was exactly what it took to calm me and staunch the torrent of tears.

But then I felt like a bigger idiot than normal, because not only had I told Drew the truth but I'd allowed myself to wallow in the fleeting comfort of his arms. It was always easier when I kept my distance, because then I wasn't tempted to believe, even for a moment, in the inherent falsehood of fairy tales. And that was all he could be—a fairy-tale prince.

I straightened away from him and climbed off his lap, drying the dregs of my tears on the hem of my T-shirt.

"Hey," he said, reaching for my hand like he wanted to pull me back down to his lap.

I skirted away from his reach and went into the bathroom to wash my face, determined not to look at him. Because I didn't want to see his concern or disgust or whatever it was that he'd throw my direction.

The cool water helped clear my mind if not my heart.

But when I returned from the bathroom, I'd hoped—however unrealistically—that he'd be gone. That he would have taken the sudden return of my cold shoulder after his soothing one as a brush-off. That he'd used it as his excuse to get the hell out of my fucked up life as fast as his powerful legs would carry him.

But he was standing there directly next to the door, his large frame seeming bigger than ever inside my minuscule apartment. He had his feet planted shoulder-width apart, arms crossed, and brows impossibly furrowed with concern. In fact, he was so close to my bathroom door that I almost ran headfirst into him.

That frown was trouble. It meant he wasn't finished with his do-gooder schtick, so I needed to head him off at the pass. I screwed up my courage and prepared to issue the final blow—something sure to run him out of my life for good.

"Thanks for bringing—"

"Did you paint these?" he cut in, not allowing me to get any headway. I must have blinked and stared in confusion, because he pointed toward the canvases stowed in my closet and said, "These paintings? Can I see them?"

I was so taken aback by his interest in my art when I'd been trying to send him on his way that I stuttered out something completely unintelligible and waved a hand toward them. It could have been an invitation to look his fill, which was counter to what I really wanted.

That was certainly how he took my incoherent mumbling. One of these days, I needed to grow a backbone and make it stick. Yeah, I'd gotten up the courage to leave my deadbeat parents when I was a teenager, but I'd run off with a guy who was more into his drugs than me. Then I'd finally left him, but it wasn't like he'd put up any sort of attempt to keep me with him—and I'd stayed for years, with him essentially ignoring me most of the time because he was too high to care, before I'd finally grown the balls to head out on my own.

That wasn't exactly a stellar track record when it came to standing my ground and putting myself first.

Drew swept the curtain to the side, not that it'd been hiding much, and took out a stack of my paintings. He carried them over to the futon and set them on the coffee table in front of him, lifting his head toward me and giving me an inviting smile. "Come tell me about them."

My feet felt like concrete blocks as I crossed over to sit beside him. "There's nothing to tell," I said, my tongue thick. The pieces in my closet were the ones I'd done most recently. I had a small space in a gallery that sold paintings by local artists. It was something Rick had helped me set up so I could earn more money. They didn't sell often, but they went for a more-than-fair price.

But the ones I had here? The ones I'd been painting lately? They weren't the sort of art anyone in their right mind would pay for. They were dark and depressing, accurate reflections of my state of mind. No one wanted that hanging in their living room.

Me, least of all.

Rick and my doctors all thought I needed to keep painting them, though. Supposedly they were cathartic—a means of allowing myself to process the thoughts jumbled up in my brain like knotted and tangled yarn. So I'd painted.

They were nothing at all like the art I had started to make a name for myself with. They were ugly and full of pain.

And now, Drew was studying them like they'd tell him everything he ever needed to know about me.

Maybe he was right.

"I don't believe that for a second," he said.

I blinked and shook my head. "Believe what?" I'd clearly lost the thread of conversation. Not uncommon for me lately. I was always floating around in my head instead of staying in the present.

"That there's nothing to tell." He inched closer to me, not stopping until his thigh brushed against mine, and he picked up the piece on top. It was a self-portrait, so the last thing on earth I wanted anyone to see.

Jagged, hateful, black lines. Hardly anything soft about it other than the fuzzy outside edges of the canvas, because there was nothing soft left in me. And tears. Lots of ugly tears.

"Like this one," he said. "I think this one says a lot. The baby floating in the tear speaks volumes."

"Yeah, but most people who would see that would assume I'd miscarried or something." Which would somehow be easier for me to bear. Because it wouldn't have been my fault, I supposed.

Women miscarry all the time. It's just a thing that happens. It still broke their hearts to lose a baby in whatever way it happened, I was certain, but it wasn't because of anything they'd done.

"But you and I aren't most people, are we?" Drew said.

And that was part of the problem. The idea that he knew the truth behind the painting, without needing me to explain it, made me want to crawl under a rock and stay there until there was no more guilt within me—which would never happen. I shook my head, because if I tried to speak, I'd break down again.

He set the canvas down on his knees and put an arm around my waist.

I cringed away from his touch. Couldn't help it. The last thing I deserved right now was someone comforting me, but he seemed more determined than ever to do so, tugging me up against his side.

"This is a lot different than any of the pieces I saw in your portfolio at the tattoo studio," he murmured.

I nodded, still untrusting of my voice and uncertain where he was headed with all of this.

"A lot more personal."

"Too personal," I croaked.

"Maybe. I guess when you do a tattoo, it's personal for the person it's going on. But this is all about you. Is that right?"

"Why does it matter to you?"

My question was insolent and ungrateful, but Drew didn't even bat an eye.

"It matters because you matter."

But that was where he was wrong. I'd stopped mattering a long time ago, if I'd ever mattered at all.

"Why are you here?" I asked. If I could figure out what he was after, what he wanted, then maybe I could get through this. But every time I thought I had the mystery of him solved, he went and flipped the script on me, leaving me floundering again while I tried to sort him out all over again.

"I'm here because I don't think you should be alone right now."

"You already said that," I snapped.

"Well, it's still true."

"But why you?"

"You have someone else who'll come hang out with you?"

"That's not the point."

"That is the point," he insisted. "That and the fact that you matter to me—"

"Why? You don't know me."

"I might know you better than you think I do."

"Yeah, right." I snorted and stood up, stomping into the kitchen. I took out a glass and filled it with water from the tap, more as a means of getting away from him than because I was thirsty. "You've known me for all of a week. Sleeping with a person doesn't do a damned thing as far as getting to know them."

But he'd followed me into the kitchen, which was far too small for a single person. Now that there were two of us in it, I felt more claustrophobic than I'd ever felt in my life. I backed up against the counter, trying to find enough space to take a breath.

Drew didn't take the hint, somehow crowding me even further and looming over me. "Okay, well, let's try this on for size. You feel like you're all alone in the world, and maybe you've been that way for so long that you've convinced yourself that's how it should be. You blame yourself for all the bad things in your life. For getting HIV. For possibly passing it on to your baby. For the fact that the baby could be suffering, and it's all because of you. You don't think you deserve anything good in life, so you're doing everything in your power—maybe subconsciously, maybe not—to punish yourself for all the bad, which only makes everything worse. Any time something good starts to happen, you hit the sabotage button, and everything starts falling apart again. So now you're in this massive downward spiral, and not only do you not see a way out of it but you're determined to stay in it. Am I getting close? Because I think I am. Because I've been there. Maybe I didn't have a baby factoring into things, but I might as well have. Because if my teammate ends up getting HIV because of me, he could transfer it to his wife. To his kids. They've got three, you know. You met them this afternoon. Dana, his wife? She was the one who asked you to watch their baby in the pool for a couple of minutes. So even if it's just Zee who ends up being HIV-positive, it'll be five lives affected. Because of me. Because of my selfishness for wanting to play a game—a fucking *game*, for Christ's sake—when I could have gone ahead and retired and not put anyone else at risk."

I stood there blinking at him in an effort to keep my tears at bay and to process what was going on. "But you said yourself that no one's really at risk if you're not practically dying. The virus dies pretty fast once the blood leaves your body."

At that, he jerked down the collar of his T-shirt, exposing the massive scar on his neck. "I *was* practically dying. If Zee hadn't shoved his bare hands on my neck when he did, which was gushing blood like a geyser, I probably would have. Right there on the ice, in front of thousands of people and Lord only knows how many people watching the game at home. The skate blade barely missed my carotid artery, and the guy had his fucking hands practically inside my body to try to save me. But that's not my point," he said on a ragged sigh.

I shook my head. "I'm not following."

"My point is that I get where you are right now. I was there not too long ago. For a different reason, maybe, but the guilt is the same. And it takes you to an ugly place where you can't see a way out other than maybe to just end things—"

"I'm not suicidal," I cut in. I wasn't sure why I needed for Drew to understand that, but right now, I *needed* it.

He looked at me like he didn't fully believe me. And why should he? Normal, sane people didn't take razor blades to their arms unless they were trying to end their lives, did they?

"I'm not," I repeated, this time with a hell of a lot more oomph in my tone. "I don't want to die. I just..." My words trailed off. After a moment, I shook my head, completely at a loss.

"You just don't know what else to do," he finished for me.

"Right. Something like that."

"I get that. Because I was there."

"And now you're not?" I asked, a fresh wave of tears clogging my throat so badly the words came out on a choke. But there was a strange note attached to them. It felt oddly like hope.

"Now I'm not," he said. "There are good days and bad days, but that's part of life. More good days lately, though. And I want to help you get there, too."

Which sounded well and good, but... "Why?"

"Because I think we can understand each other in a way that no one else is going to understand us. And that has to be a good thing, doesn't it? So I want to help you find your way to the other side."

I wanted that, too. More than I could allow myself to say, because saying it out loud would give root to that hope, and I couldn't bear to have it squashed like a bug.

But when Drew picked me up, carried me into the living room, sat on the futon, and pulled me into his lap again, I allowed it.

"Okay," I said.

He chuckled, which made his chest rumble beneath my cheek. "Okay? What exactly are you agreeing to?"

Hell if I knew.

Sixteen

Drew

ZEE WAS IN Gary Asher's office along with the whole coaching staff and what seemed like half the Thunderbirds' front office when I showed up later that week for my meeting. I'd assumed it would only be the general manager and maybe a couple of the coaches present, so this entourage caught me by surprise.

Even though this meeting was all about my future and whether or not I'd continue playing hockey, my mind had been elsewhere right up until this moment. It'd been on Ravyn and how we'd spent most of our free time together over the last few days. Much of that time had been spent in bed, but she hadn't cut herself again.

I hoped that I was at least part of the reason.

I'd been doing some Googling about cutting while she was gone to work at the tattoo shop, learning as much about it as I could. My research revealed that many people who got started cutting themselves continued to do so because the pain almost gave them a high of sorts, so it became an addictive tendency.

My plan was to give her a much healthier high: orgasms. So far, she was on board, and it seemed to be working. And really, there were far worse things we could be doing. To be completely honest, I'd rather be with her now instead of here at Thunderbirds headquarters. But she was working, anyway, and I'd promised Gary I'd be here.

Besides, if I hadn't shown up, there wasn't a doubt in my mind that London Nazarenko and Tallie Fielding would double-team me and drag me by my ears into the building.

As long as I'd known her, Tallie had always had a thing for *fixing* people. She used to focus her efforts on her brother-in-law, but these days she liked to spread the wealth since now he was clean and getting his act together.

Now that London was married to Dima, the two of them were perfect foils for each other. If one couldn't get through to someone, the other took over. Frankly, I'd rather face the music with the team than have those two in my grill again. They'd done more than enough of that over the summer when I was doing my best to pretend I didn't exist.

After shaking a few hands and greeting everyone, I took a seat. "Feels a bit like the Spanish Inquisition, boys." I raised a brow in question.

"We're not here to intimidate you," Gary rushed to say. He nodded to his secretary, who brought over a bottle of water and a selection of fresh fruit, but otherwise his focus was fully on me. "Everyone in this room just wanted to be part of making sure you know how much we want you to continue to be a contributing member of this team. We know you're still up in the air about whether you should play or not, but *we* aren't. We want you to play for many years to come."

Everyone, huh? I took a quick mental inventory, but it didn't take much exertion to realize that Mr. and Mrs. Jernigan, the hyper-evangelical team owners who were overly concerned with appearances, weren't present. I also didn't have to search my memory too hard to realize that, other than a cursory Get Well Soon card sent from Mr. Jernigan's congregation, I hadn't seen or heard from either of them since my accident.

That wasn't much of a surprise, really. Mrs. J, in particular, was all about morality. She couldn't stand the way we cursed, and she did everything possible to keep word of anything she believed to be less than savory about any member of the team from getting out to the public. Lord only knew what she assumed about me now that it'd been revealed I was HIV-positive.

A few of the journalists who'd reached out to me over the summer had tried to get me to talk about how I'd contracted the disease, but that was none of their business, so I'd declined to comment.

Maybe Mrs. J assumed I was gay, like a couple of other hockey players who'd come out of the closet during the playoffs this past year. For all I knew, she could still be living under a rock and not realize that HIV wasn't just a *gay* disease. Maybe she thought I was a drug addict and got it from sharing needles. That wouldn't go over well for the morality police. Maybe she believed I'd been the one sleeping around in my marriage. All of those things would rate me high on Mrs. J's Hockey-Playing Hooligan Meter.

But since neither she nor her husband had attempted to get to know who I was and what I was all about, they would probably never know how I'd come to be HIV-positive.

The team owners were the least of my worries, however.

I unscrewed the lid of my water bottle and took a sip, collecting my thoughts. "Okay, so everyone here wants me to play. But there are a lot more people whose opinions on this subject need to be taken into account."

"Such as?" Zee demanded, sitting up straighter.

He'd come in today wearing a suit, just like everyone else in the room other than me. Not sure why I hadn't thought of it. Maybe because I'd been far more focused on how I could help Ravyn than I was on myself lately.

Professional attire notwithstanding, Zee had the sort of look in his eye that he always got at the face-off dot, like he was ready to rip the head off the guy on the other side of the puck if he so much as dared to take a swipe at it. I'd been on the other side of that look a few times, before we'd both joined the Thunderbirds. Hell, I'd seen it a few times even in practices, too. Zee was just as intense then as he was in a game. I'd never met a guy who was more competitive or more willing to stand up for his teammates.

I just never thought I'd be the teammate he had to stand up for.

"Such as every guy on every *other* team in the league," I said, trying to keep my cool while also getting my point across.

"Bullshit," Zee shot back at me.

I could appreciate his fervor, but this wasn't something we could just close our eyes and wish away. I needed to make sure everyone in this room understood where I was coming from. "They're bound to be scared. Doesn't matter how much we know about how HIV is spread. There are still so many misconceptions out there it's ridiculous."

"Fear doesn't make it right," Doug Spurrier, the head coach, pointed out.

"And it doesn't make it legal to exclude you," Gary added. "No one can prevent you from playing."

I had a silent chuckle for myself, thinking about how Mrs. J would love to do exactly that. "Maybe not legally, but they can sure as hell make me uncomfortable for choosing to continue playing."

"Which is when the rest of the boys and I will make sure they learn their lesson," Zee said.

But that was exactly what I *didn't* want to happen. The thought of any guy on the team needing to drop his gloves over *me* didn't sit well. At all. But especially not our team captain, and that was exactly what would happen if some douche canoe on the other team tried to start something because he felt threatened because of my disease.

"We're trying to come together as a team, though," I pointed out. "I think we're set to make good strides this season with the changes Gary made in the off-season, but every time some asswipe on the other team tries to tell me where I can shove it, if one of our guys tries to pick a fight with him—"

"We will all come together as a team," Zee interrupted. "It's called closing ranks around one of our own. It's not letting anyone get away with shit when it comes to one of our teammates. This can absolutely bring us together. No, not just *can*. It already has. You just haven't been around the rest of us enough to see it for yourself, and it's going to continue to bring us together."

I rolled my eyes. "Not in the way we should be."

"Look," Zee said earnestly, leaning forward and resting his elbows on the table in front of him. "You and I both know—hell, everyone in this room does—that there are a lot of things that can happen to bring a group of players together. Getting to know each other better over these first couple of seasons has helped a ton. Playing like shit together and trying to keep our heads up has been a struggle. But there's something to be said for facing adversity as a group. The teams I've played on that have been the closest, the ones where every guy would throw down for any other guy on the team at any time? They were the teams where something awful happened to someone, and we all rallied around him. You know that, too. You've experienced it before. Not here yet, but that's already changing, whether you like it or not."

"I just—" I cut myself off, trying to figure out how to say what needed to be said in a way that they'd accept it without shooting me down again. "I don't want to be a rallying point. And I don't know if I'm ready to be the newest poster boy for HIV-positive athletes. That's a hell of a mantle to carry."

"And combined, this team has broad shoulders," Zee said. "Let us use them. We can all carry it with you."

The man wasn't going to give an inch. He was digging in his heels and refusing to budge. Damn it. But I had a grudging respect for him on that score.

"I just—"

"Drew," another voice cut in. I shot my head around to find Dr. Willie Masters, the team's head physician, staring me down. "I'm going to tell you the same thing I told you when you first filled us in about your HIV status. Everyone on this staff *and* in the league as a whole is already taking all due precautions. The likelihood of another accident taking place that's as serious as the one at the end of last season is extremely small. But even if it does happen, we're all prepared. And now, everyone involved with this team—and the league—is fully in possession of the facts."

"Not only that," Jesse Coakley, the equipment manager, said, "but my guys and I've been researching all summer, and we've got a bunch of Kevlar options for you. Neck protectors, socks, sleeves. All sorts of things to give you extra protection in case another skate comes at you at a bad angle. You can try them out during preseason and pick out the ones you like best."

"We've bought extras," Gary added, "in case any of the other guys want to wear them."

Doug nodded. "In fact, we're strongly recommending they do. The Players' Association won't allow us to mandate that the whole team wears them, but we're doing everything we can to convince all the boys that these things are for the best, just like wearing shot protectors on their skates."

"So everyone's on board," Zee said, staring me down. "Everyone but you."

Lovely. I sat there trying to come up with another argument, but the uneasy clenching of my gut was a strong indication I was out of any good ones.

Gary sat back in his chair, crossing his arms. "I don't think we've made it any secret that we've been grooming you to captain this team once Zee retires or moves on. He's been a hell of a leader his whole career, and he's done a great job of setting an example for the rest of the guys on this team in terms of how to go about their business. But he's not going to play forever. We—*all* of us, including Zee—believe you're the man to take the helm when that time comes. Prove us right, Drew."

I glanced over at Zee, trying to gauge how he felt about that.

Gary was right in that the team had made it clear that's what they wanted, although this was the first time anyone had come right out and said it to my face. That was the only logical reason they would have given me one of the *A*'s to wear since our inaugural season.

What kind of leader would I be if I ran off to hide instead of facing the adversity that came my way? I'd had it easy my whole life. My parents had been able to provide for me and get me into the best hockey programs. I'd worked hard, of course—no one got into the NHL without dogged determination and extreme effort—but compared to so many of my teammates and opponents, I'd had an easy path through life. The worst thing that had happened to me was my ex cheating and giving me HIV. Compared to so many others, my life had been a cakewalk.

When Zee met my gaze from across the room, it was with that same fierce look as earlier. A challenge. No, a dare.

Well, hell. I couldn't exactly back down now, could I?

Seventeen

Ravyn

THE NEXT TIME I went to the support group meeting, I wasn't able to disappear by holing up next to Drew and hiding in his shadow. Yeah, I'd told myself I'd never go to one again…but that was because he knew so much of the truth, and I didn't think I could face him again. But then he'd gone and made it clear he had no intention of avoiding me despite that knowledge, and I wasn't sure which end was up anymore.

While we still had more scorching-hot temperatures than cool and the leaves were still green instead of the rich reds and oranges of fall, the calendar kept inching closer to October. After his meeting with the Thunderbirds and ultimately making the decision to play hockey again this season, now Drew had to participate in training camp and other team functions.

Which meant he was busy during the day and couldn't come to the meeting with me.

His absence was both a relief and a source of terror, almost in equal measure.

I felt so sick about walking into that room alone and not having him to lean on that I almost chickened out at the last minute. In fact, I was making the return walk across the parking lot to my car when London wheeled through the glass doors in front of the building and called after me.

"Where do you think you're going?" she shouted. "I'm not signing your form if you don't get your ass in here."

I stopped and turned to face her, crossing my arms in front of me before realizing that was a defensive gesture and dropping my arms to my sides. "Forgot something in my car," I said, just barely loud enough for her to hear me.

Then I realized she had her son strapped to her chest in one of those Baby Bjorn things, and I wanted to crawl behind the wheel of my car and race out of there as fast as I could. I couldn't bear the thought of being around her and her baby and seeing how happy they were. What the hell was she doing back at work again already, anyway? Surely they would have given her a few months of maternity leave.

But she raised her brows and gave me one of those looks that said she wasn't buying my bull for a second.

I shrugged, went to my car, grabbed a tube of lip balm from the cup holder, and headed back her way.

She hadn't moved an inch the whole time, her eyes constantly on me.

"Told you I was coming right back," I muttered as I caught up to her. After unscrewing the top, I spread a sheen layer of balm over my lips so it would seem like I legitimately *had* been intending to return to the building once I'd grabbed it.

"Drew texted me this morning," she said. "He thought you might try to chicken out of coming since he wouldn't be here."

"Yeah, everyone knows me better than I know myself." The words came out as a grumble. Hating the bitchy way I sounded, I held open the door for her and waited for her to go in ahead of me.

"At least now you can prove us all wrong. Seems like a good place to start." The way she said it made me wonder what else Drew might have told her, or else maybe I really was so easy to see through.

"I'm kind of surprised to see you back here so soon," I said.

"I could say the same."

Touché.

She kept wheeling alongside me as I walked toward the conference room where the meetings were held. I supposed she intended to make sure I was safely ensconced in the room before getting back to whatever else she needed to be doing. She followed me to the table with food and drinks, grabbing a Greek yogurt and a spoon for herself while I fixed a cup of coffee. Even then, though, she didn't head out to go on with her day.

Which was more than enough to unnerve me. Did she think I was a loose cannon? Maybe Drew had told her how I cut myself, and she thought she needed to keep a close eye on me herself so I wouldn't do something stupid and bleed out all over the carpets.

I didn't know what it was, but I couldn't shake her. Even when I carried my Styrofoam cup and pastry to a seat near the back, she followed me, parking her chair right next to me. Damn it.

"They don't care that you're bringing him to work with you?"

"I'm not working today," London said matter-of-factly, like it should be obvious.

Which meant she was here because of me.

I took a sip of coffee and immediately wished I hadn't, because a massive wave of nausea bubbled up in my stomach and chest. Forcing the bile down again, I angled myself in my seat so I could look at her, doing my damnedest not to glance down at that little boy in her arms. "You don't have to babysit me. I'm here. I'm doing what I need to do to be okay. I don't know what Drew told you about me—"

"He only said he wasn't sure you were going to come," she cut in. "That's it. Nothing else."

"Then why—" I cut myself short because the baby started to fuss, and a flood of tears rushed to my eyes and my throat swelled closed. I couldn't look away as London gently bounced him in her arms, one hand patting him on the back in a gentle, soothing manner.

A motherly manner.

She was a natural with her baby, completely at ease even though several heads turned at the sound of his whimpers. Would I have been? Now I'd never know, because I sure as hell wouldn't ever have another opportunity to learn.

Within a couple of minutes, he was calm and once again sleeping soundly.

She met my eyes, hers full of fierce determination. "That's why," she said, steel resolve in her quiet tone. "Because of how you look like you're being eaten alive when you see a baby. And how you reacted the first time you came and realized I was pregnant—how you couldn't look at my belly without getting this same look in your eyes. And how you brought my wheelchair to the hospital but didn't even bother to come inside. And how you ran past me like the hounds of hell were chasing you at Drew's house that day. I don't know why you can't handle seeing anything to do with babies, but I want to be sure you get help. That's why I'm here."

I gaped at her, unable to say a word. She reached into a bag that was slung over the back of her chair and took out a pack of tissues, passing them into my hands. Only then did I realize I was actually crying, not just hoping I wouldn't.

"You don't have to tell me about it if you don't want to. But I think you should be getting regular counseling. Maybe something one-on-one instead of a group setting like this."

"I can't afford—"

She held up a hand, stopping me. "We have assistance programs in place, and I have a lot of counselors who'll work with us and whom I can highly recommend. I know that sometimes it's difficult to accept help, but I want you to let me help you."

I asked the only thing I could think of. "Why?" Seemed like I was asking that a lot lately.

But she shrugged, and after a moment, she winked. "Call it a hunch that a certain friend of my husband's wants you to be in his life—and if you're going to be in his life, I want to be sure you've got your ducks in a row. We just finally got him to a good place again, so the last thing he needs is—"

"Some crazy chick coming along to drag him back," I cut in.

"I wasn't going to put it quite that way, but yeah. Essentially." London gave me a wry smile, and despite myself, I returned it. She was an in-your-face sort, but she didn't pull her punches. I liked that.

There wasn't much I could say in response other than to nod my understanding. Especially since the counselor in charge of this meeting cleared his throat and called everyone to order. Besides, I was still trying to come to terms with the fact that she was right. For whatever reason, Drew did seem to want me to be in his life, and I was getting used to having him in mine.

I still thought he was too good to be true in a lot of ways, so I kept waiting for the other shoe to drop. So far, he'd only proven himself to be exactly what he seemed on the surface.

That wasn't going to keep me from attempting to guard myself against the inevitable letdown, but I was going to enjoy this—whatever it was—for as long as it lasted.

Especially since my sex-in-lieu-of-cutting plan was working out brilliantly, and Drew was going along with it whether he realized he was or not. I wasn't about to tell him that was what I was doing. He'd be bound to recognize the desperation of the move, and he might think I was just using him for sex.

An hour later, I'd somehow managed to survive another group session without completely losing my shit. I'd even been able to tell them a bit about myself without going too deeply into the details—name, occupation, that I'd contracted HIV from an ex who shared his drug needles.

London had stayed next to me through the whole session. I didn't know if she realized I was using her as a crutch, but I definitely had been. Much like Drew during the first couple of meetings, she was my lifeline, my connection to the small thread of sanity within me that still hadn't snapped.

Now I was following her and her baby down a long hallway to her office. She opened the door and wheeled inside, only coming to a stop once she was settled behind her desk. She powered up her computer, but when she tried to bring the keyboard tray toward her, the baby was in the way.

Before I could stop her, she had him out of the Baby Bjorn and was handing him to me. "Here, hold him for me for a minute so I can print up the paperwork we'll need for your assistance application," she said, settling him into arms that felt like shattered glass, ready to break into tiny razor-sharp shards at the slightest provocation.

I couldn't breathe. A weight settled in my throat and pressed down, down, down until my heart and lungs were compressed. I tried to swallow, but that only made me blubber and choke on my sob.

London's gaze shot up to me, calm and steady. "There's a chair to your left. Sit down." It was an order, not an invitation.

I stumbled over, cradling her son to my chest as I lowered myself into the seat with the sort of care I'd never taken for myself. "You should— I can't—"

My attempts to speak combined with the transfer into my arms were apparently more than enough to wake him up. He started fussing, his tiny fist waving around in the air while his eyes scrunched closed in distress. I shot my head up in a panic.

"Stop hyperventilating," she said smoothly. "Breathe. You're doing fine. Erik's just hungry."

"Well shouldn't you—"

"There's a bottle in the diaper bag over there," she said, pointing to a cabinet next to me and the turquoise-and-terra-cotta bag with a Thunderbirds logo on it. "Why don't you feed him while I take care of this?" Once more, this didn't come across as a question.

The chair had wheels, so I didn't have to worry about my wobbling legs. I carefully scooted over. I cradled Erik in one arm and dug around in the bag with the other. My hand finally landed on the bottle. I took it out, removed the cap, and angled it toward his near-frantic mouth. In no time, he latched on and started to suck. After a few moments more, his whimpers stopped.

I swallowed down the lump of emotion balled up in my throat, determined to get through this without falling apart.

But then he reached up with one tiny hand, and his fingers wrapped around my pinky and grasped me tight, and I couldn't hold it all in anymore. One of my tears dripped onto his forehead, and I wanted to brush it off his tender skin, but I couldn't bring myself to take my hand away from his. He was so small and strong and alive and *perfect*. Absolutely, utterly perfect.

"See?" London said. "You're holding him, and you're feeding him, and you're fine."

"I'm not fine," I choked out.

"Okay, maybe you're not fine. But you're not going to die, either. You can do this. You can be around other peoples' kids, and it won't be the end of the world. You just need practice so maybe you don't scare the kids if they're a little older. Babies probably won't notice, but toddlers? Crying on them might freak them out."

I never thought it would happen, but I burst out laughing.

Maybe I would end up actually liking London after all and not just admiring how she went about things.

Eighteen

Drew

RAVYN LET OUT one of her sexy, throaty moans—the kind that always went straight to my dick because they meant she was coming—and wrapped arms and legs tighter around me. "God, Drew, don't stop."

Stopping wasn't in my plans any time soon. Laughing, I gave her an openmouthed kiss on the side of her neck, reveling in the salty-sweet taste of her skin and the way her whole body contracted around me. I'd been able to feel other women orgasm when I was inside them before, but the sensation had never been as intense as it was with Ravyn.

Giving her pleasure was fast becoming an addiction, but there were far worse addictions either of us could have, so I'd take it.

Almost three weeks had passed since the day of the impromptu pool party at my house—a couple of weeks since my meeting with the team officials—and the two of us had spent time together almost every day. We had sex almost every time we saw each other…sometimes more than once. I wasn't a teenager any longer, but somehow, Ravyn made me feel like one.

I still didn't have a solid answer about what the two of us were to each other, but she wasn't pushing me away anymore. Even when I did everything in my power to get closer to her, she didn't fight it. Maybe she wasn't welcoming me into her life with open arms yet, but I still counted her softening toward me as a victory.

It was a Sunday evening at my house. She'd worked all day, and I'd picked her up to bring her over when she finished up. I'd intended to make her dinner once we got back to my place, but we distracted each other before I got around to it.

Food could wait.

The Thunderbirds had started back to training camp, and tomorrow night was our first preseason game against the Avs. After that, we were heading out on a quick road trip to Dallas and Arizona before returning to Tulsa for the remaining exhibition games on our schedule.

I couldn't stand the thought of leaving Ravyn behind.

Some of the guys assumed my anxiety was because I had trust issues, like maybe I thought Ravyn was going to cheat while I was gone. There was good reason for them to think along those lines, but they couldn't be further from the truth.

With Chelsea, I'd never worried about her when I was gone with the team. We'd known each other since high school, and she'd always been self-sufficient.

In hindsight, maybe she'd been too comfortable with

being on her own. She certainly hadn't needed me in the end.

I knew Ravyn was capable of taking care of herself, but I couldn't ignore the fact that she hadn't cut herself once in the last three weeks. Was it due to her having another outlet for all the emotions wreaking havoc on her mind—a sexual outlet, with me—and if so, how much? By the same token, how much was due to her making progress with the counselor she'd started seeing, thanks to London's interference?

I wasn't sure it could be quantified, but I couldn't deny I was worried. Probably more than was fair.

"Hey," she said, taking my face between her hands until I met her eyes. "I'm over here." She drew up her knees and changed the angle of her hips, which brought my attention back to her—to the present—better than anything else could have.

I let out a groan of pleasure. Her body was like liquid silk beneath me, all quiet sighs, hungry kisses, and frantic grasping. I couldn't get enough. She flitted her hands over my chest before scraping her fingernails down my back.

"Christ, that's good," I said with a ragged moan. She was so tight after her climax, and somehow softer all over.

Ravyn nibbled on my shoulder and trickled her fingers over the backs of my biceps in a way that made me quiver. "I love your arms," she said, and fleetingly, I tensed.

My arms? All right, then. For the briefest of moments, I'd fooled myself into thinking she was going to tell me she loved me. And even though I wasn't so sure I loved *her* yet, there was a part of me that wanted her to love me. Because it might mean she was coming out of her depression. Or maybe that she wanted to. But it would at least mean that she realized having me in her life was better than not having me in her life—and I wanted to become a much more permanent fixture than I was currently.

I wasn't ready to analyze that realization. Especially not while she was still moving beneath me, her hands exploring every blessed inch of my skin like it was hers for the taking. Which, admittedly, it was.

Still, the idea that she loved my arms was better than no love for me at all. I couldn't complain.

I kissed a path along her neck and jaw until our lips met again. She opened for me immediately, her tongue warring with mine in a frenzied, addictive tangle. I couldn't tell who was the aggressor between us a lot of times, and I liked that. I might like it *too* much.

In bed, Ravyn always gave as good as she got, and she always asked for exactly what she wanted.

She broke away and dropped her mouth lower, finding a sensitive spot just below my Adam's apple. The soft, wet, pointed tip of her tongue nearly undid me. But her strangled gasp and gentle sigh as her lips slithered along my skin finished the job.

The base of my spine tingled with my impending climax, and I groaned into the pillow next to her head.

She drew me down against her, her thighs trapping me around the waist and keeping us connected as I crashed back down to earth. As for me? I intended to soak up her affection for as long as she offered it, because I knew it wouldn't last long.

She had a habit of ending things sooner than I wanted, crawling out of my arms and heading off to the bathroom. And when she returned, she might let me hold her, but there was always a distance between us—

and not just on a physical plane—that didn't exist when I was inside her.

"You should keep the scruff," Ravyn murmured, her lips next to my ear. A husky laugh accompanied her words.

I hadn't shaved in a few days, which was unusual for me. The scratchiness was uncomfortable, and my mother had always insisted that a man should be clean shaven for his woman. Some habits were hard to break. I rarely went more than a day unless my team was in the playoffs. But playoff beards were a sacred tradition in the NHL, so I sacrificed comfort for my teammates.

"Mm." That was about all I was capable of saying at the moment. Especially once she started running her fingers through my hair, massaging my scalp. My entire body had been feeling the effects of getting back into game shape, but somehow her gentle touch relaxed me from head to toe. "I'll give you about three years to stop that," I said, my voice muffled in the pillow and her hair.

"Only three?"

"You could go four. Maybe a decade. I'll suffer through it."

This time, she laughed out loud. The sound of her laughter wrapped around my heart and squeezed the same way her thighs were clenching my waist, keeping me trapped. No matter how much time I spent with her, I could never get enough of it. Probably because for so long, her laughs were few and far between.

But then, long before I was ready for the moment to end, she shifted beneath me, trying to free herself from my weight pressing her into the mattress.

"I could get used to this," she said softly. "Lying together like this."

"Good. I want you to get used to it."

She stilled for a moment, blinking up at me. But then she renewed her efforts to shove me off her. "Bathroom," she said. Which I already knew. This was her routine, so the quiet moment of togetherness was over.

I rolled off of her, throwing an arm over my forehead in frustration as she scurried out of my bed and shut me out again. Two steps forward, one step back. That was how it always felt with Ravyn. And I knew all too well that this was normal. My depression hadn't been anywhere near as deep and ingrained when I'd had to deal with it over the summer. So I supposed I should be grateful that she was taking steps forward at all.

That didn't stop me from wanting more, though.

I heard her flush the toilet and turn on the sink, so I crawled out of bed and disposed of the condom, grabbing a tissue to clean myself off. The longer she stayed in the bathroom, the more frustrated I grew. Because she was leaving me alone with my thoughts when all I wanted was to be completely wrapped up in her.

That was the problem. I wanted more, and I didn't think she could give me more.

Did it make me a selfish bastard for wanting to hold her for a while after sex? That seemed backwards, but I couldn't shake the feeling that it was exactly how she might see things.

The faucet shut off, but Ravyn still didn't return to the bedroom. And I *had* intended to make us both dinner, before we'd ended up in bed, so I pulled on a pair of shorts and headed for the kitchen to do exactly that.

She might not be in my arms, but she wasn't running away from me, either. I had to keep reminding myself that we were making progress. Besides, I shouldn't be too quick to jump into another relationship, anyway. It'd only be intelligent—for both of us—to take things at Ravyn's pace.

By the time she joined me, wearing a Thunderbirds T-shirt she'd found in the closet and likely nothing else, I'd sorted and opened the mail that had been piling up for a few days and gotten some serious work done on our dinner.

My sister had sent me a few professional portraits of her daughters, which I needed to get framed and hung at some point. For now, I set them aside on the counter on top of a stack of bills and focused on the meal.

I had chicken bubbling away in a creamy tomato sauce, veggies sautéing, and pasta boiling. It might be one of five meals I knew how to make, but it definitely met my nutritional needs. And it tasted pretty damned good if I did say so myself.

"Smells good," she said.

"See? I'm not a one-trick pony. I can play hockey *and* feed myself."

"I never thought you only had one trick."

"No? What else do you think I can do?"

"I don't know." She gave me a sexy grin. "You're not too bad in bed."

"Not quite a skill necessary for survival, but I suppose it's not a bad one to have," I said with a wink.

"Definitely not." Ravyn came fully into the kitchen and hitched her hip against the counter. But then her eyes strayed to the stack of mail I'd left out with the photographs on top, and she visibly tensed.

I should have thought to put them away. After the

way she'd freaked out around my teammates' kids that day, and then her explanation as to why she had such strong reactions, I'd been doing everything I could to keep children out of the equation between us. No random visits from the guys' families. I was hyper-aware of things with Bear whenever Carter was in town so we didn't have a repeat of that afternoon. I didn't take her places we'd be likely to run into babies.

It wasn't something we'd be able to avoid forever, but there was no reason to blindly walk into a situation she wasn't ready for, either.

But instead of breaking down, Ravyn blinked a couple of times, her gaze still on the photographs, before crossing over to the other counter. She looked down at the images with a sort of determination that I'd rarely witnessed in her before glancing over at me again.

"Who are they?" she asked.

Maybe this wouldn't be as bad as I'd feared. "My nieces. That's Lucy on the left and Charley on the right."

"Charley's an interesting name for a little girl."

"Short for Charlotte. She's kind of a tomboy, though. Three years old, and she's already decided Charlotte is too *girly* for her."

Ravyn laughed. I was both surprised and relieved to see how she was taking this. No, the girls weren't here right now—we were only looking at photographs—but I just wasn't sure what Ravyn was ready for.

"Do they have different fathers?" she asked. Not a surprising question, considering Lucy was clearly Hispanic and Charley was clearly *not*. Lucy had sleek black hair and a tan that would put most beach volleyball players to shame, while Charley had strawberry-blond curls and fairer-than-fair skin that burned in a nanosecond.

"Different fathers. Different mothers, too," I said.

She hitched up a brow in question.

"My sister and brother-in-law adopted them. They both came into the foster care system at about the same time and latched onto each other, so everyone wanted to keep them together."

"Oh. That was good of them." There was no missing the hitch in her voice, but she didn't run off to hide or anything. She stayed in the kitchen with me.

"There are a lot of good people out there who want to adopt kids," I pointed out. "Melody and Shawn couldn't have any of their own. They tried for several years. Lots of fertility treatments and whatnot. Eventually, they decided that having a family was more important to them than how they came about getting their family. You know? And they looked for kids to adopt who might have been harder to place, for whatever reason."

"What was difficult about placing Lucy and Charley?"

"They weren't babies, to start. They were one and a half and two by the time Melody and Shawn met them. And Lucy isn't white. Charley might not have been too tough to find a home for on her own, but she outright refused to go anywhere without Lucy, so…" I stirred the veggies and the sauce, keeping one eye on Ravyn.

She took what appeared to be a calming breath. "So a sick baby might be hard to place, too, even if it's a baby. I mean, if someone wouldn't want a gorgeous little girl just because she's got dark skin—"

"Your son was adopted," I cut in. Letting her thoughts run away with her like that wouldn't help anything.

Her head shot up, and she blinked hard a few times. That didn't stop the tears from streaking down her cheeks. "How do you know that?"

I wiped my hands on a paper towel and turned so I could face her fully. "I don't *know* it, but I *believe* it. With everything in me." I wanted to wrap her up in my arms, but right now the temperature of the air between us made me think she'd push me away if I tried it. So, as hard as it was, I kept my distance.

"But what if I passed on the HIV and nobody knows about it?" Another tear fell from her cheek and landed on her chest, darkening the turquoise of my T-shirt.

"You dropped him off at a hospital. With a nurse. They knew you'd delivered him at home, so there's not a chance in hell they wouldn't have run all sorts of tests to find out everything they could about him."

"But we both know that HIV doesn't show up for a while, usually. It could be months later, or even years. Like your teammate. The guy who put his hands on your throat. He could have it but they might not know."

"Whether he has HIV or not, though, I believe with everything in me that they found him a good home with loving parents who are going to take care of him. Who'll get him routine medical care. Maybe they're a couple like my sister and brother-in-law, good people who couldn't have children on their own but who have a lot of love to give."

She still didn't look convinced. I doubted she'd ever *truly* be, because this wasn't the sort of thing that would ever go away even if she was certain she'd made the right choice, both for herself and for the baby.

I slipped her into my arms and pressed a kiss to her

forehead, offering what slight consolation I could. She allowed that much, so I went in for more, tucking her head beneath my chin and holding on tight.

"What you did was the ultimate act of love," I murmured. She shook her head, but I didn't give her the chance to argue with me. "It was. You knew you weren't in a position to give your child what he needed. You gave him the opportunity for a life you couldn't provide, even if it meant you would suffer."

And Lord knew she'd been suffering over this decision.

I held her for a lot longer than I'd intended to. To be honest, I wasn't sure which one of us needed it more, and as long as she didn't break contact, I wasn't inclined to put an end to it. If we weren't going to stay in bed and hold each other after sex, I wanted to get as much time with her in my arms as possible, in any way I could.

I'd always been into the cuddling side of intimacy as much as sex—maybe even more. Probably due to the affectionate way my parents had raised me. We'd been a family that was free with our hugs and kisses. I didn't know any other way to be.

But eventually Ravyn straightened herself away from me, and I turned to stir the food before something burned.

She sniffled and reached for a paper towel. "So you and your ex…"

I tensed up when she trailed off like that. I might be out of practice when it came to the early stages of a romantic relationship, but conversations about exes so soon after sex and cuddling couldn't be a good thing, could they?

"What about us?" I asked, trying to keep my tone

light.

Ravyn shrugged, but her eyes were a hell of a lot more serious than the action implied. She boosted herself up so that she was sitting on the edge of the counter behind me. "I just thought, I mean, you two were together for a long time, right?"

"You could say that." I stirred the veggies, trying to focus on dinner so I wouldn't overthink where she was going with this. "Ten years? We were sixteen when we started dating. I met her when I was playing in juniors. We married at twenty-one, divorced at twenty-six, so yeah, ten years."

More than a third of my life was with Chelsea. I'd never thought of it in those terms before, but it hit me like a brick right now. Crazy to think I'd spent so much of my life with her and I didn't even miss her anymore.

But the look in Ravyn's eyes was enough to make me lose my mind with worry. What had I done or said wrong? I didn't have a clue, and she looked like she was struggling to keep it together.

"What's wrong?" I asked, resting the wooden spoon in the skillet so I could give her my full attention.

She shook her head and shrugged again, but there were more tears pooling in her eyes and threatening to spill over. The wadded up paper towel seemed forgotten in her hand. "Did you… Did you two ever try to have kids?"

And we were back to *kids* just like that.

"We talked about it," I said evenly. "We both wanted a family, but Chelsea thought it would be best if we waited. I was still early in my career, and she said we should be settled better before starting a family."

Come to think of it, she might have been cheating early on in our marriage, so maybe she didn't actually want to have a family with *me.* I supposed I'd never know the truth now.

Either way, I was glad we hadn't gone ahead and had kids. That would have only made the eventual divorce messier, and it would have tied me to her forever, even if neither of us wanted to be. Now she could go on about her life and I could move forward with mine, and neither of us had to worry about what the other was doing.

"What about now?" Ravyn asked.

"What do you mean?"

"Do you still want kids?"

Talk about a loaded question. Especially since we still weren't officially a couple or anything. We might as well be, as far as I was concerned, but Ravyn still seemed to be gun-shy, and I didn't want to push her.

"I do," I said cautiously. "But things are complicated now. I mean, HIV doesn't transfer from a father to an unborn baby, so that's not an issue. But I can't exactly try to make a baby with a woman who isn't HIV-positive, too, without risking infecting her. And if she's HIV-positive, then there's always a risk of infecting the baby at birth, so… It's complicated." I drained the pasta, then put everything together in the big pot to combine it all, keeping an eye on Ravyn as I did. I still couldn't read her, though, which drove me crazy. "What about you?" I asked. "Do you want to have kids?"

She stared at me, her face an impenetrable mask other than her rapid blinking. If not for that, I'd think she had completely shut down on me. It was just enough to point to the fact that she was struggling with whatever emotions she was feeling. She glanced down at the photographs of my nieces for a moment before once again meeting my gaze.

"I don't think I could ever handle another pregnancy. It'd be too hard. Too many memories for me to get lost in."

Then she fell silent for so long I thought that might be all she had to say.

I was wrong.

"But I suppose there's always adoption."

Maybe she was making more progress with her counseling than I'd believed. I took down a couple of plates and glasses for water, smiling to myself. It was a good thing I was as patient as I was determined, because patience was exactly what Ravyn needed.

Nineteen

Ravyn

FOR ONLY THE second time in the last couple of weeks, I wouldn't get to see Drew today. Which felt…odd. And uncomfortable. While I was more upset about that than I'd like, there was also a part of me that was glad.

I worried that I was relying on him as a crutch. If that was the case, what would happen any time he had to leave with the Thunderbirds for a road trip? Was I doomed to go back to cutting myself as soon as he was gone or if he wasn't around for more than a couple of days? I hoped I'd come to a point where that wouldn't be the case, but I'd never know until I had at least a day or two without him.

After dinner last night and talking about things we'd never discussed before, we'd ended up back in his bed for a while. I couldn't say I minded. A couple more orgasms yesterday would go a long way toward getting me through today, as I saw it.

I tried to keep that in mind while sitting in my room and sketching a design at INKredible Ink.

Today was looking to be a rare day off, even though I was at work. After coming in a little after lunch, I'd spent a few hours restocking all of my supplies and performing maintenance work on my machines.

I didn't have any clients on the schedule for the rest of the day, and I'd already finished the designs for the ones who'd be coming later in the week, so there wasn't too much for me to do other than wait around and hope for someone to walk in off the streets or maybe call and schedule an appointment.

Rick poked his head in while I was doodling. "Looks like a slow one today."

"Mondays are always slow."

"Sometimes I think about shutting down the shop on Mondays, too, but it seems like a waste." He came into my room and sat on the chair like he would if I were going to work on him. "You've seemed better lately."

I scowled and raised a brow. He was digging for information, and I knew it. And he knew that I knew it, according to his grin.

"Amazing what some counseling can do for a crazy lady," I joked.

"Or getting laid. Whichever." He winked.

"What do you know about that?"

"Shannon and I still get it on all the time, so I know plenty about what a good roll in the sack can do for a person."

I rolled my eyes. "I *meant* what do you know about *me* getting laid—or not, as the case may be?"

"A hell of a lot more than you realize. I keep an eye on you. Been doing it since the first day you showed up in my shop with a sketchbook, asking me to teach you to tattoo." He linked his fingers and used them as a pillow behind his head, then stretched out his legs and crossed his ankles, settling in like he intended to stay for a while. "You're like a daughter to me. You know that."

"Yeah, well, my father wasn't much of an example for what a father should be, so I don't know what to do with you."

"But you had a baby of your own, so you get what the concerned parent thing is like." He didn't give me a chance to argue that I wasn't a parent, rushing on before I could get a word out. "You know I'm always going to worry about you. You know I want the best for you, and I'll do anything I can to make sure you get it. Because that's what parents should do."

I blinked back tears and traded out my black pencil for a charcoal-gray one.

Rick's eyes followed my hands, and he stared at my sketch. "Still no color, hmm? When are you gonna go back to your roots?"

I shrugged. At least he'd changed the subject. I'd been crying too much lately, and I sure as hell didn't want to do it at work.

"Maybe I need to have a talk with that guy who's driving you everywhere lately."

I narrowed my eyes at him. "What kind of talk? And what the hell does that have to do with me working in color or not?" Rick was bouncing all over the place, kind of like my new counselor tended to do, and I didn't like it. Because it threw me off. Kept me from being able to put my defenses in place.

"I don't know. You tell me. Is Muscle Man treating you right?"

I choked on a laugh. "Muscle Man?"

"Well, you tell me his name if you don't want me to make up a name for him."

"Drew," I said. "And I wouldn't know how to recognize a man who was treating me right if you bashed me over the head with him."

"Bullshit. You know what you deserve. You're just scared of getting it."

I shook my head. "What does that even mean?"

"It means you think if you reach out and ask for what you want and what you deserve out of life that someone's going to come along and rip the rug out from under you. But that's not going to happen now." He sounded so sure of himself it made me want to scoff.

But I didn't. Instead, I asked, "Why not?"

"Because you're strong enough to hold on now." He lifted my sketchbook from my hands and started flipping through the pages, easily evading me when I tried to grab it back from him.

"How the hell do you get that, when you can take something as simple as my pad away from me?"

"Good stuff in here," he said after a minute, avoiding my question. "Really good. But it's not you."

"Maybe it's the new me."

"Nah, it's not you. But you're starting to act like yourself again. Does me good to see it. So is it because of this Muscle Man—sorry, Drew—you've been hanging out with?"

"Don't go reading anything into it that isn't there just because *you* want it to be there."

"Okay. But don't *you* try to pretend something

doesn't exist when it does."

That bought him another eye roll.

"Does he deserve you?" he asked, turning serious on me again.

"According to whom?"

"You know what I mean. Is he good to you?"

Better than I knew how to handle. Rick seemed more focused on me than on keeping my pad away from me, so I snatched my sketchbook back and flipped to the page I'd been working on, giving him a look that said to keep his hands to himself.

"Maybe he is, then," Rick murmured, sitting up again and resting his elbows on his knees. "If you can't answer me, maybe it's because you've finally found a man and not a boy. Someone who's going to do right by you."

"You feel free to think whatever you want. I'm going to keep working on this."

"Mm hmm. So does he know?"

For whatever reason, I was so unprepared for that question that the shock of hearing it caused me to drop my pencil.

Rick reached over and tipped my chin up so I had to meet his eyes. He gave me a sad smile and nodded. "He knows. And he's still coming to pick you up after work almost every day. I might decide to like Muscle Man, after all." Then he gave me a quick peck on my cheek and got out of my chair. "Got to go yell at Billy again."

"What'd Billy do this time?"

"Nothing. I just haven't yelled at him in a few days. He'll think I'm sick if I don't figure out something to give him hell over." Then he winked and walked through my door, leaving it ajar.

He hadn't been gone two minutes before Dagger

knocked on the open doorframe.

"Walk-in asking for you," he said, spinning around and heading back up front again before I could ask him to expound.

Another walk-in. If this was Drew again… But no, it couldn't be. He'd had practice with the team this morning, followed by all sorts of sessions. He'd told me that since it was a game day, he'd have to go home and take a nap in the afternoon and then head up to the arena a couple of hours before game time. There wasn't a chance he'd end up here.

I quickly put away my sketch pad and pencils, tidying up the small mess I'd created, and then made my way out front to see whomever was waiting for me.

When I reached the desk, a young woman with red hair and curvy hips turned around. She gave me a tentative smile. "You're Ravyn?"

"I am."

She blinked a couple of times, then reached into her purse and brought out her cell phone. After swiping the screen and scrolling through a couple of menus, she passed her phone over to me. There was a photograph of one of my favorite tattoos I'd ever done—a watercolor mermaid in the ocean, going down a woman's rib cage, with the tail curling around the back of her waist and butt.

"You did this?" she asked me.

I nodded, trying to keep my smile in check and act like a professional, but I still felt a little giddy every time I saw that piece. It'd been a hell of a lot of work, but it was so worth it in the end. "About a year and a half ago if memory serves."

She took a few moments looking me over, like she was sizing me up, but then she gave me a curt nod.

"Good deal. Then you're the tattoo artist I want. I've been looking all over the place for more than a year, trying to find just the right person."

And I was it, based on a bold, colorful tattoo of the sort that I hadn't been able to do lately. A wave of trepidation threatened to knock me over.

Rick caught my eye from the other side of the lobby. He winked, which was all it took to bolster me up enough to get my feet under me again. I didn't know what this woman wanted. It was entirely possible I could give her what she was looking for. It was equally possible that I'd tell her I couldn't do it and send her on her way with a recommendation for someone else. No matter what, I wouldn't know unless I sat down with her and had a conversation.

So I steeled my spine and took a breath. Talking was something I could do. Maybe not anything else, but at least that. "What's your name?"

"Whitney Bayer," she said, holding out a hand.

I shook with her. "Why don't you come on back to my room and tell me what you're looking for, Whitney?" Once we were alone in my space, I closed the door and offered her a seat. "So, tell me a bit more about what you're thinking."

She glanced over at the open blinds covering the windows that looked out into the rest of the shop. "Mind if we close those, and I can show you?"

"Not at all." I got up and twisted the plastic wand thingy to close them.

When I turned around, Whitney was stripping off her shirt. I did my best not to react in any way and keep a professional demeanor. Really, in this business, I'd seen it all.

Or I thought I had.

Once her shirt was off, she reached behind her and unhooked the clasps of her bra, then let it fall forward. Without her saying another word, I understood. She'd had a double mastectomy and breast reconstruction. Scars. No nipples.

"I know maybe you're more comfortable with me because I'm a woman," I said, "but Rick, the shop's owner? He might be the better tattoo artist for the job. He's actually got a technique down for tattooing realistic looking nipples and areolas—"

"Let me stop you right there," Whitney cut in. "I didn't pick you because you're a woman, and I don't want nipples and areolas. They're gone, and they're never coming back, so why bother pretending?" She had a very matter-of-fact demeanor about her. Direct. Straightforward. I liked her.

"Okay, no nips. What are you looking for, then?"

"I want something bold, colorful, and pretty. Something no one else has." She took a seat again and crossed one leg over the other. "Something that represents beauty, strength, and peace, something about looking forward and not back. I want something only you can do."

Something I *used* to be able to do. But I kept that thought to myself.

"You have any ideas right now for what it should be?" Even as I asked the question, I took out a notepad and started jotting things down as they came to mind, images that were symbolic of what she was looking for. Butterflies, roses, dragonflies, Japanese cherry blossoms... Dragons were a possibility, depending on her preferences. And I wasn't sure how I'd fit a dragon across her chest in a way that was flattering. I glanced up and studied her body, trying to imagine it.

"So you're wanting something to celebrate being cancer free, I suppose?" I asked.

The more I could understand where she was coming from, the better I could design a tattoo that was exactly what she had in mind—even if she wasn't sure what she had in mind. This was how the collaborative nature of tattooing worked sometimes.

But I was still worried that I wouldn't be able to do something she'd like. The way I'd been so stuck in my head lately, doing a bright, bold, colorful watercolor design wouldn't be easy. I just didn't know if I could do it.

But she went and shocked me again. "Well, not exactly. I didn't have breast cancer."

I set down my pen and pad, looking up at her in surprise.

"My mother did. She died when I was only twelve. And her mother died from it in her thirties, too. I got tested. I have the gene."

"So you had a mastectomy as a preemptive measure? Like Angelina Jolie?"

She nodded. "I'm twenty-eight today. I fully intend to see forty, even though neither my mother nor grandmother did." Then she smiled at me. "I want to be able to look at myself in the mirror when I get there and smile at what I see. So I need your help."

And I'd be damned if I couldn't find a way to give her exactly what she needed.

Twenty

Drew

DOUG SPURRIER CALLED me into his office while most of the guys were kicking a soccer ball around in the bowels of the BOK Center to get warmed up. I couldn't help but feel like a naughty schoolboy heading into the principal's office, even though that couldn't be any further from what this was likely meant to be.

He was the team's head coach; I was one of his players. It was as simple as that.

"What's up, Spurs?" I asked, trying to keep it light. At his nod, I took a seat across from him.

A couple of the other coaches were in there, too, but their heads were huddled together over a laptop in the corner, leaving the two of us alone, for all intents and purposes.

The good news was that Spurs didn't mess around with me. He got straight to the point. "I'm putting you out there tonight. You're starting the game on a line with Hutch and Frisky. Don't want to make you wait any longer than necessary to shake off the butterflies. You know…rip off the Band-Aid, that sort of thing."

"All right," I said, trying to keep my shit together.

To be honest, I hadn't had the first clue what Spurs wanted when he'd sent for me, but never in a million years would I have guessed it to be this. I'd thought I'd be eased back into things. The doctors had cleared me on a physical level, but on an emotional level? I wasn't positive I was as ready for this as I needed to be.

Preston Hutchinson and Viktor Frisk weren't my usual line mates—typically, I played on a line with Zee and Gustav Gunnarsson—but in the preseason, all the forward lines and defensive pairings got jumbled up.

Lots of the guys who came to training camp were young kids just getting their first taste of pro hockey. In these games, they got to see ice time with seasoned pros, so the coaching staff and the GM's staff could discover how prepared they were to handle the big leagues. It helped the front office staff in making developmental decisions, I supposed, and gave them some guidance toward making those final cuts before the regular season got underway.

Frisky was new to the team this season. He was definitely one of those aforementioned young kids. Spurs was sending him out with me and Hutch, a couple of veteran players, probably so we could keep him calm and help him find his way out there.

Most of the lines for these first few games would look like that—a vet or two alongside fresh-faced, hyped-up, overgrown boys who would probably be sent back to their junior teams or the AHL before too much time passed. But when they went back, they'd have a much better idea of what they needed to work on in order to make the jump to the NHL level later on, because of whatever wisdom we managed to pass down to them.

Spurs didn't usually make any sort of announcement about who would be playing in a game, and definitely not about who would be starting, until well after the official warm-ups on the ice. Often not until moments before we hit the tunnel to head out there.

But for me, he'd made an exception. Maybe he realized I needed the extra time to get my head together.

Tonight wasn't normal, because it was only an exhibition game and wouldn't count toward the standings. In my mind, I knew that, but my body didn't seem to be getting the message. I'd been trying to hide my nerves, but it wasn't overly surprising to learn I'd done a poor job of it. Adrenaline had been coursing through me all day long, so much of it that I'd halfway hoped I'd be one of the regular roster players who ended up watching from the press box tonight so I wouldn't do anything stupid.

But Spurs was right, and deep down, I knew it.

I had to get this first game out of my system, and it'd be a hell of a lot better to do it when the results of the game didn't matter. If I lost my shit tonight, so what? Whatever happened, I wouldn't be hurting the team, so I nodded my agreement.

"You figure out which Kevlar pieces you like best yet?" he asked.

I shrugged. "None of them feel comfortable, but they're all a hell of a lot better than taking a skate blade to the jugular."

He let out a roar of laughter. "Fucking right. I wish

more players would wake up to the fact that taking care of their bodies out there is more important than proving how macho they are. But these things take time, and we've got to change the whole culture surrounding the game before these guys will wake up sometimes, you know?" He gave me a meaningful look.

I knew that all too well. There was a lot of truth to what he'd said about the hockey culture. In general, we were a bunch of macho buffoons more concerned with appearing manly to our teammates and competitors than with taking care of ourselves the way we should.

My mother was constantly forwarding memes via email and tagging me in posts on Facebook about how hockey players started wearing protective cups decades before anyone ever thought to wear a helmet.

But maybe I could help spark another safety measure in the sport through wearing the Kevlar sleeves and whatnot. Even if I didn't, I could protect myself—and in the process, hopefully do something to protect everyone else out there with me, so they wouldn't needlessly be exposed to my blood.

We chatted for a few more minutes before he sent me on my way so he could discuss our penalty kill units with the other coaches.

I joined the guys who were kicking the soccer ball around, doing my best to warm up my body without letting my anxiety run away with me.

An hour later, we headed down the tunnel for the ice. Hunter Fielding, our starting goalie tonight, led the boys out first, with me bumping fists with each of the guys as they went past us.

Usually, as the team captain, Zee would be the last guy out. He was up in the press box tonight, though, so for this one game, I was wearing the C and taking his place.

Finally, they were all out ahead of me. I made my way through the tunnel and stepped onto the ice to a roaring chorus of boos, louder than anything heard in this arena since the very first game of our inaugural season.

Or I thought they were boos, but all the guys skating circles around me had grins so wide their faces might crack at any moment, and they kept slapping me on the back or the helmet and saying things like "Told ya so, you big fucker" and "You were seriously thinking about *not* coming back?" and "Soak it up, bro, soak it up."

I blinked a couple of times and focused in on the fans pressed up against the glass at our end of the ice, holding up signs and screaming at the top of their lungs.

They weren't booing. They were shouting my name. *Drew*. More like *Dreeeeeeeeeewwwwwww*, actually.

I'd never expected anything like it. And I didn't have the first clue what to do with it. A couple of times in my career, the fans would chant my name like that—usually after I'd scored a big goal or some other thing that would get them behind me. Never just because I stepped foot on the ice.

Once the reality of the situation started to sink in, the only thing I could think was how badly I wanted to talk about it with Ravyn. If anyone would understand the whirlwind of emotions racing through me, it was her.

But she wasn't even here. She was at work, and I wouldn't be able to see her for hours.

The arena was full to the brim. The puck wouldn't drop for more than half an hour yet, but there were hardly any empty seats in the building—and most of the ones that *were* empty would likely be filled later by the fans currently crowding the glass to watch the warm-ups.

We might have a sell-out tonight.

In the preseason.

For a game that didn't matter.

There wasn't any good reason for so many people to be here. At least half the regular players weren't in the lineup tonight, including a lot of the bigger stars on the team like Zee, and Lord knew the T-Birds hadn't played well enough in our first couple of seasons to generate this kind of fan loyalty.

The only explanation for it was that they were here to see me. To support me as I attempted to come back from the accident I thought should have ended my career.

I hadn't felt more overwhelmed in a long time.

But we had a game to play, so I had to pull it together. Settling my helmet in place and attaching the chin strap, I stretched out a gloved hand and waved to acknowledge the crowd.

They somehow got even louder, and one of the camera guys zoomed in on me. I made a mental note to find out who he was later and beat the shit out of him, because with my mug up on the Jumbotron, you could tell I was about to cry, and every guy on the ice—for both teams—had stopped to stare.

That had to wait, though. I picked up some speed, gathered up one of the dozens of pucks with the blade of my stick, and headed for the net. Top-shelf, glove side. It went in, like Hunter hadn't even bothered.

I tapped him on the shins with my stick as I breezed past him. "Better get your head on straight before the game starts," I shouted.

"At least I'm not about to fucking cry," he called after me, grinning.

Yeah, I'd be hearing about that one for a long time to come. But I didn't care. My smile was so wide it made my face hurt.

FOR THE FIRST half of the game, Hunter played lights-out hockey. The Avs forwards peppered him with shots like they'd been waiting all summer just for that opportunity, and defensively, we weren't doing much in the way of slowing them down. That was definitely something the coaches would be on us about in the next film session, especially because the Avs weren't one of the better possession teams in the league. If we played like this against Dallas in a couple of days, you could bet they wouldn't have a goose egg on the scoreboard.

But now Aarti Nieminen, one of the two kids fighting for the backup spot this season, was between the pipes, and the guy was struggling. So far, he'd only let in one goal—and even the best goaltenders in the world would have been hard-pressed to stop that one—but the Colorado onslaught kept coming.

I was still huffing for breath on the bench after my most recent shift. We were a little more than three minutes into the third period, and a mishmash line of Dima and two newly drafted hotshots were out on the ice, with Ray "Razor" Chambers and a tall, gangly defensive prospect supposedly helping them out on the blue line. But other than Razor and Dima, none of our guys were where they ought to be, and Avalanche captain Gabriel Landeskog had just picked the enormous twig's pocket.

Razor turned on his jets and chased Landeskog, but he didn't have a good angle to do anything but prevent the Avs forward from passing the puck to a teammate. Dima rushed to get back and help out, but the other *D*—the one who'd given up the puck—was flat on his ass on the ice. One of the two junior forwards was still skating around in the neutral zone like he was hoping someone would send him a breakaway pass so he could be the hero of the day, and the other kid was so clueless that he jumped over the boards for a line change.

"Fuck!" Spurs shouted behind me, slapping my shoulder. That was all I needed to dive onto the ice and rush into the play. "Save me from fucking idiots," he was saying as I skated out of hearing distance.

Something told me that kid would be on a plane back to his junior team tomorrow. If not tonight. Seriously, a line change when the other team was roaring into our zone? That kind of shit didn't cut it even on the worst team in the league.

Nemo managed to get his blocker on Landeskog's first shot, but he couldn't control the rebound. Razor attempted to knock the puck back to me, but the rest of the Avs players had all gotten into position, and we were still in scramble mode, the tall, skinny guy just finally making his way toward the net to defend. One of the Avs *D* got his stick on the puck before it reached me.

He wound up for a slapper. I dove, flinging my stick toward the puck and praying I wouldn't end up taking a tripping minor instead. Somehow, I missed both, around the same time as the kid taking a leisurely skate around the neutral zone finally decided to join the rest of us.

Slap shot. The puck headed straight for Nemo's head, clanged off his mask, and rebounded into the corner. Dima shouted something in a garbled combination of Russian and English, heading over to help Razor dig the puck out. That left me and the two kids, both of them looking to me for direction. Fucking hell.

"You stick to Nemo like glue," I shouted to the human stick figure, using arm gestures to make sure he understood. Then I turned to the lackadaisical forward, but I doubted he was going to help us defend no matter what I told him. "You just stay the fuck out of the way," I said.

He nodded, like that was exactly what he'd been hoping I'd tell him to do. Son of a bitch, how did these kids think they were ever going to make it in the NHL?

I positioned myself high in the zone, keeping an eye on both Colorado defensemen and occasionally glancing back to the scrum in the corner. Finally, the puck squirted free, and Razor managed to tip it in my direction.

I just got a piece of it before one of the Avs *D*, and then I was off. My first thought was to get it out into the neutral zone. Once I'd managed that, I wanted to take it deep into the Avs' end so the rest of the guys on my side could get off for a change.

But that damned kid had beat me into neutral ice because this was what he lived for, and he was banging his fucking stick on the ice and shouting for me to pass it to him. There wasn't anyone close to him, so he had a legitimate chance to get off a decent shot.

If he didn't fuck things up.

If he *did* fuck things up, then the rest of my guys

weren't going to get their change in, and we'd be back to defending and trying to keep Nemo's head above water.

The truth was, I didn't trust this kid as far as I could throw him, so even if it seemed like a selfish move on my part, there wasn't a chance in hell I was passing the puck in his direction. Wasn't going to happen when the likelihood that he'd screw us all over was so high.

I held on to the puck, skirted between the two Avs *D*, who were converging on me, and surveyed my options. If I took the shot and missed, the kid was screaming toward the net to pick up the loose change. If I banged it around the boards, that'd give everyone a chance for a line change without the possibility of the Avs turning it around on us too soon. And then I could have other fresh legs out with me to help set up a cycle and generate some offense. Yeah, we were behind in this game, but the safer, smarter choice was clear.

I reached back to spank the puck into the zone, angling it toward the corner.

For some reason, the Avs goalie ignored the fact that this hotshot was coming in at full speed, and he went to retrieve the puck himself behind the net. Bad decision. Good for us, though.

The cocky kid touched the puck first, whipped it back out to me, and I slammed it home into the empty net.

Tie game. The crowd immediately came to their feet, chanting *Dreeeeewwwww* even louder than they'd done before the game. Razor and Dima caught up to me and lifted me off my feet from behind while the lanky *D* crashed into the hotshot and sent them both flailing into the boards.

Fifteen minutes to go, and we might as well be

starting over with a clean sheet. Game on.

I had no idea why I ever thought I was ready to give this up. Not a chance in hell. I'd be a miserable fucking bastard without having hockey in my life, no doubt about it.

But then one of the Avs players skated past me on my way to the bench and said, "You might have scored once, but there's no fucking chance we're letting some fucking homo with AIDS score again."

I whipped my head around to see who'd said it or if anyone else had heard it. But there were four Avs players all together in a group, and it could have been any one of them, and none of my teammates acted like anything was wrong.

Maybe it was all in my head.

Twenty-One

Ravyn

"YOU JUST MISSED seeing your Muscle Man score," Rick said, leaning one shoulder against the frame of my door. "Tied up the game. Crazy goal, too."

I blinked a few times when I looked up. "Huh?" I'd been focused on my sketches for so long that I didn't even know what time it was, let alone what the hell Rick was talking about.

I'd been working on an initial concept for Whitney, something to incorporate her ideas of beauty, hope, and strength into a design that would flatter her shape, emphasize what she wanted emphasized, and hide her scars. It was proving to be more complex than I'd initially imagined, which was saying something.

I wasn't sure I'd have anything worthy of showing

her in a week, when she was scheduled to come back for our next consultation, but I intended to do everything in my power to make it happen.

"In the game," Rick said, laughing. "Crowd's going wild, chanting his name. Who knew there were so many hockey fans in Tulsa, anyway? But you were right. Apparently his name *is* Drew, not Muscle Man. Although Billy's trying to convince everyone they're actually booing him. But everyone knows Billy's an idiot."

"You're watching hockey?"

My brain wasn't catching up. We *were* still at work, weren't we? Or had I fallen into such a daze that this was a dream? Maybe my mind was playing tricks on me, or we could have slipped into an alternate universe. But everything about *me* still seemed the same, so I somehow doubted that one.

"Dagger turned it on once I told everyone that your man plays for the Thunderbirds. There's only one client in the place, and the guys wanted to see what your Muscle Man is all about. Apparently he's the real deal. That goal was no joke. You ever watch him play?"

"We haven't exactly known each other all that long," I pointed out. "And this is his first game this year."

"Yeah, first one since that big accident at the end of last season." Rick narrowed his eyes at me, like he was trying to anticipate my reactions before I had them. "You see that yet? They showed the footage between quarters or whatever. Bunch of interviews with guys on the team, too, talking about what they remembered, how they dealt with it. Looked gnarly. He's a lucky man to be alive after that."

Lucky was one way to put it, considering how much that incident had changed his life—and not necessarily for the better.

But what did that say about me to think along those lines? I wasn't sure I liked it, so I just shook my head. I didn't know if I could stand to watch that incident. Drew had told me he could have died on the ice, and having seen that scar on his neck, I didn't doubt it. *Gnarly* didn't come close to covering it.

Rick straightened away from the doorframe and shrugged. "Anyway, I just thought maybe it'd be good for you to come out and watch it with us. Your choice." Then he headed back into the lobby.

If they'd already shown the footage from last season, packaged up in a big segment with interviews and whatnot, they probably wouldn't show it again. At least not during tonight's game. So I probably wouldn't have to see it if I went out there.

And I couldn't deny that I *was* curious to see Drew play. We didn't talk about hockey much, outside of those brief conversations when he was debating his future. Most of that had taken place during the support group meetings at the conference center, not between the two of us.

But hockey was his career. It was something he'd obviously devoted a huge portion of his life to, and I didn't have the first clue about it.

So I picked up my sketchbook and my colored pencils, and I headed out into the lobby to join the rest of the guys in watching the game.

The TV was showing a commercial break, so I decided to set myself up to keep working like I had been—because for the first time in a long time, I felt inspired. Like I could do what I was meant to do. I might not have figured everything out yet, but right now, I *wanted* to.

Rick gave me a brisk nod when I took up a seat at a big table in the middle of the room and spread out my materials. When I reached for a gray pencil, he raised a brow.

I narrowed my eyes at him in response and picked it up anyway. I was going to use color, damn it, but a bit of black and gray would only help those colors stand out. Which he knew. He'd taught me that, damn it.

Dagger took the seat beside me and shoved a water bottle in my direction. "That for your ginger lady?" he asked, pointing at what I'd drawn so far.

"Maybe. Not sure it's right yet." I liked the combination of elements, but the layout wasn't right. I had to find a way to get it to work with the shape of her body, not against her. Right now, the solution wasn't coming to me.

And until I got that part sorted out, the colors wouldn't matter. Which Rick also knew. He was just giving me a hard time.

"You'll get there," Dagger said. "Don't be so hard on yourself, and it'll come."

But then the game returned, and I looked up to find Drew's focused, sweaty face filling the enormous TV screen on the wall.

Rick had installed a gargantuan seventy-two-inch flat-screen for us. Sometimes as a staff, we all watched instructional videos about new tattooing techniques on it, and he was all about getting us the best view possible.

His dedication to our education was working out nicely for me right now, because seeing Drew in his element did a number on me.

Notably on my girly parts.

The referee-looking guy dropped the puck, and then

all of the players on the ice whipped into action. At that point, I had no idea which one was Drew anymore. They were all moving so fast, and with their helmets on, I couldn't make out his face.

"He's number eighty-one," Dagger whispered, probably sensing my frustration at not having a clue.

I gave him a sheepish grin. "Thanks." How sad was it that I'd spent almost every waking minute with him for close to a month, other than those times we were otherwise occupied with our jobs, but I didn't know even the simplest thing about his career?

I didn't like that realization. At all. Because it meant I'd been so selfishly wrapped up in my own misery that I hadn't bothered getting to know anything that was important to him.

No matter how hard I tried, I couldn't follow the action on the ice, not even with the commentators explaining what was going on. It was too fast, everything moving at warp speed.

The next time we got together, maybe instead of immediately jumping into bed, I could get him to explain hockey to me. Only I had a hunch that it would take a hell of a lot longer to explain than we could accomplish in the time it would take to reach an orgasm or two each.

Which only further emphasized how self-absorbed I'd been lately. This had to change. And soon.

Before I could blink, Drew and the rest of the guys who'd been out with him dived over the boards onto the team bench and were replaced by a bunch of other men in the same jerseys. Again, they turned into a turquoise-and-terra-cotta blur. I could hardly breathe from watching, and I was just sitting there.

My pencil landed on the sketchbook, willfully

ignored, but I didn't care. I was probably stupid to think I could focus on this design while the game was on, anyway.

There was a big hit, with one of the guys on the other team going hard into the glass. Everyone in the stands stood up, screaming and jeering in equal measure. In no time, there was a fight between the two players involved.

I did a quick check to be sure Drew wasn't the one fighting. It was someone wearing number seven, though, so I allowed myself to breathe again.

But then I wondered if he was one of the men I'd met at the pool party that afternoon at Drew's house. Not that I'd truly met any of them, since I'd run off before getting the opportunity to talk, but still. Even if he wasn't, he was one of Drew's teammates. Someone Drew knew.

My stomach churned, and I wanted to bury my face so I couldn't see. This was awful.

I'd known there was fighting in hockey, but I had no idea that there was really *fighting* fighting. This was all-out, full-on, bash-the-other-guy's-teeth-in fighting. Nothing at all like what I'd been expecting.

I couldn't look away, but I was cringing the whole time, and my stomach was doing flip-flops. When the referees finally broke the two up, the Thunderbirds player had lost his helmet, and the camera got a close up of his bloody nose as he was escorted toward the team bench. The other guy looked a hell of a lot worse for wear, which didn't seem possible.

But then I got a better look at the Thunderbirds player. It was Ethan Higgins. Huggy Bear. Carter's father. Now I *really* felt sick to my stomach. Had Carter seen that? Was he worried about his father, or did he get excited by the fighting, like so many of the people in the crowd seemed to be?

The camera panned over to the bench, and Drew was up on his feet with the rest of his teammates. They were all tapping their sticks on the boards, in an odd sort of applause. As the official took Huggy Bear past them, Drew reached up and accepted a high-five from his teammate, who dragged him in for a man hug. When they skated Huggy Bear off, Drew looked fierce and determined, and maybe a bit embarrassed.

Why would he be embarrassed?

Moments later, the game resumed. The guys were back to business, but my pulse was going a mile a minute. I'd never watched anything that was so exciting and nerve-wracking at the same time.

At first, the play on the ice seemed to all be taking place at one end of the rink. Then, in the blink of an eye, everyone shifted in the other direction, and it was a mad rush toward the opposite goal. I lost track of the puck—how the hell could the players see that thing out there, anyway?—and then a red light lit up while a deafening fog horn sounded, and everyone in the arena was on their feet screaming at the tops of their lungs.

Dagger jabbed his elbow into my ribs. "Somebody deserves to get laid tonight," he said.

Huh? I blinked in surprise and squinted at the screen. Sure enough, Drew's grinning face was in the middle of a pile of his teammates, and he had his arms in the air.

"Drew scored that one?" I asked.

"Fucking right, he did," Billy said.

That was all it took for my coworkers to decide they approved of my choice of a new friend…boyfriend…whatever he was. The guys made a bunch of crass jokes, which served as terms of endearment around here, and told me I needed to bring him around more often.

I'd just about decided their approval was solely because of Drew's status as a professional athlete when Dagger threw me for a loop.

He looked like a scary dude—covered from head to toe in ink, with piercings in so many places he seemed more metal than human, and a spiky Mohawk. But underneath all of that, he was actually a soft-spoken man. That was probably why I'd felt comfortable enough to go to him for the piercings I wanted done.

My ears, my tongue, my eyebrows…those were all places I could have handled anyone doing, as long as they practiced proper hygiene and safety techniques. But the nipple piercings? The one in my clit hood? Those are a hell of a lot more personal, for one thing, and if someone were to get them wrong, it would be really, really bad.

Which only reminded me how important it was to get Whitney's tattoo exactly right. Every tattoo was personal, but some meant so much more than others. This wasn't something I could half-ass or give anything less than my best.

But now Dagger was leaning toward me so the rest of the guys in the lobby wouldn't hear. "Especially since you two have so much in common," he said. "You and Drew," he added, probably because I looked at him like he was a crazy man.

Drew and I didn't have anything in common. He earned millions of dollars, lived in the nicest neighborhood in the city, and had a completely normal, supportive family. They'd probably had dinner together every night of his life, and I assumed his parents had gone to all of his games when he was a kid. In my mind, they were the perfect sitcom family. And he'd only gotten a tattoo because he'd wanted an excuse to see me. The two of us couldn't be more opposite if we tried.

"I don't have a clue what you're talking about," I said, "but you might have a fever or something. You feeling okay?" I reached up with the back of my hand to feel his forehead.

He swatted my hand away. "I'm talking about both of you having HIV, dummy. I'd think it's kind of nice for you to find someone else who has it. I'm sure it makes some things easier."

Like sex. He didn't have to say that part. My mind filled it in. "How'd you know he has it?" I asked.

"The video they showed. Apparently the whole world knows now. After his accident, once he recovered, they held a ton of press conferences and shit. Broke it all down for everyone—not just that he has it, but how the rest of the league shouldn't have to worry about getting it from him. I somehow doubt that they've all read up on it and believe the facts, you know?"

Wasn't that the truth? It struck me how unfair it was for Drew. Yeah, he'd talked about it that day in the support group, but the reality of his situation hadn't really sunk in for me until right now, sitting at work with a bunch of my coworkers—most of whom had never met Drew—but they knew tons of personal details about his life and health. How many other people around the world also knew that one little fact about him and then assumed they knew everything there was to know?

With all of these thoughts swirling through my head,

there wasn't a chance I'd get any more work done on my sketches until the game was over. I closed the book and put my pencils away so I could watch the rest of it. Out of the corner of my eye, I caught Rick smirking in a told-you-so sort of way.

I didn't care, though. I wanted to see what Drew was all about.

Because now, it mattered to me.

He mattered to me.

And I needed to figure out what to do with that realization.

Twenty-Two

Ravyn

DREW HAD ON a dark gray pinstripe suit, a checked shirt in various shades of blue, and a bold red tie and pocket square when he walked into INKredible Ink an hour or so after the game ended. It shouldn't have all worked together, but it did.

Maybe too well.

I'd never seen him in a suit before—usually, he was in some sort of athletic gear—but it definitely worked well on him. The jacket emphasized his broad shoulders, and the dress pants hugged his butt and thighs so tightly it had my mouth watering, and I could barely hold on to the bubblegum-pink pencil I'd been using.

Rick, Dagger, Billy, and the guys all crowded around

him, shaking his hand, saying, "Hell of a game," and generally fawning at his feet. I let them have this moment so I could pull myself back together again. He took it all in good humor, but it didn't take a genius to figure out he was searching for me through the crowd of my coworkers.

My whole body tingled with awareness when his eyes landed on me and he smiled. It should be illegal for a man to have such a potent smile and wield it while wearing a suit like that. It could make a woman's brain go foggy.

Okay, it was making *my* brain go foggy. Maybe other women wouldn't go gaga over him the way I did.

Once an appropriate amount of time had passed with him being nearly pawed by the guys, Drew made his way to my side and took up the seat Dagger had been in earlier. He looked down at my sketchbook and grinned. "Color, hmm?"

The rest of the guys gradually went back to what they'd been doing, cleaning up their work spaces or sketching out a custom design like I was, but their excitement was bouncing off the walls of the shop. It wasn't every day that people like us got to meet someone famous, so I tried not to let their enthusiasm get to me. And I *hoped* it wasn't bothering Drew. He seemed to be taking it a lot better than I was, though, which wasn't surprising.

He took everything a lot better than I did.

I tried to shrug off Drew's weighted question, even though I knew he'd think it was as big of a deal as Rick did. And I supposed it *was* a big deal for me to be working in colors again.

Recognize your victories was something my therapist was always telling me. *Celebrate them. They might seem stupid and inconsequential right now, but I promise you they're not.*

"For a special client," I finally said, glancing up to meet Drew's eyes.

"What's so special about this client?"

Everything, I thought to myself. But that wouldn't tell him anything, so I tried to do better. "Her grandmother died from breast cancer long before she was born. Her mother died of the same thing when she was really young. So she got tested and learned she has the gene, and she had a full mastectomy as a precaution."

"Wow."

"Yeah, wow is right."

He traced a finger along part of the outline. "And she wants this because…"

"These things all symbolize strength, hope, and beauty. She wants to see something that reminds her of those things when she looks in the mirror. When she's older than either her mother or her grandmother lived to be."

"Powerful stuff," Drew murmured.

And he was right. It *was* powerful. Whitney was choosing to take her life into her own hands, to move forward with purpose and determination instead of letting life drag her under.

Doing this tattoo—and spending time in her presence—might prove to be more cathartic for me than it was for her. Kind of a strange realization to have at a time like this, but there it was, dangling in front of me like a carrot. I just needed to reach out and grab it.

The same as I needed to reach out and grab what I wanted with Drew. Because here we were again, and he was asking me about my life—my day—and I still wasn't doing anything to get to know *him*. I was sitting back and allowing him to show me how much he cared about me—and yeah, I had just this second realized that was what he'd been doing all along, showing me how much he cared, which hit me like a hammer to the head—and I wasn't doing a damned thing to reciprocate.

That had to stop. Now.

"Mind if I cut out early tonight?" I asked Rick, closing my sketchbook and gathering up the supplies I'd brought out.

Drew reached over to stop me from putting everything away. "You don't have to leave work early. I don't mind waiting for you."

But that wasn't the point. The shop was still technically open for another half hour, but at this point, there wasn't a single customer in the place. No reason we all needed to stick around, especially if we wouldn't take on anything but the most basic of tattoos due to time constraints. "I'd rather go ahead and leave," I said. "I want to talk to you."

With that, Drew's eyes went wide, but he nodded.

Yeah, he was shocked that I wanted to talk to him. Right this second, he was probably running everything through his mind and convincing himself that *talking* was a euphemism for *jumping into bed*. But it wasn't. Maybe before, but not this time.

"Can I?" I asked Rick again.

Rick just shook his head and rolled his eyes.

I took that as permission to get while the getting was good.

"Two minutes," I said to Drew, but the instant I'd started packing up my things, the other guys had swooped in to get a piece of him again. He was so busy soaking up the praise from my coworkers that I doubted he heard me. By the time I returned with the backpack I was carrying in lieu of a purse, he was holding court, standing in the middle of the lobby and surrounded by the lot of them.

"Yeah, Coach wanted me to shake off the butterflies. I wasn't expecting to play until the second or third game of the preseason. These early games are usually about letting the coaches see how the prospects are developing and who's ready to make the jump to the big club. They don't put in too many vets early on. They just want to get our skating legs back under us while at the same time minimizing opportunities for injuries."

"You didn't look like you had any butterflies," Dagger said, sounding more excited than I'd ever heard him before.

Maybe I *should* bring Drew around more often. But then again, I wasn't sure Drew wanted to deal with this level of fangirling all the time. Not that they were girls, but I didn't know the appropriate term for when guys got their inner fangirl on. But seriously, if Dagger was getting this into it…

"Fucking killed them," he said. "Two goals!"

"I got lucky on that first one," Drew said. "And the second was a gift from the Avs goaltender. He shouldn't have tried to play the puck himself. He might as well have wrapped that one up with a bow for me."

"Speaking of getting lucky," Dagger said quietly, looking my way with a wink.

Heat rushed to my face, but I didn't think Drew noticed because Billy was pushing forward for his turn to bask in Drew's presence.

"Dude, so what was that fight about? Higgins just went *off*. Like, he hard-core lost his shit on that motherfucker."

Drew raked a hand through his hair. "Yeah, I don't really know. I wasn't out there on the ice, so there's no telling what was behind it." But the look in his eyes told me he *did* know. And whatever it was, he was still embarrassed about it. That hadn't been a figment of my imagination earlier.

I elbowed my way through a few of the guys, because they weren't giving Drew any space to breathe, and I wanted to get out of there with him. Now.

His face lit up when I reached his side.

I hooked my arm through his. "Let's go before Billy starts drooling on you or Rick changes his mind."

He didn't need any further encouragement. We left to a chorus of less-than-savory catcalls from the other tattoo artists present. As we turned the corner into the parking lot, Dagger poked his head out the door and shouted, "And I meant it, too, Ravyn! The guy deserves to get laid tonight."

Thank goodness we'd already reached Drew's car, because I stopped cold, pressed my eyes closed in utter mortification, and groaned.

Drew just laughed. "So I take it you guys watched the game tonight?" He opened the passenger door and waited for me to get in.

I nodded once he climbed behind the wheel. "Dagger turned it on after Rick filled the guys in about who you are. They've been giving me hell over you all night."

He started the engine and put the car in reverse, then flung his right arm across the back of my seat to back out of his parking space. His fingers danced on the top of my shoulder, making me ache for more. "You're kind of hot when you blush, you know that?"

"Don't get used to it. I don't blush much."

"Maybe I should work on making you blush more often."

"Maybe you should." I bit my lower lip as he braked to shift into drive, shocked with myself. Since when did I flirt?

He winked. "I like it when you bite your lip, too. Makes me think about doing the same."

"Maybe you can when we get back to your place."

He put on the brakes, coming to a full stop, and raised a brow. "Are we going back to my place tonight? I mean, I assumed we were, but—"

"We are," I cut in. I'd even brought a toothbrush, some pj's, and a change of clothes for in the morning, because I didn't want to make him take me home in the middle of the night if there wasn't any good reason to. "Unless you'd rather not. I mean, I know you have to leave for the road trip tomorrow—"

"I want you at my place," he said, and he sounded like he meant it. "I always want you at my place." But then he moved his arm so he could drive, leaving me to sift through what he truly meant by that. Because it sounded like he wanted me to move in with him or something.

I sulked at the loss of contact even though my plan for tonight wasn't to get him into bed as fast as we could possibly get there. But whether I wanted to get to know him or not, his touch was entirely too addictive. The next few days without having him around would be rough.

"I missed most of the game," I said, trying to figure out how to start up a real conversation with him. This was more awkward than I'd expected, which was saying something. I'd never been much of a conversationalist. "Rick got my attention sometime in the last quarter and got me to come out with the rest of the guys."

This shouldn't be so hard. We'd been sleeping together for weeks, so it *should* have been a natural thing to sit and talk about how the day had gone. But that couldn't be further from reality.

"Last quarter?" Drew said, laughing.

"Aren't there quarters? Or is it just halves like in soccer?" I racked my brain, but I was almost positive Rick had said it was the last quarter.

"There aren't quarters or halves in hockey," Drew said. "We play three periods."

"But what do you do for halftime?"

"We don't have halftime. There's an intermission between each period."

"How does a sport not have a halftime?" I asked, completely bewildered. I'd grown up in a tiny town in Middle-of-Nowhere, Oklahoma, where everyone played football or basketball. This didn't compute to me.

But Drew laughed and started explaining it. "Well, hockey is a Canadian sport, you know… We do things a bit different up there."

"Clearly."

"Maybe you should come to one of our games sometime," he said, turning from the parking lot onto the road. "Or all the time. I mean, I know you've got to work, so maybe you can't come to *all* of them, but whenever you want. Any time. I've got tickets I rarely use, unless someone from my family is visiting. I usually end up donating them to charity or giving them to one of the guys who has a lot of people in town. And I'm sure you could hang out with London or some of the other girls during the games. London could explain things you don't understand. She used to play hockey, back before her injury."

He was oblivious to my jaw hanging slack, acting as casual in asking me to come to his games as if he were suggesting that eating three square meals a day is generally good advice.

I'd been so upset with myself over not trying to get to know him, and I was so worked up about it that I was nervous, but here he was, inviting me into his life like it was the easiest thing in the world. Like it couldn't be more natural. And I supposed it *was* the natural course of things since we'd been sleeping together for a month.

He came to a stop at a red light and glanced over at me. "You don't have to come if you don't want to—"

"I want to," I cut in, and he grinned.

It was kind of a cocky grin, which made me melt. Because I'd been the one to put it there. I'd given him a reason to smile like that. And now I needed to make sure he *truly* understood what I was saying.

"I don't just want to come to your games," I said, hoping beyond hope that I didn't screw this up. "I want to get to know more about you. Your life."

I felt like an idiot saying this, like I was back in middle school and trying to talk to the boy I had a crush on, but everything coming out of my mouth made me seem like the biggest dork in school. All I needed now was a scrap of notebook paper to write *I like you. Do you like me? Check yes or no*, and my mortification would be complete.

But Drew didn't laugh in my face or make fun of me. He just turned to me and said, "Good. Because I want to get to know more about you, too." He was acting so calm and collected, like there wasn't any good reason for me to be nervous. "So you watched some of the third period?"

"Yeah," I said, trying to shove my anxiety into a corner of the closet that was my mind. "Saw your second goal. And that fight…"

The light turned green, and he took off again. "You don't sound like you enjoyed the fight."

"It's not that. I just— I kept thinking about Carter seeing his dad like that. And then I wondered if you fought much, and how I'd feel watching you in a situation like that, and—"

"I don't fight," Drew cut in. "Not if I can help it, at least."

I nearly choked on the deep breath I took then. "You don't?" Who knew I was so worried about him fighting that I couldn't breathe? But there it was. Right there for me to face and to figure out what it meant.

There'd been a lot of things like that lately.

"Not something I think is a good idea. I mean, you saw how both of those guys ended up bloody. Seems like a dumb chance to take on my part." Drew checked his blind spot and eased into traffic on the highway.

"But what if someone tries to force you into a fight?" My voice came out as a squeak. "I mean, that guy came up swinging."

"That's where it gets tricky," Drew said. "I mean, they can do that and run the risk of taking a steeper penalty, but I'm still in a fight at that point. Which is what leads to things like Bear throwing down with that asswipe tonight."

"How do you mean?"

He shrugged, but a massive ball of tension took up residence into his shoulders. He looked like he was hauling around a much bigger burden than I'd ever noticed before, and I didn't like it. He'd done so much to help me to bear the weight of my own burdens, but I didn't have the first clue how to help him with his.

I wanted to reach up and knead the tautness away, but he was driving, so that wouldn't work out too well.

"Tell me," I pleaded instead. When we got to his place, I could give him a massage and work the knots out. For now, I settled with reaching for his hand and twining my fingers through his.

He sighed, and it seemed like some of the heaviness left him on the exhalation. "It's exactly what I was afraid would happen," he said after a too-long pause. "This is one of the reasons I seriously thought about retiring, about not coming back for this season, or ever. A few of the guys on the other team were chirping at me all game about how I had no business putting everyone in the league at risk by playing."

"What?" Why would people do that? I hadn't exactly told the whole world about my diagnosis, but the few people who did know weren't treating me any differently than they had before. Rick, Shannon, Dagger…they all acted like it was no big deal.

But Drew seemed resigned to it, like it was simply how things were going to be. "That's what guys do in this league. Anything you can do to get under someone's skin on the other team, you do it. Well, they've figured out that they can take jabs at me because now they know I've got HIV, and not only will they get to me but they'll get my entire team off our game. Because my teammates want to protect me or some shit. The guy Huggy Bear lined up was probably the worst tonight. So Bear decided to make a statement."

"He fought because of you?" I asked.

"*Only* because of me. The guy's been in the league for over a decade, and I don't think I've ever seen him fight. He usually makes his point in other ways."

No wonder it'd seemed like Drew was embarrassed. I doubted anyone else had noticed, other than maybe his family if they were watching at home—everyone was focused on the two men who'd been fighting and not on him. Plus, I got the impression that Drew was pretty good at hiding these things.

But he didn't want his teammates to have to stand up for him. He felt like he was putting them in a bad position.

"He obviously thinks a lot of you, to stick up for you like that," I said.

For a long time, Drew didn't say anything. He focused on the road, changing lanes so he could exit. Once he came to a stop at an intersection on the service road, he looked at me again. I'd never seen this kind of pain in his brown eyes before. Usually, he was the one taking care of me, helping me put myself back together again. But right now, he was starting to fall apart in front of me.

"I just don't want the whole team to be worried about making guys on the other side answer for saying shit when the truth is those guys are just scared, you know? They saw what happened in that game last season, they know I've got HIV, and they're scared they're going to somehow get it from me. And I get it! I understand their fear and why they're going to act out like they are. But I want my team to worry about playing hockey. Playing as a team. I don't want the other nineteen guys out there feeling like they've got to beat some sense into the other team every time someone blinks at me the wrong way."

"Something tells me your teammates wouldn't look at it that way," I pointed out. "I mean, they threw a party for you. They clearly want you to feel like you belong."

"But if I *really* belong, why the hell do they have to drop their gloves to prove it all the time?"

"Might not be all the time."

"But it could be. This was just the first game of the preseason. The regular season doesn't even start for a couple of weeks. This was only the first chance any of the guys on the other side could have a go at me since I was carted off the ice on a stretcher. If they're already trying to get to me…"

"You think it's just going to get worse from here," I finished for him.

By now, we'd pulled into his garage. He parked the car and gave me a pained look before releasing my hand and getting out.

I followed him into the house, walking faster than I normally would because I missed the warmth of his skin pressed against mine.

Drew closed the garage door behind me, backing me up against it to kiss me. Hard. His tongue pressed against the seam of my lips, and I opened to give him access, practically climbing him as soon as his hands touched my body.

The sudden change, from talking about his worries to mauling each other in his kitchen, did a number on both my senses…and my resolve. I ripped at his tie, dragging it loose and tossing it on the floor, completely forgetting about my determination to get to know him better.

"I need you," he rasped, barely breaking the kiss long enough to get the words out.

"You have me." In so, so many ways.

And I needed him, too, more than I was prepared to

admit.

This week, with Drew gone, would be torture.

Twenty-Three

Drew

THE ENTIRE TIME I'd been playing for the T-Birds, I'd been doing it while distracted.

In my first couple of seasons here, I was trying to come to terms with a lot of changes in my life. I'd found out my wife was cheating on me, that I now had HIV, and we'd gotten divorced. I hadn't filed for divorce right away, trying to find a way to make it work out between us. Most of those things had taken place while I'd been in the playoffs with the Blackhawks—the team that had drafted me, that I'd won the Stanley Cup with, and where I had a legitimate chance of winning the Cup again every season I remained in Chicago.

But then in the off-season, I'd found out I'd been claimed in the expansion draft by the Tulsa Thunderbirds. And even though Chelsea had said she was on board with making our marriage work, and that she wanted to come with me wherever I went, that had been a lie. Because she was still cheating with the other guy. In the end, she never moved to Tulsa with me, and the divorce was finalized around the time our first season here began.

In some ways, being picked up by the T-Birds was the best thing that ever could have happened to me, even though it eliminated any hope of seeing another Stanley Cup any time in my near future. It gave me a fresh start. A new city to call home. New teammates to become friends. New sights for new memories. A new outlook on life.

Here, I had the opportunity to completely rebuild my life in a way that would have been a lot more difficult if I'd stayed in Chicago. Hell, it might have even been impossible.

So, while a lot of the guys who'd been claimed in that same expansion draft had come to Tulsa with chips on their shoulders and a belief that life was treating them unfairly, I'd arrived with a sense of excitement about what we could build here.

The newness of everything wasn't enough to eliminate my distractedness, but it had certainly helped. But instead of truly embracing the opportunity I'd been given, I'd spent a lot of that time in a fog.

Maybe it had been too many changes in my life all at once.

The only thing that had kept me sane during that time was my family. They had been my rock, the anchor that kept me grounded when my life had become a tempest.

Most of my teammates hadn't known just how fucked up my head was during those first couple of seasons.

They knew I'd recently gone through a divorce, but that was all I'd told them. Nothing about the fact that she'd cheated on me. Not a word about how I'd only discovered her unfaithfulness during a routine checkup with my doctor, which revealed I was HIV-positive. I'd kept myself closed off from the rest of the guys, determined to keep my private life private.

I hadn't done a fucking thing toward bringing this team together or helping us make the change from being a bunch of disparate parts lumped together to becoming a group truly working as a team toward a common goal.

I'd kept to myself, and I'd sat by and watched most of the rest of the boys do the same.

Zee was one of the few guys in our locker room who was making a serious, concerted effort to bring everyone together. It was high time I gave him some support in that endeavor, especially if I was going to be the next team captain, like the coaches and front office expected of me.

But now that I'd come to this realization and was ready to take the necessary steps toward that goal, I was distracted for an entirely different reason.

Because I was worried about Ravyn now that I was on the road with the team.

We'd talked every day while I was gone. I usually called her in the mornings, when I had a few minutes before practice and she was getting up to start her day. A lot of times, I called her again late at night, once I knew the tattoo shop was closed and she'd had time to get back to her place.

She sounded good when we talked. And she promised she hadn't hurt herself, that she hadn't even been thinking about hurting herself, and that if she *did* do either of those things, I'd be the first to know.

I tried to convince myself that meant she was fine and I should stop worrying about her.

But I still worried, because I couldn't get the vision of those newly healed scars on her arm out of my mind. And I wasn't fully convinced she wasn't hurting herself without me there to stop her, even though she said she was okay.

That probably said more about me than it did about her, now that I thought of it. Did I not trust her to tell me the truth? I supposed I couldn't, or I'd take her at her word and go on with the rest of my day. But what was I supposed to do with that realization now that I'd had it?

I'd been trying to get my head back on hockey, but so far, I'd had little success.

Spurs had given me the night off against Dallas, which was probably for the best for everyone concerned. We'd lost, which surprised no one, but Nemo had done a hell of a job in goal during his half of the game. The other young goalie who'd played that night hadn't fared so well. In fact, his stint in the net had been so ugly that the coaching staff had already sent him back to his junior team without giving him another chance.

Maybe they didn't want to traumatize the kid, but if that was the case, they probably shouldn't have put him in the net against one of the most potent offensive teams in the NHL.

Tonight, we were due to face the Coyotes, and I'd been hoping the coaches would grant me another reprieve. Another night in the press box could only do me good, the way I saw it. My head wasn't on straight, and I didn't want to let anyone down. Especially not myself.

No such luck.

When I walked into the locker room before the game, Spurs was writing line combinations on the white board at the front of the room. My number—eighty-one—was listed on the right side next to two numbers I didn't even recognize: forty-seven and sixty-four. Which meant I was the seasoned pro on my line for the night, whoever the other two guys were. Lovely.

Travis Royal, an insanely shy, quiet guy we all called Prince, walked up behind me to scan the board. He was in the lineup on defense for the night, also paired with some young kid. "Who's fifty-two?" he asked me.

"Hell if I know, but he's your partner for the night."

He let out a sound I couldn't interpret and headed for the arena's underbelly. "Two-touch game starting in five," he called out over his shoulder.

Which meant I had five minutes to shoot off a quick text message to Ravyn and let her know I was thinking about her. She'd be at work right now, so I doubted I'd get a response until well after the game tonight, but that didn't matter. Letting her know she was on my mind was all that was important to me.

Sitting on the bench in front of my stall, I took out my phone. I'd set it on silent earlier when I'd gone up to my room for my pregame nap. Apparently, I'd missed a few text messages in that time.

I quickly scanned through them just to be sure there wasn't anything important I needed to respond to.

One was from my sister with the latest pictures of Lucy and Charley at the park. Lucy was on the swings and Charley was climbing a kid-sized rock wall that looked a lot more daunting than I would have expected her to tackle. Both of them had grins a mile wide.

Another message was from my mother, letting me know that she and Dad had booked a flight down for the T-Birds' season opener. I'd forgotten they were planning to come down for that. Something else to talk to Ravyn about, because I wanted her to meet them. Maybe she wouldn't freak out too bad if she had enough warning.

Then Razor had apparently texted to see if I wanted to grab a coffee with him before heading to the arena. Oops. Coffee would've been good. In fact, I should probably go on a search to see where I could get a cup now. They were bound to have coffee somewhere in the arena.

The last message was actually a long string of them, all from Ravyn. My breath got trapped in my lungs as soon as I saw her name with more than a dozen messages attached.

I scrolled up to the first new text from her and worked my way down. She'd sent me some pictures of her progress with the design she was making for her mastectomy client, all full of bright, bold colors.

I actually smiled, looking at those, because she wanted to share this piece of herself with me, and because she was clearly starting to feel more like herself. Not only that, but her sketches were fucking brilliant.

But then there was a whole slew of messages with her panicking because a couple had come in, wanting Ravyn—and no one but Ravyn would do—to design matching tattoos for them after their three-week-old son had died suddenly, seemingly for no reason. Ravyn didn't think she could do it.

Because it had to do with a baby.

And because she was sure it would come out dark and ugly and full of her own pain, much like the paintings she had hidden in her apartment closet, and it wouldn't be the beautiful memorial they were hoping for.

In one of the more recent messages, she said she'd talked to Rick and that had helped some, but she really wanted to talk to me and hear my voice. That she wanted to help these people and do the tattoos for them, but she was worried she would cut herself because of all the hurt it would bring up within her to go there.

The last of her messages had been sent more than an hour ago.

Fuck. If I'd checked my phone sooner, I could have already talked to her. We could have had a good, long conversation already, and I might have been able to talk her through this. Was it too late already?

If she'd cut herself…

I pressed my eyes closed, refusing to allow myself to think like that. It wouldn't be my fault, even if it felt like it was. I couldn't *fix* her. Hell, she didn't need to be fixed. She was just depressed, and struggling, and I knew as well as anyone that depression was an illness. She needed treatment and understanding, not someone to be a knight on a white charger, rushing in to rescue the damsel in distress.

She might be in distress, but she—and only she—could ultimately get herself out of it. With help, sure, but she had to be the one to take the steps. She had to go to counseling. She had to take meds if they determined she needed meds. No one could do those things for her.

I couldn't do those things for her, no matter how much I might want to.

I dialed her number, hoping she would answer

despite being at work.

It rang twice. Three times. I was starting to give up hope when her voice met me on the other end of the line.

"Drew?" There was definitely a sense of panic in her tone.

"Hey," I said. My throat felt raw and my tongue too large to fit comfortably inside my mouth. Worry could do a number on a person. "I didn't see your messages until now. I'm sorry. I would have called you sooner."

"It's okay. You've seen them now."

"*Is* it okay?" I asked. I didn't want to be more specific than that. I didn't want to put my fears into words in case that made them come true. Probably a superstitious thought, but hockey players were superstitious by nature. Might have something to do with how often we took hits to the head or crashed into the boards. But that was beside the point. "Are you all right? You haven't…?"

"So far, so good. I'm just thinking about it. I don't *want* to, you know? That doesn't stop me from thinking about it, though. But I'm still at work, and I never do anything like that at work. Only when I'm at home."

Alone.

She didn't need to fill in that part.

I did some quick calculations. By the time we finished the game, talked to the media, got the entire team to the airport, flew back to Tulsa, and I could get home from the airport, it would be sometime between three and four in the morning.

She'd be off work by eleven.

Five hours was a long time for her to be on her own when she was in such a bad state of mind.

"Can you maybe go home with someone tonight?" I

suggested, racking my brain. "Or at least until I can get back there? I can come and pick you up once we land."

Bear walked past me, and apparently he overheard my side of the conversation, because he raised a brow in question.

I shook my head at him so he'd keep doing whatever he was in the locker room to do.

"If Rick was here, I could go home with him and Shannon. But they went to Oklahoma City for the next week. Their oldest daughter is having a baby any day now."

"But you said you'd talked to him."

"I did. On the phone. He called me as soon as he saw my messages."

Shit. "And you can't go home with any of the other guys from the shop?"

"We don't have that kind of relationship," she said, and I didn't doubt it. Ravyn wasn't the sort who invited many people into her life. She kept her distance. And I wasn't sure I'd want her going home with one of them, anyway. I didn't know any of them well enough to trust them with her.

"Does Ravyn need a place to stay?" Bear asked, plainly ignoring my earlier head shake. "There's a key under the potted plant in my backyard. Left it there for the dog sitter. She can go to my place, and you can pick her up when we get back."

"Hold on," I said to Ravyn. Then I angled the phone away from my mouth so I could get rid of him. "She's got somewhere to stay. She just shouldn't be alone right now. That's all."

I assumed he'd go on about his business, but he took a seat next to me, claiming the bench at Preston Hutchinson's stall.

"What about going to stay with one of the WAGs?"

She didn't know any of them to speak of, other than London, and I doubted she wanted to spend hours with a newborn baby. Bad idea.

She'd briefly met Dana Zellinger, but Dana had a three-pack of little ones running around.

Tallie Fielding would open her door to Ravyn in a heartbeat, but she was chasing around a one-year-old daughter these days.

I didn't know Tori Chambers well enough to ask. Or any of the other guys' wives, either. That was one of the problems with me keeping my distance since joining the team.

None of those sounded like very good options considering the reason Ravyn needed to be around other people right now.

I shook my head. "Don't think that's a good plan right now. She doesn't really know many of them, and the ones she's met before have kids."

He nodded, with a thoughtful, serious expression. "No kids right now, huh? What about overactive, overly friendly puppies that might have a problem with peeing from too much excitement?"

I was about to try to brush him off again, but then I thought better of it. Maybe I didn't know Bear all that well, but he did owe me after dropping off his kid and puppy at my place that day with no warning. And if Ravyn went over to hang out with Snoopy when she left work, she wouldn't be alone. In a situation like this, puppy love might be better for her than anything. That dog would love her unconditionally, probably wagging his tail for days and licking her into submission.

I'd never thought about hurting myself, but I couldn't imagine anyone wanting to do something like that with a puppy showering them with affection.

"You sure you wouldn't mind?" I asked.

"Nah. Besides, Snoopy needs some company. And he'll let me get to sleep a hell of a lot sooner if he's had someone to jump and drool on for a while before I get home." He stood up. "Key's under the potted plant by the back door. The gate's not locked. Tell her to be careful where she steps and I'll clean up any pee I find when I get home, so she should just go get some love from him. Guest bed's made up if she wants to sleep, but that little fucker is going to insist on being under the blankets with her, so she'd better be prepared for that. He'll rip the shit out of my carpet and howl so loud she'll never be able to sleep if she tries to shut him out."

"Got it. Thanks," I said, but he was already stalking off.

"Is he serious?" Ravyn said into the phone.

"So you heard all of that?"

"Every word."

"Well, he's serious," I said. "And I think it's a good idea."

She was quiet for longer than I would have liked, but then she made a humming sound. "I think so, too."

"So you'll go over there when you leave work?"

"I will."

I rattled off his address and promised I'd meet her there as soon as physically possible.

We talked for a few more minutes, but not too long because she had to get back to work and I had to get ready for the game. But by the time I hung up with her, I was breathing a bit easier.

She might have thought about cutting herself, but she hadn't done it yet. And she had actively reached out to me and to Rick. She was looking for alternatives. She'd been up front with me when she'd thought about hurting herself.

Maybe she was finally starting to come out of her depression. She might not be in the clear yet, but she was trying to get there. And there wasn't any good reason for me to doubt her. She was proving the opposite, actually.

No more needless worrying about her when I needed to focus on my job. It wouldn't do either of us any good, and she deserved better than to have me constantly hovering and assuming the worst.

The two-touch game was in full swing by the time I made it out to join the rest of the guys. Prince headed the soccer ball in my direction as soon as I arrived, and I had to back up a few steps to catch a piece of it with my toe, sending it straight back in his direction.

"You're late," Prince said, but he took his eye off the ball for a half a second to do so. That was half a second too long. It hit the ground, and he closed his eyes and dropped his head back in defeat. "Well, fuck."

"At least my head's in the game," I said.

And I meant it.

Finally.

Now I needed to figure out who numbers forty-seven and sixty-four, my line mates for the night, would be. Might help if I knew their names.

Twenty-Four

Ravyn

I FINALLY FELL asleep last night on Ethan Higgins's couch with a warm puppy snuggled on my chest, and now I was waking up with a warm man lifting me into his arms. "Hi," I murmured, curling up against Drew in a pose that mimicked how Snoopy had been sleeping on me.

He'd apparently removed his tie after leaving the airport, but he still had on the shirt and jacket he'd worn when they left Phoenix after the game. The silky feeling of his shirt against my cheek was like a drug to my soul. The powerful muscles underneath it even more so. All he'd done was lift me from the sofa, but I felt more thoroughly cared for than I could ever remember feeling in my life.

I was too out of it—and too content, now that Drew

was here—to complain about anything, including about being woken up. To be honest, I wasn't sure I'd been asleep for very long. My thoughts had been running away with me the whole time I'd been at Huggy Bear's house.

Only Snoopy's insistence on incessantly licking all the tears from my face until I finally stopped crying, and then sleeping on top of me (which, in turn, kept me down where he wanted me, so he could lick more if necessary), could account for the fact that I *had*, eventually, nodded off.

In the few weeks since the last time I had seen this puppy, he'd nearly doubled in size. Which only meant that he had twice the strength to make me do what he wanted. Not that I'd had it in me to fight him, but the licking *had* been a bit more than I'd bargained for. He hadn't stopped until my tears had turned to laughter, and even then his excitement knew no bounds.

"Sorry it took me so long to get here," Drew said. He had at least two full days' worth of scruff covering his jaw, and I couldn't stop myself from reaching up to touch it. Hell, I didn't *want* to stop. I'd meant it when I told him that he should think about keeping the scruff. It was delicious. *He* was delicious. The scratch against my palm was both abrasive and comforting—because it meant he was really here, and this wasn't only happening in my dreams.

I shook my head. "Don't be sorry. You have a job to do. A life to live."

I was still shocked by how much I'd missed him. The team had only been gone for four days, but it felt like a month had gone by. A month of being alone. A month of having no one here to prevent me from cutting, other than myself.

But it hadn't been a month. Only four days. I'd reminded myself of that so many times it ought to be tattooed on my skin.

"Thanks again, man," Drew said, carrying me toward the front door.

"Any time," Huggy Bear replied.

I was still half asleep as Drew opened the passenger door of his car and set me inside. Good thing we didn't have to go far to reach his house. The two minutes or so it took to get there was enough to vaguely wake me up. I climbed out on my own and met him at the door.

One strong hand landed on my hip as he guided me inside, carrying his suitcase in the other. I shivered at the contact, desperate for more of his touch, almost as desperate as I was for more sleep.

"Come on," he said, leaving his bag on the floor in the kitchen. He guided me back toward his bedroom. "Why don't you go get cleaned up? I'll bring you something to change into."

I nodded, too physically and emotionally drained to do anything more than that.

Drew nudged me toward the bathroom, and I took a few minutes to wash all the puppy slobber off my face and brush my teeth. He joined me by the time I was finishing up, having already removed his jacket and belt. The buttons of his dress shirt were undone, giving me a glorious view of his undershirt hugging his broad chest.

I had to kiss him. It'd been too long, and I needed his lips on mine as much as I needed my next breath. Taking his shirt in my hands, I hoisted myself up to my toes and dragged him down to meet me halfway.

His lips crushed against mine with the same sort of desperate hunger I felt, and he hauled my body against him. Being in his arms this way again was like coming home. At the same time as he angled his head to take the kiss deeper, I opened my lips on a whimper. He took the opportunity I'd provided and thrust his tongue inside my mouth. It was almost like he was trying to claim me, to mark me as his. At the moment I was more than all right with the idea.

I felt his kiss all the way to my core. In no time, I was not only wide awake but frantic with the sort of need that had been building for the last several days. Drew was my new addiction, and I needed to feed it.

But all too soon, he broke away and set me back from him. "Sorry. Didn't mean to maul you like that."

His lips were as kiss-swollen as mine felt, and his eyes were dark with lust.

"What if I want to be mauled?" I demanded, my lungs trying to remember how they were supposed to work.

"Sleep first," he said.

There wasn't a chance in hell I'd be able to sleep now. Especially not once we were lying in bed. His skin on mine. The familiar, comforting weight of his arm draped across my waist. I'd never be able to get my mind off of *him*.

I pouted my displeasure, but he ignored me, his face taking on a business-like expression. He tugged at the hem of my shirt. Like an obedient child, I lifted my arms and allowed him to strip me. But when he innocently brushed the side of my breast with his hand in the process, my body's response was anything but *obedient* or *childlike*, particularly after that kiss.

I needed more.

I needed Drew.

I let out a groan and nuzzled into his arms, splaying my palms over his abs before he could replace one shirt with another. The telltale sign of his erection pulsed against my belly. His need for me was just as strong, even if he was trying to hide it.

There was no hiding that kind of heat, though. His scent wrapped around me, settling into my senses and soothing my nerves.

It would be entirely too easy to get lost in him. And for some reason, I didn't think that would be a bad thing.

"I need you," I said, inching my hands up his chest to lock on to the back of his neck. My fingers delved into the hair hanging over his collar, and I rocked my hips toward him in invitation.

But he just stood there, holding me, his strong hands stroking my back and sliding down to cup my ass in a move meant to comfort, not to arouse, even if it did exactly the opposite of what he intended.

In an effort to get him to loosen up, I let my hands roam all over his torso. My fingertips found the deep vee heading down south. I teased the lines and the soft, taut skin surrounding them until his abs jerked against me.

"You need sleep," he murmured, his chin resting on the top of my head, but his breathing was turning ragged and harsh—just the way I liked it.

"I need you more than I need sleep." And to further emphasize my point, I dropped one of my hands down to rub him over his pants.

An involuntary moan bubbled up in his throat. "I'm trying to take care of you right now, Ravyn."

"This is another way you can take care of me." And a way that I could take care of him, whether he wanted to see it that way or not. Plus, it was the way that made the most sense. For both of us. At least to me, it did.

I released his fly and, in a single move, tugged down both his pants and boxer briefs. Removing it all at once would give him less opportunity to block me, in case he tried again. I had no doubt that once we got going, he'd be more than happy to continue.

His dick bobbed in greeting, hard and hot and fully on board with my plans even if Drew hadn't caught up yet. I dropped to my knees and took him into my mouth, drawing a groan from his lips when I traced the underside of his cock with the tip of my tongue.

He backed up against the counter, bracing himself against it with his hips and one hand, the other cupping the back of my head with gentle pressure. "Fuck, that's so good," he said when I swirled my tongue around his head, then took him all the way to the back of my throat. I followed that up with a strong pull of suction, and was rewarded with his balls tightening in response.

Resting one hand on his powerful thigh, I added the other to my efforts and worked him over. He started pumping his hips toward me, tender but insistent movements as his head fell back.

"I love your mouth," he rasped, but I already knew that because of the way he was responding, the grunts and groans, the hardness and heat.

Changing things up a bit, I stroked his length with my hand and gently lapped at his balls. Might have been too soon for that move. Drew sucked in a breath while his sac tightened, preparing for his climax.

But apparently it was exactly what he needed in order to get him fully invested in my plan. The next thing I knew, he was dragging me to my feet, cupping my face with both hands, and kissing me so hard it felt like he was trying to crawl up inside me.

And I wanted him to do exactly that. I needed to feel

him inside me. I fumbled with my skirt and panties, trying to get them out of the way because I couldn't wait much longer.

He released my face and broke the kiss long enough to rip the material down my legs, kneeling before me. My ankles got tangled in the fabric, and I couldn't kick it free, so I grabbed hold of his shoulders and held on for dear life. He tried to tear them away from me, but it was no use. Laughing, he gave up. But on his way back up my body, he settled a hand over my pussy, one finger easily slipping into my wetness while his thumb stroked tight circles around my clit. "Hell, baby, you're so wet." His forehead dropped down against mine. It was enough to steady me while he drove me toward climax.

I was *this close* to coming all over his hand, but that wasn't what I wanted. I wanted the connection of our two bodies. The closeness I could only feel when he was truly inside me. "Fuck me, Drew. I need you to fuck me."

In response, he flung open one of the bathroom drawers, fumbled around until he came up with a condom, ripped the wrapper open, and unrolled it over his length. And then he spun me around and bent me over the counter. With a solid thrust, he was fully inside me.

My sweat-damp arms on the cool marble countertop, I met his gaze in the mirror. I'd never seen anything hotter than the look on his face as he watched us. Mouth parted. Eyes dark and glinting with need. Sweat on his brow. Muscular arms flexing as he brought my hips back to meet his thrusts.

He slid one arm around my waist, easing his hand up my abdomen to my breasts and bringing my back into a fuller arch. He angled his forearm across my chest, that hand latching on to my opposite shoulder while he lowered the other to circle my clit. "Touch your tits for me, baby. I want to watch you touch yourself."

I was too far gone to do anything other than exactly what he told me. Secure in his grip, I reached up and lightly pinched my nipples, getting a corresponding pinch to my clit almost as soon as I did it. My whole body clenched from the sensation, especially my pussy, and Drew groaned in pleasure. I rolled my nipples between my thumbs and forefingers, and Drew matched that motion with my clit. His eyes stayed focused on my hands and breasts, so he could repeat the ministrations down below, all the while driving up and filling me like I'd never felt before.

Drew dipped his head and placed openmouthed kisses all along my neck and jaw, working his way toward my mouth. I let my head fall back, and his tongue met mine. He sucked my lower lip between both of his, ending it with a slight nip of his teeth.

I cried out. Not in pain, exactly. It was a good sort of pain, a sudden jolt that was gone before it could seep into me and take root. The sort that made every muscle in my body clamp down, sending me to the very edge of a powerful climax.

Drew must have sensed how close I was, because he nibbled on my lower lip again at the same time as he pressed down with his thumb over my clit hood piercing.

And I came apart. It was too much. Too much sensation. Too many pleasure points. Too much emotion coming at me from too many sources, all at the same time.

I went completely boneless in his arms as he thrust

into me a few more times and came with a harsh grunt, his mouth pressed to my cheek while he held me up.

Somehow he still had the strength to pick me up and carry me to his bed. In the back of my mind, I knew I shouldn't lie there with him right now. I should stay in the bathroom and clean myself up. I should take a few minutes to calm down, because getting too close to him right now could open up a can of worms I wasn't ready to open.

But he settled me in his bed, and after dealing with the condom, he climbed in beside me. He wrapped one arm around me, tugging me to his side. Without even thinking about what I was doing, I rested my head on his shoulder.

And he held me.

He held me like it was the only natural thing we could possibly do.

He held me like you see in the movies, with perfect couples and perfect lives.

He held me like a man who might even love me.

He rested a hand on my hip and stroked my cheek, planting soft kisses on the top of my head and saying things that didn't make sense in my current state.

"I hated not being here for you," he said after a minute, once my mind was working again. "I hated that you were alone. I don't want you to have to face these things alone."

But I'd been alone for so long I didn't know any other way to be. My parents had too many children and not enough time for me. Together with my five siblings, we'd shared a run-down house with two other families. Lots of kids. No supervision, because all of the adults were always at work. I'd grown up in a house where I'd been surrounded by people but felt completely alone.

They hadn't even made an effort to stop me when I'd run off with Jax. They hadn't tried to get me to come back. It might have been a relief, actually. One less mouth to feed.

And when I'd been with Jax for all of those years, he'd needed his drugs more than he'd needed me. I'd been gone for more than a year, but I doubted he even realized I'd left him, beyond not having my wallet to raid whenever he needed another fix.

I knew how to be alone.

What I didn't know was how to let someone else in, even though Drew was somehow managing to make it happen, anyway.

He tipped my face up toward his and kissed me.

This kiss was unlike any kiss we'd ever shared before. It was soft and sweet. It was tender. His lips gently brushed mine, over and over again, while he caressed my cheek.

This kiss broke me.

Twenty-Five

Drew

ONE MINUTE I was holding Ravyn, kissing her, and trying to figure out how to tell her I loved her—something I'd only come to terms with on the flight back to Tulsa, while talking to Zee and Bear—and the next minute, she was sobbing uncontrollably and ripping herself away from me.

She rushed into the bathroom and slammed the door closed before I had even managed to untangle myself from the blankets and get out of bed. Just as I reached the door, I heard her turn the lock.

Fuck! This wasn't how this was supposed to go.

"Ravyn?" I tried the knob, just in case. But as expected, it didn't budge. I rested my forehead against the door and listened. She was definitely still crying, but then she turned on the faucet. The rush of water drowned out any sounds I might have otherwise heard.

When she finally shut off the water, I tried again. "Ravyn, please open the door."

"Why?" she asked. Her voice cracked, and I could swear I heard her hiccup.

"Because I want to talk to you."

"You can talk."

"I need to *see* you." I needed to hold her, too, but I'd start with just being able to see her face. That would be a hell of an improvement over talking to the door. And it'd tell me a lot more than any words she might say, because I was finally learning to interpret her facial expressions.

But she didn't unlock it. She didn't answer me for quite a while, either, and when she did, it was to say, "I can't do this."

She might as well have kicked me in the kidneys. I'd thought she was making progress, maybe starting to come out of her depression, and now she might as well be heading right back to square one. Or at least that was how it felt right now. It *might* not be quite as bad as that, although I wouldn't hold my breath.

Hard to know for sure, since she wouldn't open the door and let me hold her.

"Did I do something wrong?" I asked, barely recognizing my own voice because of how pained and strained it sounded. She'd all but demanded sex, so that couldn't be it. The only thing I could think was that I'd tried to cuddle with her afterward.

If that was truly the problem, and she wouldn't ever be able to let me hold her after we were intimate, I didn't know how to deal. Getting or giving the cold shoulder after sex wasn't in my makeup.

"No. It's not you." She sniffled, immediately followed by a fresh wave of sobs.

"Then let me help you," I pleaded. "Whatever it is. You can tell me about it, or not if you don't want to. I just—" Needed to hold her. That was it. I needed to hold her, and until I could, I'd be an utterly worthless wreck. Maybe that meant I needed to turn in my man card, but I didn't care.

I was about to give up and stalk off to the kitchen to make some coffee—no chance I'd be getting much sleep any time soon—when Ravyn unlocked the door and cracked it open.

Her nose was red and puffy, and her face was splotchy from crying. Reflexively, I held out my arms for her even though I doubted she'd come into them.

She surprised me by doing exactly that.

"Hey," I said, tucking her head under my chin and wrapping my arms around her so tightly she might not be able to breathe. But I needed the comfort of comforting her. "I've got you. Whatever it is, whatever's wrong, I've got you."

She shook her head. Her soft dreads tickled my chest.

"Will you at least tell me what's going on?" I asked. "I might not be able to fix it—"

"No one can fix it," she cut in.

Which was possibly true. She and I both knew that there were things in life that couldn't be undone. "Okay, but it'll help to talk about it."

Again, she surprised me, this time by nodding. She pulled away from me, though. Reluctantly, I let her out of my arms. She walked over to the bed and climbed under the covers, so I followed her. She held up the blankets, waiting for me to get in.

I didn't mess around, taking the opportunity she'd given me because there was no telling how many more chances I'd get. We lay on our sides, facing each other. I brushed away her tears, leaving my palm resting on her cheek, my fingers sinking into her hair, because I needed to have contact with her.

She blinked a few times, and I feared she might have changed her mind.

"They had pictures of their baby," she said finally.

Her voice cracked so hard it made *my* chest seize up, but I remained silent, waiting for her to get it out—however much she needed to—in her own time. She blinked again, but another tear made tracks down her cheek. I swiped at it with the pad of my thumb, but another quickly took its place.

"He was so tiny. But he was perfect. Lots of blond hair so light it was see-through. Ten fingers and ten toes. Eyes too big for his face. And I just—" When she broke off, the pain ripped through her so hard it made her body tense up into a ball, and I wondered if she was talking about this couple's baby, the one who'd died—or her own baby, the one she'd given away.

Feebly, I tried to dry her tears again, but they were flowing so fast now that she was drenching the pillow beneath her.

"Every little thing makes me think of him," she sobbed. "And then I'm right back where I started, and I can't do anything because I'm racked with guilt and worry, always wondering, never knowing."

She tried to bury her face in the pillow, as if she could hide from me, but that wouldn't work. This was as real as she'd ever been. Even though it made me physically ache to see her like this, I knew it was exactly what she needed. I stroked her cheek, slipping her hair back over her shoulder so it wouldn't get caught in her tears, then slid my hand over her shoulder and down her arm until she met my eyes again.

The moonlight shining through the windows glimmered in her wet eyes, her cheeks, bouncing off the sheen of sweat covering her bare skin. It made her seem almost ethereal.

"My baby had soft blond hair like that. Not anywhere near as much as this one, but it was so fine and light, like if I blew on it too hard, the hair would float away like dandelion fluff."

"How long did you have him?" I asked, resting my hand on her hip.

She was still a bundle of nerves, but she was starting to soften beneath my touch. "Only a few hours. Rick helped me clean him up and then drove us to the hospital. I wrapped him up in two of my towels to keep him warm, because it was freezing outside and I didn't have any baby blankets."

"Towels are good. You took good care of him."

"But these people—this couple that came in, Jason and Karen—they did everything right, and their baby still died."

"Sometimes that happens. Just like sometimes we do everything right, and we still end up getting HIV."

She stared at me for a long time, blinking those big eyes at me like she was looking for the secrets of the universe in my gaze.

I didn't have any answers for her, and we both knew it.

"His name was Tanner," she said, sniffling again. "Their baby. The one who died. They want a tattoo of a baby swaddled up in a blanket or something, with his name on it. And angel wings." She was still struggling to talk, but it seemed like the worst of this round of tears might be slowly coming to an end.

"Tanner's a good name."

She nodded.

"So these tattoos…they're doing it for closure? So they can move on but not forget?"

"Something like that."

"Did you ever name your baby?"

"No."

"Not even just for you?"

Ravyn shook her head, but she kept her eyes on mine.

"It might help. You could paint something—just for you—and put his name on it. Just a thought."

"Wouldn't that be like letting myself off the hook?"

"Wouldn't letting yourself off the hook be the only way to move forward?" I countered.

Her expression was pouty, but she didn't immediately brush me off.

"Did you ever think about keeping him?" I asked, trying a different tack.

"All the time. Right up until the moment I climbed out of Rick's car at the hospital."

"So you must have thought about names. I mean, if you went that long being undecided, you had to have thought about the future."

She nodded solemnly.

"So what names did you think about?"

"The one I kept coming back to was Devon."

"Devon's a good name, too. Devon Penn. I like the sound of that."

"Even if I paint something, though, and give him a name," she started, and I breathed a bit easier. Because it meant she was at least thinking about doing it. Maybe it wouldn't work, but how would she know if she didn't try? "I still won't *know* that he's okay."

I inched closer to her on the bed, tucking my left arm beneath her pillow. "So it sounds like we need to find out whatever we can. So you can have some resolution."

"There's no such thing as closure in a situation like this," she said.

I was afraid she was right about that. But I wanted to do whatever I could to help her find some semblance of closure anyway. Whatever that might be.

Twenty-Six

Drew

I STARTED MY quest with London. There was always the possibility that she wouldn't have any answers for me, or that I wouldn't like the answers she *did* have, but she had a degree in social work, she was constantly surrounded by counselors, and she seemed like a good jumping off point. If nothing else, she could probably point me in the right direction for wherever I needed to go next.

The team had the day off after getting home so late last night, so once Ravyn headed off to work around lunchtime, I texted Dima and asked if I could drop by to see his wife. He agreed without even questioning why I'd want to see London and not him.

He answered the door in nothing but a pair of faded jeans and huge, dark circles under his bloodshot eyes, glowering at me. "You wake baby up, I chop you up and make you into puppy treats for Bear's dog."

I was going to laugh, but the look in his eye warned me not to.

"Got it," I said. "I'll be quiet. Just need to ask London a few questions."

Then he led me into the kitchen, where London was busy putting together a salad for their lunch. Dima stalked off, somehow not making a sound despite his heavy footsteps.

"Hey," she said, glancing up. She looked just as exhausted as her husband.

"Baby keep you two up last night?" I asked, trying to make polite conversation.

"He's not sold on the idea of sleeping at night and being awake during the day," she answered dryly.

I winked. "I thought Dima was the baby whisperer." The seat next to her wheelchair was empty and waiting for me, so I sat.

"Either his technique only works on Harper Fielding or only on baby girls and not baby boys or only on babies with colic or *something*. Maybe it's just that Erik's determined to put Dima through hell because he loved another baby first. I don't know. All I'm sure of is that no one in this house is getting any sleep, and I doubt we will be anytime soon. Want something to drink?" she asked, wheeling to the fridge. She took out a bottle of water for herself and glanced over her shoulder.

"Water would be great."

She tossed a bottle in my direction before wheeling back over. "So what's up with Ravyn?"

"Why do you assume it's something to do with Ravyn?"

"Because you've never once come over to see me, and because she's like a ticking time bomb."

I winced at that description.

"Okay, maybe that's a bit harsh," London said. "I'm trying not to be such a bitch, but it's hard when I'm not getting any sleep. Anyway. Spill. Tell me why you're here so I can feed one of my babies before the other wakes up and demands to be fed." She picked up her knife again and resumed dicing a tomato.

Again, I bit my tongue to avoid laughing. No one but London could call Dima a baby and get away with it.

Those two had an interesting relationship. They antagonized the hell out of each other, but in the end, they made it work. But I wasn't here to worry about their relationship or to analyze what they saw in each other.

I opened the bottle, took a sip, and cut straight to the point. "If someone were to surrender a baby—"

"Surrender a baby?" London cut in, her knife clattering to the table. "Like with the safe-haven laws? Is that what she did?"

But she didn't wait around for me to answer that question, which was good, since I had no plans to respond. This wasn't about me letting the whole world in on Ravyn's secrets. It was just about helping her find the answers she needed for closure.

London pressed her eyes closed for a moment, then picked up her knife again. "Never mind. I shouldn't have asked that. But that's what you mean, right? About the safe-haven laws?"

"Yes, like if someone surrenders a baby to the hospital or to police."

"Got it. Go on."

"So *if* someone were to surrender a baby, is there any way for the parent to find out anything about what's happened? I mean, if the baby's been adopted or who the parents are or…?"

"Or anything," London finished for me, with a sad look on her face.

"Right."

"Okay. Loaded question, but here goes. First off, I'm not an expert, and I don't know everything there is to know about this subject. My community center is not a safe zone under the safe-haven laws, so all I can do, if someone comes and wants to do something like that, is direct them to places that *are* safe zones, like hospitals, fire stations, and the police department." She fell quiet, then, and emptied her diced tomatoes into the salad bowl, then picked up an avocado.

"But…" I prompted.

"*But* I am almost positive that they won't ever tell her—well, the biological parent, or whoever surrendered the baby—anything."

"Never?"

"Never. Once the parent has left the premises, the baby is officially a ward of the state. When the kid is eighteen, they can initiate the process to find their birth parents if they want to. But depending on how much information the birth parents left when they surrendered the child, that may be extremely difficult, if not impossible."

And knowing Ravyn the way I did, I doubted she'd told the nurse anything that could be used to identify her if he did want to find her someday. I'd have to ask to be sure, but she wasn't very forthcoming with *any* information under normal circumstances. And when she was worked up or upset over something? She shut down and closed everyone out.

That didn't bode well for Devon someday being able

to find her, if he even wanted to. If he didn't want to, there wasn't any chance of her ever knowing even the simplest things about him.

At least not if London was right. My gut told me she was.

"So what happens to these babies when they've been surrendered?" I asked.

London cut the avocado in half. She whacked her knife into the pit before giving it a twist and pulling it out of the center. "If the baby needs medical care, that's the first thing they'd do. In Oklahoma, they can only be surrendered when they're three days old or younger, so they're always the newest of newborns. As soon as everyone is satisfied that the baby is healthy, they'd begin the process of finding an adoptive family. With newborns, that rarely takes very long."

"So by the time the baby is six or nine months old, he or she would be adopted?"

"I'd guess it would happen before a month goes by, to be honest. Maybe the red tape wouldn't be completely finalized yet by then, but the child would be in a stable home within days, and would likely remain with that family permanently."

"Okay. Thanks."

In the distance, I heard the baby start fussing.

"Unless you have anything else to ask me," London said, "you should go. I won't let Dima bake you into puppy treats, but he could probably do some significant damage before I managed to stop him."

"Duly noted," I said, getting to my feet. I winked and took my water, then headed for the door. "Tell Dima I'll see him at practice tomorrow."

She nodded and waved me off, so I left and closed the door behind me.

I didn't go home, though. Instead, I headed for Hunter's house. Tallie's father was a partner at a local law firm, and I hoped she could help me find someone there who could give me answers. They might not be better answers than what London gave me, or even *different* answers, but it was worth my while to ask.

Tallie answered when I rang the doorbell, grinning from ear to ear. "Hey, Drew. You actually just missed Hunter. He's spending the afternoon with his new backup goalie. Meeting of the goalie guild or something, he said." She had on a bright-red apron that said *Caution: Extremely Hot* and had a silicone spatula in her hand.

"It's actually you I'm here to see," I said.

"Well, get on in here while the gettin's good, then." She winked and took a step back so I could join her.

Before I got through the door, an adorable curly-haired munchkin came racing my way at full speed. I caught Harper before she could dart past me, lifting her high in the air and spinning her around until she giggled.

"Not so fast, little missy," her mother said, rolling her eyes in my direction. "Good thing Mr. Drew's got good reflexes. She went straight from taking her first steps to *running* everywhere. And she's a heck of a lot faster than me. I can't tell you how many times she's gotten away from me when I'm garage sale shopping with Tori."

Harper ignored her mother and patted my cheek to get my attention. "Go go," she demanded, pointing toward the door. She nodded and blinked big, serious eyes at me. This little girl meant business, and she was determined to make me into her accomplice.

"We're not gonna *go go* anywhere," Tallie said.

"We're gonna *stay stay* and bake cupcakes."

Harper's eyes went comically wide. "Cup cup?"

"Yes, cup cup. You can help me ice them like a big girl if you stop trying to run away." Tallie headed back into the kitchen, and I followed, carrying her daughter. "Seriously," Tallie said, "you'd think we tortured her or something. She wants to be anywhere but where she is and to do anything but what she's doing. Her favorite thing in the world right now is to go go, and she doesn't even care where."

"That's probably normal for a kid her age, isn't it?"

Once we reached the kitchen, I set Harper in her high chair. The tray was covered with Cheerios, and she immediately shoved a handful of them in her mouth, then spit them out. "Cup cup!" she demanded.

"They have to bake bake first," Tallie replied, laughing. "Hold your horses."

"Horsey? Go go!" And just like that, Harper was bouncing in her seat and trying to figure out how to climb out of it.

"Would you mind buckling her in?" Tallie asked me, as she was already back to work on putting cupcake batter in paper-lined muffin tins.

"I'm on it if you can help me out with something."

"As long as you don't need me to function at a much higher level than toddler brain, I'm your girl."

Lucky for me, I'd spent enough time around my nieces that I knew how to strap a kid into a few different types of seats. Within a few seconds, I had the belt secured around Harper's waist and she was shoving Cheerios into my mouth—the same ones she'd just spit out only moments before.

I laughed and moved out of her reach before she got any more bright ideas, taking a seat on one of the barstools across the counter from Tallie. "So I've got a problem," I started.

"A girl problem?" Tallie reached for an ice cream scoop and used it to measure batter into the lined cups.

"Not exactly, but kind of. I have to say, though, you sound strangely excited by that prospect."

Her eyes lit up, and she grinned. "I've been wanting to set you up on a date for a long time. You have no idea. I have this girlfriend from college who'd be *perfect* for you, and I wanted to introduce you over the summer, but Hunter told me I needed to butt out and let you do things in your own time."

My eyes crinkled with laughter. I couldn't help it. "I'm touched," I managed to get out between big belly laughs that got Harper cackling with glee.

"Tori and I started planning it as soon as—well, you know." She had to mean the accident. I nodded, and that was all she needed to keep going. "Anyway, London's told us you seem to have a thing for this tattoo artist. Purple-haired chick? I saw her at your pool party. She's cute."

"Cute's one word for her."

Probably not one Ravyn would appreciate, but she'd be even cuter if she got all indignant over being called cute.

"So I was hoping you were dating her," Tallie said, taking a spoon and scraping it along the side of the virtually empty bowl, then passing it over to her daughter. "And Hunter seems to think you might be. All the guys do, actually."

"What, is it gossip central in our locker room?"

"Isn't it gossip central in every locker room?" Tallie winked. "Even if it's not, the WAGs keep the gossip flowing. We live for this shi— *stuff*."

I shrugged, because I wasn't sure what Ravyn would have to say about whether we were dating or not—we weren't, in the traditional sense, but sleeping together for a month seemed to put our relationship in the *serious* category.

"So you need help with Ravyn?" Tallie asked, turning around to put the cupcake pan into the oven and set the timer. "What kind of help? Romance or…"

"Legal," I said. "It's more your father's help that I need."

Harper took that opportunity to start flinging the remaining Cheerios all across the kitchen, so Tallie took her out of her chair and set her on the floor to run around. Harper didn't run far; she came straight to me, lifted her arms in the air, and demanded, "Up up!"

I picked her up and set her on my knee, getting another tiny fistful of Cheerios shoved into my mouth as a reward for my compliance. "Mmm," I said, winking down at her giggling face.

"Harper, you cut that out right now, you hear?"

The little girl only laughed harder.

"She's fine," I said. "I don't mind." I kind of liked it, actually. Kids were sweet and uncomplicated. Right now, everything else in my life was as complicated as it could be.

"Legal?" Tallie repeated. She took off her apron and hung it from a hook on the wall. "Is she in some kind of trouble?"

"Not exactly. But I need a few questions answered. London already gave me some answers, but she doesn't know everything there is to know about this matter."

"And you need to know more," Tallie said.

"Right."

She scowled and planted her hands on her hips.

"Well, damn."

"Damn?" I repeated, trying not to laugh.

"I'll hook you up with Daddy. That's not a problem. But here I was hoping you were coming to me for romantic advice or something. You got my hopes up, and now you're letting me down. That's rude."

I grinned. "Hit me. What do you have?"

"Yeah? You mean it?" Her eyes lit up mischievously. This couldn't be good.

But still… "Yeah. I'm all yours. Help me out."

"Stay right there." Tallie hustled down the hall and up the stairs.

While she was gone, Harper decided to get my attention again. She patted me on the cheek until I looked down at her. "Go go?" She even cocked her head toward the door, like a dog would.

"I don't think your daddy would be happy with me if I ran away with you. And your mommy would miss you."

She laughed. "Go go!"

"Harper Paisley Fielding, you'd better not be go going anywhere!" Tallie called out on her return.

I shook my head solemnly. "Sounds like that's a no no."

Harper cackled again. At least she took rejection well.

When Tallie came back into the kitchen, she handed me a brown paper bag and took her daughter. "There. Go spoil your girl. You've got candles, bath bombs…all sorts of good stuff. Put on some sexy music. Hell, you could join her in the bath, too. That'd be good. Oh, and I texted Daddy while I was upstairs. He said to give you his direct number at his office. He can probably answer your questions over the phone, depending on the specifics, and most likely he won't charge you because you're a friend. And because I begged. And because I've got him wrapped around my finger. And I might have threatened to keep him from his granddaughter if he didn't do what I wanted."

"You're the best," I said, climbing down from my stool.

"Don't you forget it. And bring her around sometime. The girls all want to meet her."

I laughed on my way to the door. "I'll try. She's not much of a joiner."

"All the more reason to bring her to meet us. We can initiate her."

"Is that code for garage sale shopping?"

"It's code for get her ass around us so we don't have to hunt her down."

"I'll see what I can do." But first, I needed to make a phone call.

Twenty-Seven

Ravyn

IT WAS STARTING to feel normal to go home with Drew every night after I left work. The most surprising aspect about that was the realization that it *still* felt normal after I'd completely fallen apart in front of him last night.

Probably because he didn't treat me any differently. He'd seen me at my lowest, and now he was looking at me the same way he always did, with an odd mix of curiosity, hunger, and a lot more caring than I deserved.

"How was work?" he asked, passing a grilled turkey and Swiss cheese sandwich across the counter toward me.

I hadn't adjusted to his desire to feed me all the time, but there was no getting around the fact that I was ravenous tonight. I'd been working on Whitney's design when I should have taken a dinner break, so I hadn't had a bite to eat since lunch—and it was almost midnight.

I tore off a bite with my fingers, ruminating over how terribly domestic we seemed to be becoming. When had this happened? It wasn't exactly overnight. It'd been more of a gradual shift in our relationship from casual sex to not-so-casual sex, and now to…what? I wasn't sure.

I carried my plate to the dining room and took a seat. Drew joined me, a couple of beers in his hands. He opened mine and set it in front of me before sitting directly across the table.

"Thanks," I said after I'd swallowed my bite. "Work was fine. No dead baby tattoos today."

I felt his smile all the way to my core. It warmed me from the middle out to my fingers and toes, leaving me tingly, like a good alcohol buzz. But I hadn't even taken a sip of my beer.

"Glad you can make a joke about it," he said.

"I have to. If I don't…" There wasn't any point finishing that statement. He'd already seen what would happen when I couldn't laugh things off.

"So, who did come in today?"

"A couple of Tri Delta girls from University of Tulsa came in and got matching tattoos of their sorority symbol. I swear, I've never heard so much giggling in my life."

Drew's grin somehow widened even further. "I had my fair share of giggling today, too."

I raised a brow. "Oh, yeah?" He'd told me this morning that he was going to a teammate's house today. I couldn't picture a bunch of big, burly hockey players sitting around and *giggling.*

"Went to visit a couple of my teammates' wives."

I tried not to recoil at the idea that he'd gone to see their wives and not the guys. But they were married, after all, so I doubted there was anything going on to upset me. That didn't stop me from feeling a twinge of jealousy.

But Drew would never cheat. And we weren't officially an exclusive item, so it wouldn't even be cheating. Still, after what had happened with his ex… No, that wasn't him. I had no reason to be jealous at all.

Maybe I was more invested in *us* than I'd thought I was.

He took another swig from his beer, going on like he was oblivious to my discomfiture. "Hunter and Tallie's little girl is a riot. Tallie says you need to come around, by the way."

"Come around?" Why would I need to *come around*?

"To hang out with the other guys' wives and girlfriends," Drew said, like it was the most natural thing he could ever say, even though I nearly choked on my food due to shock.

Which meant he thought of me as his girlfriend.

And *they* thought of me as his girlfriend.

But was I? And did I want to be?

Yes.

The answer hit me like a battering ram, particularly after my moment of envy. I wouldn't have told Drew all those things last night if I didn't want to be with him.

Hell, I'd never before told anyone the name I'd chosen for my son, not even Rick. I'd never said it aloud, because giving it voice made it feel too real.

But I'd told Drew that my son's name was Devon.

I didn't know what his new family had named him,

but he was Devon in my heart. And now, Drew knew he was Devon, too. And that he'd had the softest blond hair. And that I'd almost changed my mind a half dozen times in the few hours that he'd been *mine.*

Telling Drew these things had to mean I wanted more from this relationship than I'd previously been allowing myself to believe. I swallowed hard and took a sip of my beer, letting the smooth, malty flavor envelop my mouth for a moment.

"Do you want me to hang out with them?" I asked.

He shrugged. "It's up to you. But I don't think it would be a bad thing for you to get to know the guys and their wives, you know? I mean, they're a part of my life, and so are you." Again, he made it seem like there was no other way things should be.

"I'm not good with people," I pointed out.

"I think you're better with them than you give yourself credit for. And I think the more practice you get, the easier it'll be for you."

Practice. How pathetic was it that I needed to *practice* having relationships?

But he had a point, even if it was one I had difficulty conceding.

"I suppose it wouldn't be the worst thing that could ever happen to me," I said dryly.

"I'll tell London. She knows how to get in touch with you, so she can set something up."

"So what were you doing today?" I asked. He'd asked about my day. Time for me to reciprocate, since it seemed like we were doing this domestic, relationship thing. I picked up the sandwich and took another bite.

"Trying to find out what information we could learn about Devon."

My stomach churned, and I wished I hadn't eaten a

bite. I set the rest of the sandwich back on my plate and pushed it away, praying that my stomach would settle down before I upchucked all over his house.

"There's nothing we can learn," I forced out.

"Not much," he agreed. He sounded way too chipper, considering he'd just brought up a subject that he knew would send me into a tizzy.

I pushed away from the table. I needed to leave. My car was still at Ethan's house, because we'd slept too late this morning to go back for it before I had to get to work, so Drew had driven me both ways.

But his house wasn't far. I could walk. I *would* walk, because my lungs were starting to close off on me, and my heart felt like it was going to shatter again, and I couldn't be here.

But Drew put a hand on my elbow before I reached the front door. "Wait," he said gently. Everything about him was gentle. The way he held my arm, with just enough pressure to keep me from leaving but not enough to cause me any discomfort. The way he urged me back against him and pressed a kiss to the top of my head. The way his breaths pressed his chest against my shoulders. "Don't run away," he murmured, and it was enough to break me again, like that kiss had broken me last night.

But that was what I always did. I ran.

I'd been doing it my whole life, and it had never—not once—left me in a better place than I'd been before I took off. Because no matter how fast I ran or how far I went, *I* was still with me. I couldn't get away from myself.

I forced myself to stay put, the words of one of the doctors from the loony bin echoing in my mind. *You think you're crazy, huh? Well, you know what they say the definition of crazy is, right? Doing the same thing and expecting different results.* I'd been running my whole life and blindly hoping that somehow, some way, things would turn out differently.

And of course, they never did.

Now that I wasn't actively trying to get out, Drew's grip changed. His fingertips danced along my shoulders and upper arms, a light touch that soothed me more than I ever would have expected.

"You're not going to leave?" he asked after a moment.

I shook my head, not trusting my voice.

His arm came around my waist, an anchor in the storm being waged in my mind. "So can I tell you what I found out today?"

"I'm not sure I want to know," I croaked.

Because if there *was* anything I could learn, any tiny nugget about Devon, what purpose would it serve? I'd still walked away from him. I'd given him up.

I wasn't sure which would hurt worse—never knowing anything or knowing only a tiny bit but being unable to learn the rest.

"I think I should tell you anyway," Drew said softly. The warmth of his body wrapped around me, somehow seeped into me. Melting me against him. Turning me into putty, to be molded by his hands.

My eyes stung with tears, so I blinked a few times, trying to keep them at bay. But I took a deep breath, leaned into Drew's offer of comfort, and nodded. If he knew something, I needed to know it. Then I'd have to find a way to deal with this new knowledge, whatever it might be.

"You're mostly right," he said. "You can try to find out information about Devon, but no one will tell you anything. They can't. Legally, you gave up all rights to any knowledge about him the moment you walked away from that nurse. But someday, when he's an adult, he can try to find you if he decides he wants to."

"There's no way for him to find me, though," I spluttered through the tears that had forced their way through.

"There could be. You know what hospital you took him to. You remember what the nurse looked like, right?"

Drew didn't wait for me to argue with him or to confirm what he already knew—that I did remember her face, as clearly as I remembered the crinkle of Devon's nose when he cried and the way his tiny fingers had gripped my pinky and refused to let go when I passed him into her arms. I didn't just remember her face—I knew her name: *Tricia Patterson, R.N.* My breath caught in my throat and formed a lump.

Drew ran his hands up and down my arms, soothing me and bolstering me in the same motion.

"You could find her and give her any information she asks for. Maybe you didn't give it to her then, but you can do it now. Your name. How to find you. Your medical history. She can't tell you anything about Devon, but she can be sure the right people know what they need to know about *you*. And she'll remember you, so she'll be able to line you up with the right baby. I know she will. You're pretty unforgettable."

So even if they didn't already know that I might have passed HIV on to him, they could know now. And they could test him now. And if the tests were inconclusive, they could test him again and again and again, and they could treat him properly, whether he was HIV-positive or not.

Drew was right. I didn't know why I'd never thought of it before. I'd run into the brick wall of their refusals to give me any information about my son and taken that as the end of the story.

But maybe it didn't have to be.

I spun around in his arms, looking up to find his serious eyes pinned on me. His brows drew together with concern.

I couldn't blame him. He had to be thinking I might fall apart again at any moment like I had last night. I wasn't proving to be the most stable person in the world, which made me wonder more than ever why he'd want to be with me.

But this, more than anything else, proved he did. He'd spent his day finding a way for me to get closure.

"Have I ever told you how amazing you are?" I asked through my tears.

He kissed me on the forehead, tightening his arms around my waist. "Come on. Finish eating, because I have more plans for you tonight."

"Plans? Like going to the hospital?" Because now that the idea was in my mind, it was the only thing I could think of. The only thing I wanted to do. The sooner I could get there and find this nurse, the sooner I'd be able to breathe again.

"We can do that tomorrow," Drew promised. "It's kind of late for that tonight. This is something else." He broke away from me and took my hand, then led me back over to the table. "Sit. Eat. I'll be back in a few minutes." Then he took off down the hall toward his bedroom.

I *was* still starving, and now my stomach was full of excitement instead of dread and guilt, so I picked up the rest of my sandwich and finished it off.

A few minutes later, Drew came back to join me. He'd taken off his clothes other than his boxer-briefs, showing off his chest, abs, and those amazingly strong arms. There wasn't any point in pretending I didn't enjoy the view.

He dropped his head down and kissed me on the cheek before reaching across the table for what remained of his beer. "Ready?" he asked.

"For what?"

"You'll see. Bring your beer." Then he laced his fingers through mine and led me back to his bedroom. Or more accurately, to his bathroom.

The lights were out, and he had lit candles spread throughout the bathroom. The soft light bounced off the mirrors and reflected off the water in his massive garden tub. The tub I'd been eyeing every time I was here but hadn't dared to get into because it seemed like such an indulgence, and I'd never been one to indulge.

Drew dipped his head from behind me again, kissing a trail along the tendons in my neck. I shivered.

"What's this about?" I asked. My voice came out all breathy and sexy, even though it was confusion and nerves causing it to seize up more so than me trying to pull off the part of the seductress.

"Tallie mentioned it might be a good idea for me to spoil you," Drew said between kisses. "I thought she had a point. Because I doubt you've ever been spoiled."

That would be a safe bet to take.

He reached around in front of me and started undoing the buttons of my shirt, and the whirlwind of emotions coursing through me over the last hour took yet another sharp turn—this time heading straight toward lust.

Or maybe even love. *Do not pass go. Do not collect two hundred dollars.*

Drew crushed his mouth to mine, and I welcomed his tongue inside as we worked together to get rid of all our clothes. He carefully tied my dreads up on top of my head so they wouldn't get wet and helped me into the tub. It was steaming hot and deep enough I could soak every inch of my body.

I reached for him to drag him in with me, but he winked and shook his head.

"Not just yet," he said.

Then he took out his phone and turned on some music. "Wicked Games" by Chris Isaak bounced off the walls surrounding us as Drew reached into a small brown paper bag and took out what looked like an orange tennis ball. He tossed it into the water, and it started to fizz and give off the most delightful, sexy scents.

"Now I'm ready," he said.

I leaned forward as he climbed in behind me, not that he needed the space. The tub was more than big enough for the both of us.

Once he settled into place, he drew me back against him, nestling my hips between his powerful thighs and resting my head against his chest. I tipped my head back for another kiss. It was deep and slow and languorous.

It was perfect.

And this time, I didn't feel the need to run and hide. Because Drew had already shown me that even when I fell apart, he was ready to catch as many pieces as he could and hold on to them with his big hands until I was able to glue myself back together again.

Twenty-Eight

Drew

THE DAY BEFORE our season opener, Gary Asher dropped a bomb on the team. He pulled off a last-minute trade: my regular line mate, Gustav Gunnarsson, had been sent to the Islanders in exchange for an American hotshot right wing named Hayes Lennon.

All the hockey insiders said it was an absolute coup for the T-Birds. The Isles had to make a move in order to get under the salary cap, so they ended up getting the short end of the stick in this trade, apparently. The truth was that Lennon was a true top-line winger, unlike Goose, who'd been filling the role reasonably well for the last couple of seasons, considering he would be a much better fit on the Islanders' third line.

The other truth about Lennon was that he was an egotistical asswipe who had never been much of a team player on any team he'd been part of. Stories of locker room brawls with teammates and other similar incidents had made their way throughout the league.

Gary made it clear that Zee and I—as Lennon's new line mates, in addition to being the two primary leaders of the team—were responsible for keeping the son of a bitch in line and making sure his antics didn't screw up what we'd been building.

Quite a tall order, if you asked me, and that was even before meeting him.

He and his girlfriend flew in that afternoon, the same as my parents did. Gary and Spurs both went to the airport to meet Lennon and help get him settled in a hotel until such time as he could sort out his housing situation.

Ravyn and I were at the airport at the same time to welcome my folks in.

We'd gone to the hospital and found the nurse, like Tallie's father had recommended. Mr. Roth had even come with us so he could help all of us, including the nurse, feel comfortable that everything said and done was completely above board and legal.

Ever since then, though, Ravyn had been improving dramatically with her depression. She was opening up to me more. We'd actually gone on a few real dates, instead of just hanging out at my house and jumping into bed together every chance we got.

And now, she was starting to see all the ways she could fit into my life.

I'd tried to let her take it at her own pace, but today things were escalating because of my parents' arrival. I couldn't exactly put them off, and I'd told them about her, so they expected to meet her.

She was nervous as hell at the moment, and I

couldn't say I blamed her. I mean, *I* knew my parents were awesome, but she didn't have the first clue about that other than what I'd told her—she'd never experienced anything firsthand with them to prove my claims.

Given her history with her own parents, it couldn't be easy to believe that some families were actually like what you saw in sitcoms. Mine sure had been. Plus, she'd never really done the whole meet-the-parents thing before, or at least not in a very long time, and the only positive parental figures in her life were Rick and his wife.

Her anxiety was only compounded by having my coach and general manager trying to make small talk with her while we all stood at baggage claim.

"Have you met Dana Zellinger yet?" Gary asked her, his hands tucked into the pockets of his slacks as he rocked back and forth on his feet.

She sent me a slightly panicked look.

I squeezed her hand and turned to the GM. "A couple of times. Ravyn's starting to come to a couple of games, getting to know the other WAGs."

"Dana's a good one to get to know," he said, either oblivious to the fact that I'd been the one to answer when he'd questioned Ravyn or simply trying to ignore her discomfort in order to put her at ease. "She's going to be putting together an auction for our Hockey Fights Cancer night. I'm sure she could use your help with that. All the players' wives and girlfriends get involved."

Spurs winked. "Not just the players' wives. They always drag the coaches' wives into things, too, and probably half the front office."

"It's a real team effort, on and off the ice," Gary agreed.

"I'll be sure to find out what I can do," Ravyn said quietly, but she seemed like she was trying to crawl into my side and disappear, so I knew she was getting to be overwhelmed.

We'd started small, in terms of bringing her around the team.

She already knew London because of the support group, and she'd briefly met a few others that day at my pool. But now she was starting to get together with some of the rest of them. She'd had a day of garage sale shopping with Tallie and Tori while Hunter did a daddy-daughter day with Harper.

The next time Carter flew down to spend the weekend with his father, we'd invited the two of them and Snoopy over to hang out at the pool—not the whole team, this time, but just a few of us—even though it was getting to be too cold for any of us but the puppy to get in the water.

As far as I was concerned, it wasn't just about Ravyn getting to know the people in my life, either. One night, we'd invited Rick and Shannon over for dinner, and another time, Dagger had come with Ravyn to one of our exhibition games. It happened to be one that the Jernigans attended. The look on Mrs. J's face when I'd walked out of the arena with my arm around Ravyn's waist and a guy with a spiky Mohawk ambling alongside us was one I wouldn't soon forget. I wished I'd had a camera at the ready, because that was one expression I doubted I'd ever be able to replicate.

A big crowd started to head our way, which meant one of the two flights had landed. I caught sight of Lennon in the crowd. Couldn't miss the guy, actually. He was six foot four and solid muscle, so he stood a head above just about everyone around him. The guy had a shock of overly long blond hair, and he was screaming bloody murder at the petite blonde rushing to keep up with him.

I couldn't make out what the guy was saying, but it didn't matter. She was in tears, and the fact that he was berating her in such a public way made him a Grade A douche canoe in my book.

I didn't like him before I met him, but there wasn't a chance in hell I'd change my mind about him now.

"If you'll excuse us," Gary said to me and Ravyn, concern drawing his brows together.

Yeah, he should be concerned if this was the kind of player he thought he should bring in to take the T-Birds to the next level. But then he and Spurs rushed over to defuse the situation before the team ended up in the news again for all the wrong reasons.

The good thing was this meant Ravyn didn't need to try to impress those two anymore. Now she could restrict her worrying to the thought of meeting my parents.

"He's your new teammate?" she asked.

"Apparently so."

And at the moment, Gary and Spurs were essentially standing between Lennon and his girlfriend, like they were protecting her. Good Lord, what a clusterfuck this trade was going to be.

I had half a mind to go over and help out, but it seemed like they were getting things under control. And besides, Ravyn didn't need to be in the middle of all that, especially with the way her anxiety was practically seeping out of her pores.

"I should have cut off my hair and died it a nice, tame brown," she said.

"Why the hell would you do something like that?" I

demanded.

"Because then I wouldn't look like quite as much of a freak. I'd still have the tattoos and piercings, but…"

"But nothing. I like you exactly the way you are. And my parents will, too. Besides, I've already shown them pictures. It's not like they don't know."

"Seeing pictures of someone with purple dreads isn't the same as seeing them in person."

"Stop worrying," I said. I tugged her into my arms and hugged her to calm her down. That was something I'd been doing more and more lately. Whenever she got too worked up about anything, I'd hold her hand or hug her, something to be in physical contact with her. So far, it didn't seem like she'd caught on to my reasons for doing it, and it appeared to be working. Plus, it meant I got to touch her more often, which was always a boon in my book.

"You do realize that I don't know how to not worry, right?" she said, laughing. The laughter was a good sign. A very good sign. It didn't mean her worry was gone, but maybe I'd managed to alleviate it somewhat.

But she wouldn't have to worry much longer, because my parents were making their way toward us with huge smiles on their faces.

"Come on," I said to Ravyn, squeezing her hand and heading over to meet my folks halfway. "They're here."

She stumbled along beside me, muttering, "Oh shit."

"It'll be fine," I promised just before my father dropped his carry-on bag on the ground and wrapped me up in a massive bear hug.

Mom essentially did the same to Ravyn. I probably should have warned her that we were a touchy-feely sort of family, but it was too late now. She was going to have to sink or swim. Good thing I'd seen her swim through any number of other situations that would have sunk a lot of people.

"Look at you!" Mom said, patting Ravyn on the cheek. "Even prettier in person. I never would have guessed your hair would be so soft!" She probably had no clue that what she was saying could be seen as offensive, but it didn't look like Ravyn was taking it badly. She was in too much shock, to be honest.

And then Dad took over where Mom had left off, lifting Ravyn off her feet, while Mom took her turn with me. They told us about their flight, and we caught them up on the ongoing draught in Oklahoma—it had been close to a year since we'd had any decent rainfall—while we waited to collect their checked bags from the conveyors.

On our way out to the parking lot, we had to go directly past Gary, Spurs, Lennon, and his girlfriend. The situation there was still as much of a mess as before, even if the son of a bitch was no longer screaming loudly enough for everyone as far away as Dallas to hear him.

"So that's your new teammate, huh?" Dad said once we were outside. "The one who's supposed to be so great for your team?"

"Not just my new teammate. My new line mate, too, if everything goes down the way Gary said it would." I guided them toward the SUV I'd rented for the duration of their visit since my car was just a two-seater, wheeling both of the larger checked bags behind me.

"He's a real treat," Dad said.

We reached the SUV, and Dad and I loaded all of the bags into the back while Mom and Ravyn climbed in. Apparently, Mom took the opportunity of having Ravyn all to herself to start up a conversation. In my rearview mirror, I caught the panicked look in Ravyn's eyes when Mom said, "So Drew's told us all about you."

Because, of course, that was a loaded statement. And while my mother might assume I'd told them everything there was to know about Ravyn, that couldn't be further from the truth. Her secrets were her own for as long as she wanted them to be.

"Not exactly *all* about her, Mom," I said, putting on my seat belt while Dad did the same and laughed.

"Well, no, not everything," Mom conceded. "But more than enough to be going on with."

"What Marcie means to say," Dad put in, turning his head toward the two women in the back, with a full eye roll evident in his tone, "is he's told us you're an artist."

I tried to catch her eye in the mirror, hoping to convey through my gaze that she didn't have anything to worry about. If she didn't want them to know she was HIV-positive, they didn't have to know. If she wasn't ready to tell anyone else about Devon, I wasn't going to be the one to break that trust. It was entirely up to her how much to tell my parents, my friends, her friends…

She visibly swallowed, and I winked. I barely caught her slight nod before she turned a smile toward my father. "Did he mention I'm a *tattoo* artist?"

"Not *just* a tattoo artist," I added, winking at her in the rearview mirror. "Ravyn also does watercolors. She's got a spot in a local gallery where her paintings are displayed and sold."

"Actually," Mom said, "I seem to recall Drew telling us he got a tattoo himself."

"Hey, now!" I complained. "This wasn't supposed to be about all the things I've done wrong."

"Your mother didn't say you'd done anything wrong by getting a tattoo," Dad said.

"But honestly, Drew," Mom said, fully in Mom-voice, "didn't you think it was a bad idea because of the HIV?"

"Actually, it's completely safe, as long as the tattooist is using proper hygiene techniques," Ravyn put in.

"Is that so?" Dad asked. He winked over at me. "Whaddya know? Learn something new every day."

And just like that, Mom stopped giving me a hard time over getting inked. To be honest, I got the impression that she'd just gone off on that tack to help Ravyn feel more comfortable, to bring her into the conversation more. And it had worked brilliantly. Just one more reason I adored my parents.

The more time I spent with Ravyn, and the better I came to understand how bad things could be with parents who weren't as loving and devoted as mine, the more thankful I was for them.

Mom angled herself in the backseat so she could look fully at Ravyn. "Did you do it for him, then?" Not that she needed to ask that. She already knew the answer, because I'd told her back when I first got it done.

"I did." Ravyn sounded a hell of a lot more relaxed now that they were talking about things she was comfortable with. "In fact, that was how he convinced me to spend time with him. He came in as a paying client, so I kind of *had* to be around him for a while, whether I wanted to be or not."

Both my parents burst out laughing, and Ravyn smiled—a big one that went from ear to ear.

"And we all know what a chore that can be," Dad said when his laughter subsided.

See, they love you. Just like I do. Those words were on the tip of my tongue. But now wasn't the time. The first time I told her I loved her shouldn't be such a high-pressure situation for her, with my parents sitting there to see her reaction.

I didn't have a clue what her reaction would be. All I knew was I needed her in my life, and while she'd made a ton of progress, I couldn't be sure how she'd take my declaration.

But at least now she could see for herself that she'd be a welcome part of my family.

I really had hit the parenting jackpot.

And the girlfriend jackpot, too. But now I needed to make Ravyn see it.

Twenty-Nine

Ravyn

DREW'S PARENTS STAYED in Tulsa for most of a week, only flying back to Victoria a day before the Thunderbirds were due to leave for another road trip. This one was going to be a long one, too. Eight days. I couldn't deny I was nervous about how I'd handle being on my own again for so long, because Drew had become my rock.

In the time that Mr. and Mrs. Nash were here, they'd started to join him in that. Maybe they were pebble-sized rocks and not big boulders like he was, but they were still starting to become comfortable fixtures in my life. His mother even made sure I had their phone numbers and email addresses before they left, and she told me to call them anytime.

And while they were here, Drew got his sister and brother-in-law, Melody and Shawn, on Skype. We had a big family talk with them and the girls.

Yes, *we*. They'd included me, despite my protests.

But now, Lucy was demanding tattoos, and Charley wanted dreads. Her parents agreed to braids, and I sent them some of those wash-off fake tattoos, with a promise that I'd get some special ones made up just for her. Ones that I would design. For now, that seemed to satisfy everyone.

I was still in awe that I was included as part of the family, and none of them had acted like I didn't belong.

The girls, in particular, wanted to talk to me more than anyone else. I was sure it was because I looked funny. Drew insisted it was because I was an artist, and his nieces loved to color.

By the time we ended the Skype call, both girls had proclaimed they wanted to be Ravyn for Halloween this year, and Melody and Shawn were thanking me for getting them off the hook for buying or creating two more Elsa costumes, like they'd had to do last year.

My counselor and I had a plan in place for Drew's road trips. It included daily phone calls with Drew, spending time with London and some of the other WAGs on the days I didn't work, and snuggle-and-play time with Snoopy whenever I needed a dose of companionship but didn't feel up to being around kids.

Ethan—I just couldn't keep calling him Huggy Bear, even though that was what his teammates called him—had agreed that I could let myself in as often as I wanted while the team was gone. The dog sitter was only coming twice a day, so he wanted me to burn off some of the puppy's energy and take him outside a time or two. Actually, he'd begged me to stop by every night when I got off work. Puppy potty training wasn't going very well.

All in all, it seemed like a reasonable plan. One I could work with. It might not be perfect, but when had life ever been perfect?

But for now, Drew and I were alone at his house. It was both the first time it'd been just the two of us in almost a week and the last time we'd see each other for more than a week, and neither of us could keep our hands to ourselves.

We'd barely returned from taking his parents to the airport five minutes ago, and we were already getting naked and sweaty. Drew latched his mouth on to one of my breasts and suckled, and there might as well have been a line that ran from there straight to my clit.

I moaned and squirmed beneath him, reaching for his hard-as-steel dick. "I need you inside me." Who knew that going almost a week with no sex could turn you into a demanding, sex-crazed fiend?

But even though he let me stroke him, he didn't hurry up and do what I begged him for. In fact, he looked up and met my eyes, his full of a mischievous gleam, and grinned. "I'll get there. But first, I want to make you come a time or two with my tongue. I want to drive you crazy tonight."

"Too late to get on the crazy train," I said, even as he reached between my legs and slipped two fingers inside me. "I'm already there. Loony bin, remember? No need to drive me there when it's where I live."

He growled in answer, giving me a fierce look even though he didn't stop what he was doing. In fact, if anything, he only made me crazier with need, pressing the pad of his thumb against my piercing down below and rubbing tiny circles there. He didn't argue with words. How could he? His mouth was otherwise occupied with licking a feverish path down my abs, but his expression argued plenty. Drew didn't like me calling myself crazy. We'd been over this a few times, and he refused to budge.

"Sorry. No more crazy talk," I promised.

But then I couldn't say anything else at all. He went around my belly button with his tongue a few times, fucking me with his fingers until my hips bucked and my breath hitched. Who knew the belly button was an erogenous zone? Not me, until now.

His hot mouth inched lower, but he didn't go straight for my pussy. He licked a line down the inside of my thigh to my knee and back a few times. By the time his tongue landed where I wanted it, I was already a whimpering pile of goo. It only took a couple of well-placed licks and a good pull of suction, and I was coming all over his face, my body quivering and going boneless.

He left a hand in place as he inched his way up my body again until he could kiss me, long and slow and deep. I tasted myself on his tongue.

Drew, however, was anything but *boneless.* I wanted to give him the same kind of pleasure he'd just given me. Turnabout was only fair and all that jazz, right? As soon as I could remember how to use my muscles, I reached for him.

"Nuh-uh," he murmured against my lips, his thumb drawing lazy patterns over my clit and brushing insistently against my piercing.

"Drew." The word came out as a whine. For good reason. I wanted him inside me. I needed that deep connection.

For me, it wasn't just about the orgasm. Sex was

great, but sex with Drew was one of the most intense things I'd ever experienced. Because he mattered. And he made me feel like I mattered, too.

I tried again, and this time I was able to wrap my fingers around his length. His heat pulsed against my palm. I wanted to feel him pulsing inside my body.

He climbed over me and settled himself between my thighs, and I thought he was finally giving in. But he dragged his hands up the sides of my ribs, not stopping until he'd lifted my arms over my head. He pinned me like that, pressing my hands to the headboard with one of his strong fists holding both of my wrists, his hips pressing mine to the mattress.

I ground myself against him in an effort to get on with things, but he laughed and shook his head.

"Not yet, baby. Soon."

"Now."

"Not until I tell you something first."

There wasn't a damned thing he could tell me that would come close to taming the heat he'd built in my body. I sulked and rocked my hips against him again, earning a pained groan when I made contact with his cock.

He slowly shook his head. "You're killing me."

"You started it."

But still, he didn't get on with things.

I let out a groan of frustration. "What on earth do you need to tell me that can't wait?"

He stayed just as he was, cupping my cheek with his free hand, for so long I thought he must have forgotten what he'd wanted to say.

But his eyes. God, his eyes! He was staring at me with such intensity and reverence. I might melt from the heat of his gaze.

His lips met mine. Soft. The kiss was barely there and gone too soon, like a flutter of butterfly wings. It was a kiss meant to break down all my defenses, leaving me open and vulnerable and raw.

It worked.

"I just need you to know something," he whispered, his lips hovering only a hairsbreadth above mine. The warmth of his words landed in the cracks in my armor, filling them up.

"What?" My question came out like a puff of air and got trapped in the tears stinging my eyes.

Drew kissed one of my eyelids, then the other. That was enough to make the waterworks flow. Good grief, why was I crying? Other than being a freaking bundle of nerves lately, always on the verge of tears. But there was no good reason for my emotions to overwhelm me right now.

He kissed my wet cheeks. Then my lips again. The salty taste tickled my tongue.

"Do you have any idea how beautiful you are to me?" he asked.

"I swear to God, if that's what you stopped in order to tell me—"

"I need you to know that I love you," he cut in, silencing me before I could argue with him by planting another kiss on me. This one was harder. Needier. Over way too soon.

My lips felt delightfully swollen when he broke away, and I blinked at him a few times, trying to gather my wits.

"I love you," Drew repeated. "I've been in love with you for a while, but you've been dealing with so much, and I didn't want to overwhelm you, so I've been waiting to tell you. But I don't want to wait any longer.

I need you to know, because we never know what's going to happen. And because it's killing me not to tell you every time I see you. And because I don't want to leave tomorrow without you knowing how it's going to rip my heart out to walk away from you, even though I know I'll be back in a week and you'll be just fine while I'm gone. So I love you. And I get that love isn't a very comfortable thing for you to tal—"

"I love you, too," I cut in before he could make any more excuses for me.

I blinked away my tears, in shock that the words had fallen so readily from my lips. I couldn't remember the last time I'd told someone I loved them. That wasn't ever anything Jax and I had said to each other. I *did* love Rick and Shannon, and I knew they loved me, but it wasn't something any of us ever spoke aloud. The only person I'd said those words to in more than a decade was Devon, and I'd said it right before handing him over to a woman and then walking out of his life.

But I wasn't going to walk away from Drew. And I didn't have a fear that he would walk away from me, either. If that wasn't proof that I was starting to find an internal sort of peace, I didn't know what would do it.

Drew's face took on a cocky, sexy smile. He bit his lower lip, which gave me ideas about doing the same. "You do?" he asked, his voice going deep and husky. "You're sure about that? Because you don't have to say it just—"

"Shut up and kiss me," I said, rolling my eyes.

"Impatient." He flicked the end of my nose with a finger, following it up with a kiss. *On the nose.* Not what I'd meant at all.

"That's not the kind of kiss I want," I groused.

"Hmm." He brushed his lips over mine in the most

excruciating tease. "You know what I love most about having you like this?"

I wriggled beneath him, which caused my piercings to drag against his skin—a move that I knew from experience would drive us *both* wild. "My piercings," I joked.

He nipped my lower lip, much like I wanted to do to his, and grinned. "I *do* love your piercings, but that wasn't what I meant. I love that you ask for what you want. Hell, you *demand* it. You always have, since the first day we met. You remember that?"

There wasn't a chance in hell I could have forgotten that. I still didn't know what had gotten into me that day, when I'd all but insisted he take me home and fuck me. "I'd love it even more if you'd *give* me what I want right now," I said, pouting. "You gave it to me, then." And it'd turned into so much more than I ever would have imagined.

"As you wish," he said, claiming my lips in another scorching kiss.

He'd just gone *Princess Bride* on me again. And I knew he meant it, too. Because Drew loved me, and he'd never been one to do anything halfway.

He took his time about it, but I didn't mind. Because for the first time in a long time, I had something to look forward to. Not behind.

I used to be scared of the future, of the unknown, of whatever life had in store for me. Because in my experience, it could never be good. I'd gone from one awful, horrible thing to the next, which was bound to be even worse somehow. But now, I didn't see things that way. Being with Drew, I wanted to see what the future held.

Thirty

Ravyn

HALLOWEEN WAS CREEPING up on us, which meant Thanksgiving and Christmas weren't far off, either. Christmas would come with its own set of challenges for me this year, but I was becoming more confident that I could handle them. Especially with Drew by my side. And while Halloween wasn't one of the holidays that most couples think of when they talk about their various firsts, it was going to be the first holiday Drew and I spent together.

He had big plans for us involving a costume party with a bunch of his teammates, complete with us wearing a couple's costume.

Our debates over what, specifically, we should dress as had been numerous and heated, but in the end we'd landed on dressing as Bob-Marley-esque Rastafari.

He'd found some crazy dreadlock wig for himself, and we were going to spray paint my hair black to match—after testing a single dread first, to be sure it would wash out. Add in some brightly colored tie-dyed rags, and we should be good to go.

At least there weren't going to be any kids at this particular party. I'd been spending more and more time with the other guys' wives and girlfriends, which meant spending time with their kids. And while I could honestly say I hadn't experienced a panic attack while holding one of their babies, there had been a few times I'd needed to spend several hours alone with my watercolors afterward in order to recover.

But this Halloween party wouldn't take place for a few more days, and I had other things on my mind at the moment.

Such as the fact that Drew was coming back from his road trip today, and I'd get to see him tonight after his game. It'd been way, way too long. But I'd managed to get by on my own just fine. Better than fine, actually. I'd only gone to Ethan's house for a puppy fix because I wanted to play with the puppy, not because I was falling apart.

But seeing Drew wasn't the only thing on my mind. There were also the matching watercolor baby-footprint-with-wings tattoos I was finishing up for my grieving clients. We'd decided to go with the sorts of soft, baby colors you'd find in the yarn aisle at a craft store, blues, yellows, and greens, primarily, with a hint of lavender thrown in for contrast.

His was already done. He'd gotten it on his chest, directly over his heart—much like my adoption symbol tattoo. I'd worked *Tanner* into the lines of the wings.

You could read it if you knew it was there, but it wouldn't be obvious to the naked eye.

I was in the midst of inking the final bits onto his wife's tattoo, but I was having a hard time not crying all over her while I did it. She'd chosen to get the design on her belly, directly over the place where Tanner had spent nine months growing inside her.

"It's where my battle wounds are," she'd said, indicating her stretch marks and the scar from her caesarian. "This is the only place it should be."

I certainly couldn't fault her logic.

The whole time I'd been working, the three of us had shared stories from our pregnancies, from their three weeks with Tanner, and from my three hours with Devon. Rick stopped in every now and then. Sometimes he cried with us. Other times, he just stood back and watched.

I'd been afraid, heading into today. Afraid I wouldn't be able to ink the design on their skin without falling apart. Afraid I'd chicken out entirely.

But in the end, there wasn't anything to be afraid of here. Inking these matching tattoos had turned out to be the most cathartic experience I could have ever hoped for.

I took a moment to dry my eyes and blow my nose, changing into a fresh pair of gloves before going back in for a final pass over the last section. I knew there wasn't any chance I could spread HIV through tears or snot, but I couldn't be too careful. These two had open wounds on their skin—wounds I'd just inflicted—so being overzealous was my only reasonable option.

I set my machine down and sat back to give the fresh ink a final once-over. Then I looked up into her eyes and smiled. "I think we have it. Want to see in the mirror?"

She gave me a watery smile and got out of the chair. But when I led her over to the floor-length mirror, she dragged me into her arms for a bone-shattering hug, sobbing on my shoulder. "Thank you."

She still hadn't released me when her husband wrapped us both up in his arms as well. In no time, we were having a massive cry fest in my work space.

And it felt good.

Eventually, we broke apart. I bandaged them up and went over their aftercare instructions before sending them up to Dagger so they could pay.

Once they were on their way, I tried to dry myself off and get my head back in the game. Because I wasn't done for the day. Whitney was due to arrive any time now so I could show her the final designs I'd come up with and we could get her officially on the schedule.

Rick popped his head into my room and leaned a shoulder against the doorframe. "Best fucking tattoos I've ever seen you do," he said, his voice rough with emotion.

"Because it meant something," I said, shrugging off his praise.

"That's exactly why it's so good. You're a hell of an artist, Ravyn, but when you have a vested interest in the art you're creating…" He shook his head. "There's nothing like it. You put the rest of us to shame. That's when it goes from being a *job* to being a *calling*."

"Yeah, but I still have to pay the bills, so…"

"If you keep putting out work like that, before much longer, you'll be able to pick and choose your clients. You can choose to only work on the ones with stories you can connect to or who want designs you're desperate to work on. Like your cancer chick."

That was the dream, of course. Everyone wanted to be in a career that they *loved.* Every artist wanted to create only the art they were desperate to create, but they had to balance that with the commercial aspects. Sometimes, doing what we loved wasn't what sold, so we had to do what sold, too. Or *instead.* I shrugged, determined not to get my hopes up even though that was exactly what Rick was trying to do.

"I'm proud of you, Ravyn," he said gruffly. "I know it hasn't been easy, but you're doing it."

"Doing what?" I asked, cleaning up my space so I'd be ready for Whitney when she arrived.

"You're climbing out of the hole you've been living in." And with that, he walked out of my space, leaving me to ponder his words.

Had I been living in a hole? Yeah, probably. A dark one. A lonely one. And for so many years, I hadn't even been able to see the sun. There'd only been the darkness.

But now… Now it was like the clouds were starting to part overhead. There were still thunderclouds on the horizon, and I knew it wouldn't be perfectly sunny all the time. But at least I could see the light, and I knew there was more on the way.

I buried my head and got back to cleaning up. The chair needed to be thoroughly wiped down and disinfected, and I needed to tidy up all my ink. Before I knew it, there was a knock on my open door.

I whirled around, expecting to see Whitney. Instead, Drew's big, sexy frame filled the doorway. I grinned, dropping everything so I could head over and feel his strong arms around me.

"Hey! What are you doing here? I thought you'd be heading home for your pregame nap around now."

He obliged me, of course, picking me up off my feet for a kiss that left me wishing we could sneak out right now, or maybe hurry to the bathroom for a quickie. But Whitney would be here any minute, so sex was out of the question.

Damn it.

"Seeing you was a hell of a lot more important than getting a nap. It's all about relaxing, anyway, and nothing would help me relax if I couldn't lay my eyes on you right now."

"You just missed my baby tattoo couple," I said. I took out my phone and scrolled through the pictures so I could show him.

"And you're okay?" he asked slowly.

I shrugged. "I cried. A *lot.* They cried, too. Everyone cried. But they got their tattoos, and a few tears never hurt anyone."

He planted another kiss on my forehead, but Whitney came up and knocked on the window before we could do anything else. Good thing I hadn't seduced him into a quickie.

"You ready for me?" she asked.

Drew backed away, letting Whitney come into the room. "You're still coming to my game tonight, right?" he asked.

"As long as Rick is serious about letting me have the night off."

"He's serious!" Rick called from somewhere in the general vicinity of the lobby. "And he might let you have more nights off for his games if they start to win, too. Because you could be their good luck charm or something."

Drew winked. "I'll have to see what I can do about that." But then he closed the door to my room so

Whitney and I could have some privacy.

"He's hot," she said appreciatively.

"He is." I might have been blushing. Because Drew wasn't just hot; he was *mine*. "Now, you ready to see what I've come up with?"

"I've been ready for a long time."

I took out my sketches and laid them on the table for her, but then I looked up and laughed. Because Drew was standing on the other side of the window holding up a sketch that Dagger must have drawn.

He deserves to get laid, it read, surrounded by hearts and flowers and dragonflies.

Drew waggled his brows comically, pointing at the sign.

I nodded. "Later."

That caught Whitney's attention, so she turned to look and burst out laughing, too.

"Promise?" he asked, his voice muffled by the closed door between us.

"If you score, then you'll *score*."

"Ultimatums now, huh?"

"Yep," I replied. Not that I had any intention of holding out on him. Because like he'd said to me before he left—we didn't know what would happen. I fully intended to take whatever life threw at me and hold on to it with everything I had.

And right now, life had thrown me Drew.

I wouldn't be throwing him back.

Epilogue

Drew

I WAS TOWELING off after a grueling practice when Zee came up to me with a goofy grin on his face. Spurs had just put us through a hell of a bag skate. In last night's game, the whole team had shit the bed, so we definitely deserved it—but I couldn't for the life of me figure out why Zee would be grinning like that.

"Just got the results of the latest blood work," he said. "Still negative, just like I told you I would be." They'd been testing him regularly ever since the final game of last season, and every time his test came back negative, I was the first person he told—even before Dana.

I held out a hand to shake. "Glad to hear it." Hell, *glad to hear it* didn't even come close to how I felt about it every time he gave me news like that. Inside, I was dancing a jig.

I wanted to get home to be with Ravyn so we could celebrate, but I wasn't so sure she'd be in the mood for a celebration. Tomorrow was Christmas Eve. Which meant it had been a year since her baby's birth. I was fully prepared to spend the next few days holed up in my house with her crying all over me. Because this was what I'd signed up for when I'd gotten into a relationship with her. The good and the bad, the laughing and the crying. All of it.

For the most part, she was doing amazingly well. But there were probably always going to be things that would trigger her depression. That only proved to me how deeply she was capable of loving, though. If she didn't love that baby so much, it wouldn't hurt her as much as it did to not have him in her life.

I was a hell of a lucky man to be the one she'd chosen to give her love to, and there wasn't a chance I'd forget it anytime in the next millennium or so.

"Anyway," Zee said, drawing me in for a bro hug, where he was slapping me on the back. "Hope you and Ravyn have a good Christmas."

"Same to you and the family," I said.

Zee and the rest of my teammates didn't know how hard Christmas would be for Ravyn, and I didn't want to bring them down by pointing out that it might not be such a great time for everyone. Some things just needed to stay between us.

I finished drying off and getting dressed, then made my way home.

Ravyn should be there waiting for me to get back. She'd spent the night, and since she didn't have to work for the next several days, I'd left her in bed on my way to practice.

When I came through the door, there was no sign of

her anywhere. Hadn't she gotten up to eat, at least?

"Ravyn?" I called out.

No answer.

I headed into the bedroom. She wasn't there. The bed was made, like she hadn't been there at all.

Well, damn.

I took out my phone to text her and find out where she was, but there was a message waiting for me.

Actually, it was a picture.

Of Ravyn with a puppy. And it wasn't Snoopy, either. They were standing next to one of the paintings she had for sale at the gallery, and it had a big "Sold" sign hanging over it, and she was grinning from ear to ear. The pup was scrawny, scruffy as all hell, and looked like it might have fleas, but Ravyn was as happy as could be.

Instead of responding, I dialed her number and headed back into the living room to sit on the couch.

"Hey," she said, answering on the first ring.

"Did you adopt a puppy?"

"We did," she replied.

We.

Now, I could have gotten upset that she'd made a decision for us without consulting me, but I was too busy internally doing a Tarzan-chest-pound move over the fact that she'd made a decision for *us* to bother being mad.

Because it meant there was an us.

I still couldn't get over the fact that she loved me.

"So why did we adopt a puppy?" I asked, my amusement threatening to choke me with laughter.

"Because so many of my paintings have sold this month that the gallery asked me to double how many I provide them with, which meant I had some extra money lying around. And because I get lonely when you're gone on road trips, and I feel guilty about stealing Ethan's puppy all the time. And because it seemed like a better next step for us than jumping straight into adopting a kid."

"So this is like a trial run or something?"

"Or something," she agreed, laughing.

"So where is our puppy going to live?" I didn't want to push, exactly, but Ravyn already stayed at my house more than her apartment—even when I was gone with the team—and I'd asked her a couple of times to think about moving in with me.

She fell quiet, which meant she was thinking hard. "Where do you think he should live?" she asked after a moment.

That was an easy question for me to answer. "I think he should be with you. And I think you should be with me."

"Hmm," was all she said.

Hmm? What the fuck did hmm mean in a situation like this?

"Can you open the front door?" she asked then.

"You're here?" I was already on my feet, though, and racing for the door. When I opened it, I burst out laughing and dropped the phone into my pocket. Because I clearly needed my hands for other things—like taking the massive pile of art supplies out of her hands before it all collapsed on the puppy she was leading on a leash.

"I figured you were right," she explained. "And maybe it's time for me to move in."

Hell yes, it was time. Past time. I hauled her stuff into the dining room and tossed it on the table while she picked up the puppy and got a million puppy kisses.

"How much more do you have?" I asked. "I can get Bear or some of the other guys to help."

Ravyn walked into my arms, which was exactly where I wanted her to be. "The rest can wait. There's no rush."

That was true. Because I intended for us to have forever.

The puppy stretched up and licked my face, getting his tongue in my mouth. I was laughing too hard to gag, especially because he was wriggling so much and wagging his tail so fast. That little guy couldn't have been happier, and it was impossible to be anything but happy when seeing him.

"So where'd you find him?" I asked.

"In a box on the sidewalk by the art gallery. It said *Free to good home.* Whoever had put him in there, they'd just left him."

"They'd left him like that? Things like that piss me the hell off. Makes me think of how Bear said they'd found Snoopy tied up in a garbage bag on the side of the road."

"I know," she said. "But I figured we could be a good home for him. And besides, I've been there before. They probably aren't bad people. They just know they're not the right people for him right now."

And it hit me. She probably felt like she'd done the same thing. But Ravyn had given her son to someone who would make sure he was taken care of. She hadn't dropped him in a box and left him, hoping someone else would come along and take over. It wasn't even close to the same thing.

"So we can be his people instead," I said, shoving all of that aside for now.

"Exactly."

I kissed her on the forehead, and the puppy tried to get his tongue in my mouth again. "Any idea what you want to name him?"

She backed up for a moment, and her brows drew together. "I was thinking about Devon."

Holy hell. "Do you think you can handle that?"

She blinked a couple of times, but it didn't stop the tears from pooling in her eyes. Still, she nodded resolutely. "I think it'll be good. And this is perfect timing, too. It'll be a good way for me to remember him, and to prove to myself that I'm capable of taking care of someone other than myself. Maybe not a baby yet, but *someone*."

"You take care of me," I murmured.

She chuckled and rolled her eyes. "That's debatable. I'd say the opposite is true."

"We take care of each other," I insisted. "And now we can take care of Devon together."

"Yeah? You mean it?"

"I do." And then I felt something that distinctly resembled a flea bite on the side of my neck. I slapped my skin, then gave Devon a thorough once-over. "And I think it's time we get started on that. First item on the list is a flea bath."

"Have you ever given a dog a flea bath before?"

"Nope." I took out my cell again and sent off a quick text to Huggy Bear to see if he had any dog shampoo he could bring over. "We can figure it out together." And if all went according to plan, we'd be figuring it out together for a very long time to come.

Roster

Name	Position	Nickname	Number
Travis Royal	Defense	Prince	2
Ben Schuster	Defense	Shoo	3
Vyacheslav Zherdev	Defense	Slava	5
Ray Chambers	Defense	Razor	6
Ethan Higgins	Defense	Huggy Bear	7
Alexei Petrov	Center	Petro	8
Eric Zellinger	Center	Zee	9
Anton Dobransky	Left Wing	Doberman	13
Dmitri Nazarenko	Left Wing	Dima	14
Isaac Johnson	Defense	Ike	16
Ludvig Andersson	Left Wing	Luddy	17
Chris Richards	Center	Richie	18
Hayes Lennon	Left Wing	Haymaker	19
Mike Oslow	Right Wing	Ox	23
Victor Frisk	Center	Frisky	27
Nathan Cochran	Defense	Nate	28
Hunter Fielding	Goal	Hunter	31
Aarti Nieminen	Goal	Nemo	33
Preston Hutchinson	Left Wing	Hutch	39
Jacob Dresden	Right Wing	Jake	41
Andrew Nash	Right Wing	Drew	81
Seth McCormick	Right Wing	Mac	93

About the Author

Catherine Gayle is a USA Today bestselling author of Regency-set historical romance and contemporary hockey romance. She's a transplanted Texan living in North Carolina with two extremely spoiled felines. In her spare time, she watches way too much hockey and reality TV, plans fun things to do for the Nephew Monster's next visit, and performs experiments in the kitchen which are rarely toxic.

Books by Catherine Gayle

Breakaway
On the Fly
Taking a Shot
Light the Lamp
Delay of Game
Double Major
In the Zone
Holiday Hat Trick
Comeback
Dropping Gloves
Bury the Hatchet
Home Ice
Smoke Signals
Mistletoe Misconduct
Losing an Edge
Ghost Dance
Dreaming Up a Dare
Game Breaker
Rites of Passage

Twice a Rake
Saving Grace
Merely a Miss
Wallflower
Pariah
Seven Minutes in Devon
The Devil to Pay
A Dance with the Devil
Flight of Fancy
Rhyme and Reason
Thick as Thieves
An Unintended Journey
To Enchant an Icy Earl
Wanton Wives

Made in the USA
Columbia, SC
18 January 2025